PENGUIN BOOKS

PEACE WORK

Spike Milligan was born at Ahmednagar in India in 1918. He received his first education in a tent in the Hyderabad Sindh desert and graduated from there, through a series of Roman Catholic schools in India and England, to the Lewisham Polytechnic. Always something of a playboy, he then plunged into the world of Show Business, seduced by his first stage appearance, at the age of eight, in the Nativity play of his Poona convent school. He began his career as a band musician but has since become famous as a humorous script-writer and actor in both films and broadcasting. He was one of the main figures in and behind the infamous Goon Show. Among the films he has appeared in are *Suspect*, *Invasion*, *Postman's Knock* and *Milligan at Large*.

Spike Milligan's published work includes *The Little Potboiler*, *Silly Verse for Kids*, *Dustbin of Milligan*, *A Book of Bits*, *The Bed-Sitting Room* (a play), *The Bald Twit Lion*, *A Book of Milliganimals*, *Puckoon*, *Small Dreams of a Scorpion*, *The Mirror Running* (a book of poetry), *Transports of Delight*, *The Milligan Book of Records*, *Games, Cartoons and Commercials*, *Badjelly the Witch*, *Dip the Puppy*, *The Spike Milligan Letters* and *More Spike Milligan Letters*, both edited by Norma Farnes, *Open Heart University*, *The Q Annual*, *Unspun Socks from a Chicken's Laundry*, *The 101 Best and Only Limericks of Spike Milligan*, *There's a Lot of It About*, *The Melting Pot*, *Further Transports of Delight*, *Startling Verse for All the Family*, *The Looney: An Irish Fantasy*, *The Lost Goon Shows* and *It Ends With Magic*. With Jack Hobbs, he has also written

*William McGonagall: The Truth at Last* and *William McGonagall Meets George Gershwin*. His unique and incomparable seven volumes of peace/war memoirs are: *Adolf Hitler: My Part in His Downfall*, *'Rommel?' 'Gunner Who?'*, *Monty: His Part in My Victory*, *Mussolini: His Part in My Downfall*, *Where Have All the Bullets Gone?*, *Goodbye, Soldier* and *Peace Work*. To celebrate his seventieth birthday Penguin published a special edition of his first novel *Puckoon*. Spike Milligan received an honorary CBE in 1992.

SPIKE MILLIGAN

# PEACE WORK

## PEACE/WAR AUTOBIOGRAPHY
## VOL. 7

PENGUIN BOOKS

PENGUIN BOOKS

Published by the Penguin Group
Penguin Books Ltd, 27 Wrights Lane, London W8 5TZ, England
Penguin Books USA Inc., 375 Hudson Street, New York, New York 10014, USA
Penguin Books Australia Ltd, Ringwood, Victoria, Australia
Penguin Books Canada Ltd, 10 Alcorn Avenue, Toronto, Ontario, Canada M4V 3B2
Penguin Books (NZ) Ltd, 182–190 Wairau Road, Auckland 10, New Zealand

Penguin Books Ltd, Registered Offices: Harmondsworth, Middlesex, England

First published by Michael Joseph 1991
Published in Penguin Books 1992
3 5 7 9 10 8 6 4 2

Printed in England by Clays Ltd, St Ives plc

# HOME

Indeed, we won the war, but I lost five precious years. I was to mourn and still do, the physical break-up of my family; it was a sort of time-warp Belsen. As my ship left Naples harbour – it was the cool end of autumn – the year 1946; time, like the ship, was slipping away, an azure twilight glazed the Campania, lights enumerated along that seemingly timeless shore, now lifeless, Vesuvius was turning into a faded amber silhouette. I stood aft on the promenade deck, seamen still fussed around the ship's limits, other passengers leaned out at the rail. I watched the oncoming pollution, as they tossed their cigarette ends in the sea.

Goodbye, here was I saying 'Goodbye to all that' though I was only twenty-eight, here I was saying goodbye, I hated goodbyes, they gave me the same haunting sadness every time. Wherever I had put down emotional roots, it was painful to bid it adieu; I am still haunted by all the homes I have had to leave. What was it like to live in a cottage in a village in the sixteenth century, and never say goodbye to it? Is the modern social pattern of unending change and movement the cause of two modern diseases, insecurity and dissatisfaction? How lucky Thomas Hood was to be able to write:

> I remember, I remember,
> The house where I was born.

I don't even know what mine looked like! I stayed on deck, smoked a Capstan 'full strength', one of my last NAAFI-issue cigarettes. On the portside, we passed what were then isles of magic memory, Capri and Ischia, scarlet and bronze in the

5

sunset; the sea was turning to ink, our propellers churning up a Devonshire cream wake, the ship's siren sent out a long mournful departure note – it echoed across the bay.

Eddy Molloy, who had been below, joined me; he'd run out of cigarettes, sure enough, 'I've run out of cigarettes,' he said. In the 'Central Pool of Artists' he had been known as Virgin Pockets as no human hand had ever entered there for money. Ashore, somehow he had the franchise for the weekly NAAFI Ration. He would sell anything, half of Italy was walking the streets in overcoats made from his army blankets. When asleep, one only had to whisper 'How much?' in his ear, he would leap to his feet and sell you his bed. 'Yes, I've run out,' he reconfirmed, puffing away; 'I've got to cut down,' – on mine I hoped. 'It's getting chilly,' he said and all his blankets ashore. 'I've got a nice cabin,' he said. I waited for him to sell it to me. It was dark, better go below before he sells me a torch.

The four-tone dinner xylophone had gone, 'First dinner sitting,' called the white-uniformed steward.

'I'm first sitting,' said Molloy, referring to his seating card.

Good, I was second sitting.

'Why don't you change to first?' he said. 'No, wait, I'll change to second.'

So while I waited he did. We sat at the purser's table, or was he sitting at ours? Mr Greenidge. 'Yes, twenty years with P & O and Union Castle, "nearly" torpedoed twice.' He was a man in his middle fifties, or a woman in her late sixties, a repressed homosexual with a wife and one daughter. He was possibly the first human gynandromorph*.

Next to him, Eileen Walters, Queen Alexandra Nursing Sister – a fine, cheery, plump, sweaty matron, passing forty, at great speed, and mostly uphill. 'I came out via the Cape, on the er – the er.' Oh dear, she can't remember. Never mind, she came out on the SS *The-er*.

Two officers at the table, one in mufti, Carlton D'eath, tall in a rigid Eiffel Tower way, saturnine, his jet eyes incredibly close together, a forceps delivery I'd say. Before we had finished soup, he let slip he was Coldstream Guards and

*I don't know.

ex-Eton. I heard myself saying I was a Lance Bombardier and ex-Brownhill Road School, Catford, 'Not many people can say that, you see the school burnt down,' I concluded.

There was Captain Manning O'Brien, a wayward romantic Irishman, who had produced some of our shows at CSE* Naples; how does a man who claims he was dropped with fellow drunk Randolph Churchill into Yugoslavia to 'organise' Tito's guerrillas and Alcoholics Anonymous get posted back to an entertainment unit and Alcoholics Anonymous? His first effort was to call a parade. 'Any Irishmen here?' he said. Two of us held up our hands. 'You four step forward,' he said. 'We need schum more – hic,' he shed. It was only 8 a.m. His 'show', Shamrock Review, was unbelievable. The entire cast were untrained Italian POWs. Their sallow complexions done over with a pale make-up, red lips, pink cheeks and the occasional red wig, each one dressed in green breeches smothered in red shamrocks (red?). Every victim had been taught the songs parrot-fashion. The curtain went up on a tableau of an Irish village, harps, jaunting cart, shillelaghs, and the opening chorus 'Begin The Beguine'. Efforts had been made to para-chute him back to Yugoslavia, or Greece, or anywhere. He ordered drinks for the table, and I think for the chairs as well. 'God, you should have seen Tito and Randolph together,' he said. I said how sorry I was not to have.

'Apropos of that,' our Matron said, 'I met General Mont-gomery;' had I? No, the nearest I got was General Motors. Colonel D'eath too had met General Montgomery and Chur-chill, but was loath to mention they fired him – he ended his 'career' as a military prison governor in the Dolomites.

'Ah yes! the ship!' she remembered. 'The SS *Ascanius*, it was the worst ship I *ever* travelled on.' With her on board it must have been. My travelling companion Eddy Molloy was eyeing her up and down, it was quicker than going across, she was a large woman – plain, but sexually attractive, to Molloy that is. It would be like sleeping with a side of beef, even a football side.

Finally, Captain The Reverend Father Peter Fairchild,

*Combined Services Entertainment.

Château des Aygalades

Army Chaplain with the 'Jocks', was 'Going home at last,' sixty-one, quite old to have been in a war; going home was Dundee. 'It's a nice wee place,' he said in a slow drawl. 'It's been a long time, fourrr years.' He went on to say, 'Aye, fourrr is a long time.'

Five is longer, I said.

'Aye, five is longerrrr,' he agreed.

You can't argue with a man of God, but Molloy, 'I ain't bin 'ome for twelve, I was servin' in India.'

'Oh aye, twelve is a verrry long time.' Something else was going to be very long, this bloody trip.

Thankfully, we didn't stop at Malta, I think Malta was thankful too. We docked at Marseilles; ashore for the evening with Molloy and Matron Walters, I had last come ashore at this port in the arms of my mother* in 1919. I knew we had been billeted at the Château des Aygalades, was it still standing? It

*It Ends With Magic . . . (Michael Joseph, 1990) for full story.

was, so let's go see. French taxis—when I mentioned the place he threw his arms in the air, I waited till they came down, '*Mon Dieu, sacré bleu, etc.*' It was *très distance*. He believes the world is flat, outside Marseilles you fall off, but he will risk it for twice the fare.

So, a voluble driver plus thirteen kilometres. He wants to know, 'Why are you going there?'

'It's a nostalgia – I was here when I was one.'

'When you were one what?'

'A baby.' (Silly man.)

'A baby? . . . well, now it is an old folks' home.'

I didn't get out of the taxi, it was just, well, I don't know. What *was* I doing there, never go back they say, well, I had. I would be a lifelong nostalgic fool.

That evening Matron Walters, Molloy and I sat in an *estaminet*, 'Café du Port', at a dockside, redolent with Gauloise and fish. My mother told me, that distant day in July, 1919 she and my father too had drunk wine in a dockside café, was this the one? Never go back. My God, Molloy has let go a Butlers*, (Butler's revenge) and he's looking at me.

*Dominion Monarch* sailed at midnight, by which time Molloy had been rogering the lady who had met General Montgomery. I had fallen asleep trying to read *Le Matin*; I could read the date in French fluently, le 2nd, de November.

Evenings, after dinner, were spent in the saloon; the decor was appalling, someone thought pink, green, black and blue curtains and carpets were acceptable. 'Yes, we have a lady who does our decor,' said Mr Greenidge, 'she worked for Hardy Amies.' Not for long I'd say. We played cards, at the insistence of Molloy we terminated whist and played pontoon.

'Oh dearrr,' said the Reverend Fairchild, 'I shouldn't be playing carrrrrds,' as he cleaned us all out.

'You sure you never played this before?' said Molloy.

'Oh no, no, neverrr,' said the holy man, 'it's more than my job's worth,' and pocketed the winnings which did look more than his job was worth.

The days were sunny but cool, the evenings were starry and

---

*Breaking wind silently and looking accusingly at someone else.

cold. Winter started as we reached Gib, very brief, we docked at 6 p.m. 'Will passengers please return by midnight,' said the notice. What about the bloody *crew*! It was *they* who were being driven back crammed into horse-drawn landaus, insane with Spanish wine and vomit; did the victorious Trafalgar fleet really bury their dead here? They must have missed this lot. I think our ship left the Rock with only the captain on duty.

The event of the voyage! Ta-raa!!! The Captain's cocktail party, first-class passengers only – 'Fuck 'em – we'll still go,' said Molloy. At the party was Colonel Philip Slessor, 'Saw your act at the Bellini Theatre, jolly good, you going to do it back home?' Yes, I was going to do it back home and her name was Lily Dunford. 'Haw-haw-haw,' he said. 'Jolly good.' I next met Slessor at the BBC, a good place for unemployable people to go.

In Biscay unexpected calm weather, cold, brisk walks around the promenade deck early mornings. Lascars sanding the decks, seagulls overnight, where from? Took picture of porpoise.

Coming towards me, rather bearing down, Matron, doing her constitution, white plimsolls on chubby legs. While down below in his semen-ridden bed, Molloy is recovering from her. 'Good morning, Mr Milligan,' she warbled, 'change in the weather.'

'Yes,' I grinned in time-honoured clichéd reaction.

'Did you see my porpoise?'

Yes, I said, still with the fixed grin.

'He was up there a moment ago,' she pointed a suturing finger forward. 'Oh, he's gone, never mind,' she said, 'he's bound to show up.'

'Yes,' I said, and away she went; she really was a very nice woman. I wished her and 'her' porpoise well, he in the deep Atlantic, she on the ship, if only it were the other way round, oh God, here she comes again.

'Seen him again?'

No – grin.

'Well, I must be getting below.'

Yes, she must, I insist, right down to the very keel then out through the bilges! Why did I hate ordinary people? If only she

Head of Christ by Leonardo da Vinci, bought in a shop in Naples

had said, 'Good morning Mr Milligan, I had a good shag last night, nothing like it for a good night's sleep.' If only.

'See you at breakfast,' she yodelled as she heaved a door open and went.

Yes, I wanted non-clichéd conversation. 'Good morning, Captain, like to join me for nine-a-side porridge? Good; better get your knee clips and quoffle spoons, or would you rather a twosome with cronk-plates?'

The night before Tilbury, the Cordon Bleu gourmet dinner turned out Cordon Brown. Six out of ten to the chef for trying and ten out of ten to us for eating it, Basically roast beef, but! not two but *three* veg! However, we were well served with red Chianti; amazing how wine transforms a meal, that night it transformed me, I was such fun, as Molloy told me next morning. 'Yes, they put you to bed after you did the white-eared elephant.'

My father, Leo, trick riding in Belgaum, India

No, did I do that?

'Yes, not only but also early days of aviation.'

Never mind that, did they clap?

We would dock at high tide – mid-morning. I packed my lone suitcase, with a few war souvenirs, some purchased in Napoli, a drawing of the head of Christ by Leonardo da Vinci – after two thousand years of standardised Jesus, he was something different, a *Jewish* Jesus.

After two years away I had precious little to show for it: an Italian medal intended for a victory in Egypt, a pocket Belgian .32 pistol, my webbing belt and £80.

Weather was chilly as we moved slowly to berth, I had no demob overcoat – I sold it in Bologna to an Italian footballer, he was a top goalscorer, 3. Military Police and Customs came aboard from the pilot's boat, we queued in the Saloon with our documents – documents, bloody documents, paper, paper everywhere and not a bit to read! 'Milligan,' the passport officer reads my name, 'I knew a Leo Milligan in the Indian Army, any relation?'

'Yes, he was any relation, he was my father.'

'It's a small world,' he said.

'Yes, I nearly fell off it,' I said.

'Yes, I remember he was a very good horseman.' Indeed he was.

His name was George Guy, my name was Spike Milligan, he had befriended my father back in 1919 on leave from India and got him a job as Tally Clerk at East India Docks. 'Good luck,' he said as he stamped the passport. Down the gangplank to the gloomy, unwelcoming luggage sheds, with equally gloomy people. Since I last saw England it had gone prematurely grey, or had I been disorientated by the sun of Africa and Italy?

Molloy is up the platform waving and pointing at a carriage. What a great mime artist he was. 'It's a non-smoker,' I said.

'Fuck 'em,' he said; the likes of him would proliferate in the land and become football fans.

Shock horror, Matron Walters has joined us. 'Oh, I don't mind if you smoke,' she said, followed by England's only porter, a little tiny chap, who couldn't reach the luggage rack – or didn't want to.

Molloy took them and with eyes popping got Matron's two bursting cases on the rack. 'Wot you got in there, pianos?' he said.

'Oh, you'd be surprised,' she twittered, eyelashes flickering.

'God, it's a wonder I'm not ruptured,' he said, lighting up a cigarette.

'Do you know?' said Matron. 'The first operation I attended was a rupture,' she giggled; 'when I saw it I fainted.'

To add fuel I said, 'I suppose you're used to it now.'

'Yes, I've seen a lot of it,' she said.

I daren't look at Molloy.

Two middle-aged officers with luggage struggled into the compartment, they were both portly, with heavy army over-coats. The rack was now a-glut with luggage. After the traditional struggling and straining and the 'Is anyone sitting here,' silly sods, they could *see* there was nobody sitting there, they sank into their seats. The platform is a criss-crossing of civvies, and servicemen, two soldiers are carried by on stret-chers. 'Now that's how I'd like to travel,' said Molloy. The guard's whistle; we are leaving for lovely London. One portly officer leaned towards Molloy. 'I say, this is a non-smoker you know.'

What does politeness matter?

'Is it annoying you then?' says Molloy, accelerating the puffing regretfully; simmering with hatred, he stubbed it on the floor. Picking up the stub he made a great display of straightening it out before pocketing it, true grit, as most of the stub now was. I don't recall much more of the journey and I'm glad.

# 3 LEATHWELL ROAD

At Waterloo I took the tube through the rush hour to London Bridge – being very sunburned, I turned a few girls' heads, the bodies would have to wait. St John's Station where I alight, now where the hell was 3 Leathwell Road, what *was* a Leathwell? It doesn't appear in any dictionary or place name – okay, let's say it was a 'well' but what *is* a leath? Who are these creeps who choose our street names? Yoxley Approach, Zenoria Street, Yabsley Street, Cronk Avenue, Gonson Gardens, *Gonson*? GONSON? Who, where, why???? By asking a hundred people who were each 'a stranger round here', I arrived at Leathwell Road, a terrace of factory workers' houses that backed on to Elliot's Factory and a shunting yard.

I had not informed my parents of my return, I wanted it to be a lovely surprise; it was, for me, they were away. It was evening, cold and foggy, a Mrs Hicks, the lodger, answered the door on the chain, a shivering old Victorian in black, 'Yerss, they are awaine.' Who was I, how did she know I was their soldier son Terence back from the wars? 'Oh, I done know, you might be anybody . . .' I showed her my passport, my army paybook, my bank statement, my laundry list, my scar on my right shin, I sang God Save the Queen, finally I was allowed past this centurion who was heartbroken I wasn't a rapist.

I walked down an unlit passage, the only light from the landing above. In the gloom I fell down a half step. I'd never said 'Oh fuck' in the dark before. Groping, I opened a door,

N°3 Heathwell Road.
Deptford
Some time in 1946 Mr & Mrs L A
Milligan moved into this house.

1746

lino was crackling underfoot, I struck a match, what a terrible thing to do to an innocent piece of wood. By its light I saw a twin-mantled gaslight; pulling down a tabulated metal chain, I applied the match. Soon the room was an unearthly green, a small rectangular room, against the wall a dining table covered with a blue cloth edged with little dangling balls. Into the opposite wall was let a magnificent black iron stove – with the faintest glow of fire from under kitchen peelings – a large, bulging, blue moquette armchair and, above me, a triple drying rail, hung with underwear; it could have been 1880. I wished it was, I wouldn't be here. Outside I found a coal box, and made up the stove, I rustled some tea, and toast from mildewed bread. In this setting I stared into the fire, sipped tea, and suffered the trauma of having left behind what was the good life . . .

This was home! Off the front passage there was a 'parlour' and a bedroom with my parents' double bed covered in a pink padded eiderdown, which inevitably slid off in the night as Molloy had done. The WC was outside in the garden; upstairs next to Mrs Hicks was a back bedroom twelve feet by twelve with a single bed, this would be mine, all mine! The time was 10.30. In the kitchen, I boiled two eggs for dinner, fiddled with the battery-operated wireless, it was Harry Roy and His Band, with Ivor Moreton and Dave Kaye – all very hot-cha-ma-cha-cha; having heard new players like Miles Davis, Charlie Parker, Charlie Christian, this all sounded dated. Harry Roy, 1939, and the world I knew would be coming to an end. A week-old copy of the *Daily Herald*, which suggested how long my folks had been away; wouldn't it be silly if they'd gone to Naples to surprise me, oh ha ha ha eh?

I lit the gas in my little bedroom, unpacked my worldly goods, put them in a small chest of drawers, and hung my clothes in the wall cupboard that flanked the Victorian fireplace, the grate filled with red crepe paper. The fog had increased in density and so had I; I drew the flimsy curtains on my window. I was in bed, smoking; I had left in 1940 – all the while my head lived in 1939 and the years up to it, in those Thirties' days I was in a dream, I learned the guitar – to knock out chords like D9th & 11 & 13 made me feel giddy at their sound. Eddy Lang was God, then I heard Crosby, a vibrant light baritone, different from the appalling English nasal singers like Brian Lawrence, Kitty Masters et al. I *had* to sing like him, and by God I *did*, I won Bing Crosby contests.

Bing Crosby Cup won in a crooning contest at the
Lady Florence Institute, Deptford

Local bands like the New Era Rhythm Boys had me sing with them – there was no money in it, I did it just for kicks so I got nowhere*, but loved it, couldn't wait to put on my 50/- tailor's suit, Brylcreem my hair and get on to the mike at Ladywell Baths to sing 'Temptation'. My friend Geoff Smith recalls those days:

*Brockley.

*On the evening I was present at the Ladywell Baths when you were asked to sing a number with the band, I do not recall any hesitation on your part. You sang 'Temptation' in a Bing Crosby style. He was all the rage at the time and you received quite an ovation, partly because this was a tricky song. When leaving these dances, you found leaflet distributors outside advertising coming dances in the district. They must have wondered who the young unknown singer was, and where from.*

Next morning I slept late, mild 'ship lag'. I bumped into Mrs Hicks on the landing, what do you say to someone you don't know? 'Good morning,' I said, and with all the warmth of old England she said, 'Morning? huh, more afternoon.' A few letters were on the mat, 'Captain L.A. Milligan, Mrs Florence Milligan.' Food! I found some Shredded Wheat, the milk had just gone off – not enough, by adding mounds of white sugar I neutralised the taste – tuned in the wireless. News is all about rationing, no one's getting enough of.

## RESTARTING THE TRIO

What to do? First I had to contact Bill Hall the violinist from our trio – 6 Legard Road, Highbury. After a spaghetti of buses and trams, through grey, grotty, postwar streets, I was knocking on the door of a Victorian terraced home, had I gone in a circle? It looked like 3 Leathwell. A dying female circa 1880 opened the door, 'Oo?' she said. 'Spike Milligan.' What did I want? I didn't want anything, I wanted to see Bill Hall, her son, 'Ee's out gettin' some fags.' Could I come in and wait or rape her? Grumbling, she let me into the kitchen of 6 Legard Road, with identical laundry overhead.

Seated in an identical blue moquette armchair was Bill Hall's father Albert. 'Oh yes, Spike Millington, Bill told us you might be cummin', didn't 'ee Vera?'

The living dead Vera said, 'Yer, but I dinn knowed wot 'ee looked like, 'ee could 'ave been anybody; I done like lettin' stranglers in.'

'She means strangers,' said Albert.

A dog has appeared, an old English mongrel with a huge nose. 'It swooled up when the cat bit 'im – here, Rex, Rex, good dog.' Good dog Rex, good dog, ignored him and started to sniff my balls. It happens not only in working-class families, I was at a black tie dinner with Lady Nethersole – among the guests were Kenneth Tynan, Sir Bernard Miles, Field Marshal Montgomery – post-dinner a poodle was released under the table and sniffed all our balls.

The front door slamming announced the return of Bill Hall. 'Oh, 'ello,' he said with a smile, his lips parted, a cigarette stuck to the bottom. We shook hands, 'When you get back?'

I gave him chapter and verse, spicing it up with Molloy's extra-marital bunk-ups – Bill frowns, looks at dying mother and puts his fingers to his lips. 'Shush! me muther,' he whispers; 'me muther is in the back kitchen making a "nice cuppa tea", I don't want her to hear about Molloy's bunk-ups, it's bad enough 'er 'earing about mine.' Hall and I are making arrangements to get our postwar career started. We have to get an agent. 'Fosters,' says Bill; 'Fosters are the biggest.' I like big agents, they're easier to see. Bill has Johnny Mulgrew's address, 13 Linden Gardens, Notting Hill Gate. Park 3535, thank God a phone!!! We'll leave all messages there.

We have an appointment with Leslie MacDonnell, one of the agents at Fosters' agency in Piccadilly; fancy, *me* in Piccadilly! I remember before the war simple-minded me thought of Piccadilly in the same distant terms as Moscow. Piccadilly, oh no, that was where special people went, the toffs, you had to dress up to go there – have money – I recalled my father did a speciality song and dance:

> Picc-a-dilly – London West
> That's the place – that I like best
> There's the place to drive you silly
> Willy-Nilly dear old Picc-a-dilly.

But the army, the war and Toni Pontani had changed me, now I would go anywhere with or without money, mostly without.

# WORK

Hall and Mulgrew met me in Lyons Corner House, Coventry Street, at eleven. We sat around, the Nippies flitting between tables, 'Pot of tea for three, please Miss.' A palm court trio are playing a medley of tunes from Ivor Novello's *Perchance to Dream*, which was showing at Wyndham's Theatre. ''E can write tunes can't 'e,' said Mulgrew with witty smile.

'Never mind,' said Hall, 'if we are as popular in England as we were in Italy, mate – we might be in the dibs.' As a prophecy it was a disaster. All this time Harry Secombe was appearing at the Windmill in a nude review; he was the one with clothes on, though had he been offered more . . .

Being there gave us ingression to the stage door in Archer Street – 'Yes?' said the Stage Door Keeper. 'I've come to see Mr Harry Secombe.' I thought the Mister bit made me sound respectable, whereas all I wanted to see was birds' tits. Harry took me to the 'green room', where all the girls were in dressing gowns; yes, yes, yes, yes, he liked it here, yes, yes, yes, all the girls, yes, yes, yes, was he allowed to stand in the wings, yes, yes, yes, yes, he had to get on the stage, was he going blind, yes, yes, yes. He gets me a free seat; doing comedy at 11 a.m. can't be easy. I watch with popping eyes, and aroused loins, as naked women, NAKED WOMEN, a tableau, 'Spring In Arcadia'; the nudes stay stock still as the waiting onanists vibrate our row of seats, the only moving entertainment on stage is *premier danseur* Peter Glover, who is leaping everywhere to the Spectre de la Rose. Curtain.

Enter one who a while back was a Lance Bombardier in a hole in North Africa, he comes on like a dynamo carrying a table and shaving kit – 'Everybody's got to shave,' he says. He is hypnotically funny – the energy could light a city, in eight explosive minutes he's finished, a few wankers laugh, and they've got five more shows. Between shows, Harry and I visited Poppa Allens, a first-floor 'club' on Windmill Street, others from the Windmill were Jimmy Edwards, Frank Muir, Michael Bentine. 'Have a drink, Spike,' said Harry, over the moon at being in the West End. He was on £20 a week, and I wasn't.

It was Harry who gave us an introduction to the nightclub circuit. The first one was the Florida in Carnaby Street; it was six phone-boxes square, the 'house band' was the Ike Isaacs Trio, unbelievable Ike was at school with me in Rangoon, they took one corner, the bouncer Mike Noonan the next, the rest were customers. We appeared in a serving hatch. It was our first appearance in England, and by God we tore 'em up folks, oh yes, here was an unusual comedy act, literally in rags but playing like the Hot Club de France. We were soon inundated with work, we did the circuit: the Blue Lagoon, Panama, ending up in Edmundo Ros' Coconut Grove, featuring his and Syd Phillips' bands. We were kept on for an extra week. Rawicz and Landau came regularly to see us, so did Eugene Goosens and Eileen Joyce.

Syd Phillips took us on one side, he couldn't manage two, and said, 'Now listen, I'm going to make a lot of money out of you boys.' Another disastrous prophecy. Syd was Jewish, how did he go wrong? What did we do in the day? To start, I was living with my parents, who weren't at home when I had returned from the war, and the surprise was extended. They had been staying with 'Aunt Nance in Sittingbourne, whose husband is a builder you know,' so when they got back from Aunt Nance in Sittingbourne, whose husband was a builder you know, I was out. I left a note saying I was 'back from Italy and was now in Catford' visiting Aunty Kath, whose husband was an insurance agent you know. So during the first days I was back, I tried to revive 1939. I had to see Lily, Beryl, Ivy and anybody but! Lily Dunford had been unfaithful to me, she'd married!!!! So had Beryl Southby and Ivy Chandler, yes

Publicity postcard drawn by Bill Hall

married, but to someone else! Why hadn't they waited for beautiful me – me with my five times a night, had they all forgotten the one and threepenny seats at the Rialto, Crofton Park? Those dinners of egg, chips, tomatoes, bread and butter and pot of tea for two in Reg's Café – opposite Brockley Cemetery? *And* I used to change my hair oil every three-hundred miles. Very well, they'd regret it – in gloom over the loss of Lily I wrote this bizarre letter of farewell, which I never posted:

*Dear Lily,*

*Remember this – one day in years to come, you will cry – cry for the fool that you were and are – cry for me, Lily – remember that – No one will ever love like me – You will come back to me one day. Love has many children – one is called HATE – you will smile when I say 'I hate you – want to kill you – see you with your face blue and black and the eyes I love to see – sightless.' I mean that – all that. To finish this – I will make you hate me – hate me till your mind is full of poison – hate me till it hurts –*

*And I will still love you.*

*Goodbye, Lily.*

God, what a monster! No wonder she didn't marry me. Ex-soldier kills ex-girlfriend, paints her face black and blue then does her in. When I read the letter after forty years, it made me wonder what kind of person I used to be. Well, for a start, I liked to choke and blind people. I could have been another Neville Heath; help!! When I eventually booked a room at 13 Linden Gardens, I discovered the previous occupant had been the murderer Neville Heath himself, I mean, who else could he be? ''E was a real gentleman, 'oo would 'ave thought it of 'im?' said Blanche the lady cleaner who 'did the place'. Dear Blanche, about forty-five, with a face that could have modelled Palaeolithic man – she was still a virgin. 'I still got it – an' no one's 'aving it,' mainly because no one wanted it.

I wasn't earning, so I had to budget, to-ing and fro-ing from 3 Leathwell to London was boring and expensive so I moved to 13 Linden. Aren't we strange. Two years away from home, come home, leave. It was one room with sit-up bath, top floor at back, it was £1.15.0 a week with breakfast, usually a kipper. If you stand in Notting Hill High Street next to Lloyds Bank, look up, you can see the window of my bedroom.

Margo, the landlady, was a short, plump, prettyish, mid-forties, dark, feline, very rouged with dark red lipstick. She reminded me of Theda Bara, in that she was dead. Margo spoke so slowly, people dozed off in her presence. She lived in the basement in Stygian gloom with the smell of cats and Mansion polish, a widow, but there came into her life a humpty-backed lodger, Mr Len Lengths, an insurance broker who 'worked from home'. He was about five feet six inches, an inch taller than Margo, he had a face like Charles Laughton's and Boris Karloff's superimposed on his, he wore pebbledash glasses which magnified his pop eyes, giving him the countenance of a man being garrotted, yet Margo was attracted to him. She had him down for supper and while there he had her down for screwing.

'What does he see in her?' I said.

Mulgrew, who is evil, says, 'His hump turns her on.'

'Hump, my arse,' said Hall, 'I bet he's got a huge chopper, lengths by name, lengths by nature.' How did Hall deduce this?

'Listen mate – admit the number of good-looking wimmin with ugly blokes, well, it's a big prick, wimmin will stand anything as long as the bloke's chopper is big.' All these theories seem to clash with medical evidence, but neither Margo nor Lengths had heard of them. All we knew was he wasn't paying rent.

Yes, what did we do in the day? One time at the Windmill canteen, Harry introduced me to 'Jimmy Grafton who owns a pub'; he was to figure in my life in those immediate postwar years. He had served as an officer in the infantry and was at Arnhem. He was now serving behind the bar; he had, somehow or other, become a scriptwriter to Derek Roy, a would-be comic appearing on *Variety Bandbox*, so Jimmy had an 'in' into broadcasting.

Michael Bentine introduced Harry to Jimmy, as Harry

recalls, 'Mike told me of this pub in Strutton Ground where I got a drink after hours, and somehow Jimmy became my manager and scriptwriter.' He started back to front by me telling him what bloody awful scripts Derek Roy had, and Jimmy said, 'Well I write them'. A strange start to a forty-year relationship.

## HACKNEY EMPIRE

'I've got a week for you at the Hackney Empire,' the words fell from the mellifluous lips of Leslie MacDonnell, our agent, sitting behind his desk at Piccadilly House, Piccadilly Circus.

We were overjoyed, I could see our name in lights. Mac-Donnell then added, 'I've arranged for Val Parnell to see you on the Monday performance.'

*Val Parnell*!!!! This was something. If Parnell was coming to see us, MacDonnell must have thought pretty highly of us; for giving us this break, Bill Hall proffered his thanks, 'Ta,' he said.

I burst out laughing. 'Bill,' I said, 'Ta? Ta? Excuse him, MacDonnell, Bill is a man of few words and that was one of them.' I then thanked MacDonnell more formally, 'Like this, Bill,' I said. I knelt in the grovelling position, my head on MacDonnell's shoe, 'Oh a thousand thanks, oh great wise one.'

MacDonnell was highly amused. 'Is he always like this?' he said.

'Only when the money's right,' said Mulgrew, pulling me away. 'There, there boy,' he said, patting me on the head and feeding me pretend sugar lumps. So to the big time.

'Oh, we'll be there* son,' said my dad when I told him. My parents, especially my father, were very proud, he having been a stage performer. 'I never knew you had it in you,' he said. I told him I myself had never had it in me, but I had had it in other people, the opposite sex, well that's where they were at the time.

*At home.

25

That fateful Monday night, the night of February the 3rd 1947. Heavy snow had been falling, it was very cold – up to then it was the worst recorded winter in living memory. Our dressing room was on the fifth floor. 'They must think we're bloody eagles,' said Mulgrew humping his double bass. Dressing room six feet by ten: a cracked mirror with dabs of greasepaint, a surround of forty wall bulbs, three fused, a leaking washhand basin – 'Warning, do not stand in the sink, one of the girls did and was TERRIBLY INJURED'. It must have been something to see. Before the show started we peeped through the front curtain. My God, there were only three people in and two of them were Val Parnell. Even by curtain-up there were only twelve customers. Serious. The pit band struck up. I strolled on the stage alone, started to tune my guitar, Bill Hall runs on backwards as though being cheered on – he collides with me – looking directly at me he places the hair of the bow over the string and with the bow underneath the violin saws through 'Organ Grinder's Swing', until then a popular tune, during which Mulgrew brings his bass on. The diminutive audience don't laugh, one person applauded, which made it sound even worse, in the box we could see the chair-oscuro figure of Val Parnell. We went through our repertoire, after each number there was the lone clapper. In desperation I ad-libbed, 'Please sir, you're spoiling it for the other people.' This got the only laugh of the evening, it would go on to be the only laugh of the month. We died the death. The pit band played us off with 'Where's That Tiger?'; if I'd have found it I would have shot it.

We stood there in the gloom. 'Never mind, lads,' said the Stage Manager, 'it's Monday, they'll be better by the middle of the week.'

'They're not staying here till then are they?' I said, always cheerful Spike.

We sat in our dressing room. In silence, in unison, we lit up a cigarette. 'Where the fuck did they get that audience?' 'It's the Nazi Party.' Never mind eh? Val Parnell had seen us, he knew a good act when he saw one. We never heard from the bastard again. Tuesday night only eighteen people in, the next night it snowed heavily. 'This'll kill the business,' said the manager.

On the Saturday night we did well; why, oh why did Val Parnell come on a Monday? 'He's a perv, that's why,' said Mulgrew. 'I bet he feels little girls' bicycle saddles.' However, from that week we received £75! Who would have dreamed such wealth existed! It meant £25 each, but each of us had to pay £2.10.0 commission. Mulgrew rolled his wages into a tight roll then wedged it into his wallet with a rubber band around it; I think he was marinating it.

## A DREAM OF GRANDEUR

The story that follows tells of the bitter experience of a bass player who basically had the arse out of his trousers, even someone else's trousers. This first week's wages went to Mulgrew's head. He had met a girl – Elsie, I remember was her name; she had enormous bosoms that promised pneumatic bliss, it appeared as though a giant hand had grabbed her bottom half and squeezed it all upwards. Mulgrew was besotted with all three of her. Every night after the show, she waited at the stage door, and he whipped her away from A to B – that is, stage door to bed. By the time I arrived back at 13 Linden Gardens, groans and steam were coming from under his bedroom door. I would send a prayer to help him through the night. On the Sunday I was up at the crack of one in the afternoon. Sunday was the one day we didn't get breakfast, so I made tea and toast on my gas ring and did my accounts for the week.

There was a faint tapping on my door; there after a good night's coitus stood the wreck of a man in the Robbie Burns manner. I sang at him as he tried to shush me.

> They were fucking in the hallway
> They were fucking on the stairs
> Yer could nae see the carpet
> For the xxxx and curly hairs.

27

'Ssh! She'll hear you,' said the wreck of a man whom I recognised as the remains of Johnny Mulgrew. 'Ha, you got any tea?' he said.

Ha – yes, so I boiled up a pot for him and his wee lassie. That night we repaired to the Coach and Horses (now alas demolished). Here Mulgrew's attempts at the grandiose failed. What he had done, the little Scottish nana, was to cut thirty strips of the *Daily Mirror* to the size of pound notes. These he rolled into a wad, then wrapped his twenty-five one-pound notes around them. This looked very impressive until the following Thursday when, at the same pub, well oiled, he forgetfully peeled off his last two pounds to reveal the *Daily Mirror*; it didn't stop there, he peeled off two *Daily Mirrors* – the barman said, 'I'm sorry, we only take the *Express*.'

My brother Desmond, like all males in a sexual trauma, is to get married; Pixie Roberts of Devon is the one to get it. I'm to be the best man, thank God I've got that new suit made by the tailor in the Circus Maximus in Rome – what a heritage for a suit!!! Why didn't I choose Royal Purple? The wedding took place at St Saviours RC, Lewisham, with the reception at Chiesmans (now Army & Navy) where the entire Milligan family assembled.

## 5 MAY 1947

Phone for me from Leslie MacDonnell, thank God! 'Spike, I've got a few dates for you.'

Dates? Where is he, Arabia?

'We have a week's variety for the Trio!'

Oh boy! We're on our way. 'Thank you, Leslie. I'll tell the boys.' First week is in Beautiful Sunless Blackpool – Hollywood with flat 'ats.

So we proceeded to do the No. 1 dates, something my father would have given his right arm for. Why he wanted to do a one-armed act I'll never know. It seemed as though I personally was like a gramophone needle stuck in a groove. Life was like moving but standing still, 1939 was hard to recapture; on stage I wasn't crooning, or looking like Robert Taylor – no,

Sergeant Desmond Milligan marries Miss P. Roberts at St Saviours, Lewisham, with me as best man

I was in rags, with a grotesque make-up, and ridiculing the music we played. It was the liberties we took with the music that got us our applause – but 1939 it wasn't; it was digs like 356 Hagley Road, Birmingham – poached haddock in milk for breakfast, lunch in a café, dinner was Arrggg!!! Cold Collation!

One show a night, matinées Wednesday and Saturday. Friday night, the agents came in, Lew Lake, Joe Collins, to suss out the acts; from it a Joe Cohen got us some work after the show at working men's clubs. Everyone changed in the same room. We shared with a lady act. Cathy, the cowgirl (Will lasso your heart), say forty-one, but not in front of her. I watched fascinated as she put make-up to cover the varicose veins on her plump legs. 'I should have the operation, but I'd be laid up fer a month, I can't afford that.'

Bill Hall felt sorry for 'Poor Cowgirl', he said. He felt so sorry for her he took her back to her digs and screwed her. Bill! All those veins like snakes crawling up her legs. Don't worry

The wedding group, from left to right: Kathleen Thurgar née Milligan, sister of Captain L. A. Milligan; Alfred Thurgar; Terry Thurgar; William Milligan; bridesmaid; vicar; Desmond Milligan;

Mrs Pixie Milligan; bridesmaid; me; Mrs Florence Milligan; Joseph Milligan. This was the last photo of the Milligans all together. Not present was Bert Milligan.

Spike, you couldn't see 'em, she had her elastic support stockings on. Ah, *l'amour*! It was in these very digs, 356 Hagley Road, the landlady had caught Sir Donald Wolfit at it on the marble washstand with his leading lady. 'It's all right, Mrs Cartwright,' said the steaming actor, 'it's . . . it's only my sister.'

The afternoons of those distant days were spent at a cinema. I remember seeing Danny Kaye in *The Kid From Brooklyn* and thinking, I should be doing that . . . that was me up there. I realise now that while I was young, vigorous, good-looking and a natural clown I should have gone just for that, it was the right time for my type of clowning – but fear of unemployment, inherited from my mother, kept me with the Trio, at £25 a week I could save, but what for? In any case I always felt I had no talent outside of music; I came from a family who were basically working class, who had left the poverty of London's Poplar and Woolwich, then suddenly were with the Indian Army in India – servants, free quarters, free rations, horse riding, shikar, polo. Despite this, I remember my family thought of anyone above the rank of Sergeant as 'Superior'. I didn't think I could do *anything on my own* – because I was working class. When I think of the number of idiots I said Sir to because they had a posh accent. Oh, what did class do to me? I could have been a Scholar, University, hell . . .

## BLACKPOOL

Ah yes, Blackpool in May, the season was just starting, we were on the bill with Dorothy Squires and Billy Reid. Her song 'The Gypsy' made her top of the bill. To avoid legal proceedings I'll say no more. We travelled up to Blackpool from Euston.

> The train for Dagarees – isn't – stopping at
> Gadernedring-Gritshate-Kandarella-Mish-
> Pasth-plan – thank you

and other such announcements. It was the days of Third Class.

We are joined in the carriage by Clapham and Dwyer, who are on their way to somewhere. 'You'll love Blackpool,' said Clapham; 'you'll have seven sunless days, tripe, onions and bronchitis. What? You're closing the first half? – then get out as soon as you can. You see, it's beginning of the season, locals go to the theatre to kill Londoners, next month is when you get the good audiences, they know how to clap, half of 'em have got it . . .'

Before the war I had seen their act at the Hippodrome, Catford, along with Gertie Gitana.

'Ah, Catford, England's answer to Karachi,' said Clapham. 'You know what they say about Catford? . . . They don't say *anything* about Catford, you know why it's called Catford? In 1598 all the dead moggies were rowed across a ford, and sold to gypsies to make boots for the Army, Navy and the Airforce.'

'They didn't have planes then,' I said.

'Ah, but they didn't know that,' he grinned. The man was a mass of pro. stories. 'Yes, we were on the bill with little *Davey Kaye* at Aylesbury, I remember. The food at the digs was terrible, and Davey being kosher hated the food. On the last night, a rabbi brought Davey an oven-ready kosher Beth Din duck. He took it home and said to his landlady, would you take this duck, chop it up, boil it, put it into a mincer and make soup? She said yes. He said, I thought you bloody well would. On went Clapham, the story of Joe Church, in digs in a bitter winter, the loo at the bottom of the garden – taken short in the wee hours, he pulled a large fern from its pot, crapped in it, then put the plant back. Two months later he got a telegram – 'We know what it is – we know who did it but for Christ's sakes tell us where it is!'

Well, I had never been to Blackpool before. We arrived at the station during a May thunderstorm, an almost monsoon rain – it looked bizarre to see families arriving, mothers in floral frocks, children carrying buckets and spades. On the deserted beach little groups of donkeys stand in the rain, their attendants wait under mortuarial umbrellas, the sea looks like liquid dysentery – and possibly is. We have arrived Sunday night, we have to be here for band call Monday.

We have been recommended digs with Mrs Walters, 106

Hornby Road. It's one of a Victorian terrace – all the windows are steamed up. A sign: 'No hawkers or circulars'. 'I'll ring,' said Hall, 'I know about these things.' No, she mustn't see him first – if they see him first!!! I am the most handsome, *I* will ring, so I ring, and ring – doing that is one way to find it's 'out of order'. The door opens, it's the landlady. 'I thought I 'eard sommat at door, there's bell's broken.' Yes, she should be standing outside saying it. The sign outside said Hazelhurst Hotel, inside it isn't like a hotel. 'That's the name of the sign,' hissed Mulgrew.

''Ow do,' she greets us, 'I'm afraid after the last lot it's rent in advance.' (The last lot were Borra Minovitch and his Harmonica Rascals.) Of course, Mrs Walters, you bloody cow; both Mulgrew and Hall, both boths, borrowed from me to pay. 'There's one single and one double,' she led the way.

The hall was a polished brown lino bordered by a Greek frieze, green lincrustra ran the length, up to a staircase with a floral carpet restrained by polished brass stair-rods. 'You register 'ere,' said she indicating a desk squeezed against the wall leading to the kitchen, from which came smells of cabbage and death.

Behind the desk sat the daughter Hazel (Hazelhurst Hotel geddit?), a little sex bomb that was about to explode. 'Just write your name there, luv,' she said. Eighteen, blonde, blue eyes with all the expression of a manatee, looks like Grace Kelly, but dead. 'I'll fill the rest in.' Oh yes, fill it in darling. 'What's the number of your car?' She looks up. 'Ee,' she says, 'you look like Robert Taylor.' The number of my car is LNER*. 'Oh, you silly,' she says.

''Urry up, 'azel,' says Mother. 'Tea's coming up.'

Travelling salesmen are coming down the stairs. As one passes he says, 'There's no paper in the loo, Mrs Walters.'

'Hungry buggers,' says the landlady as they rush past her into the dining room.

We check our rooms, the decor was 1930, and the beds made at the same time, and those padded eiderdowns, pink! Argggh, green counterpane, Arghhhh! The whole room with yellow

*London and North Eastern Railway.

34

washbasin! 'Not bad for £2.10.0 for the week,' said Hall, who himself looked like a portable slum.

'No, it's not bad, but it's going bad,' said Mulgrew, pulling hairs out of the sink, then stubbing out his fag in the soapdish.

Our bedroom looks out on to a garden full of sheets drying in the rain. We went down for high tea. The dining room is full – 'Someone's bound to leave soon,' she says – I suppose standing in a hall can be entertaining. An old man was wheeled out by an older woman. 'Is it night or day?' he said.

'Day,' said his tormentor, 'day – I'll tell you when it's night, watch the light bulbs.'

'It's not a bad tea,' said the Wretch Hall as his teeth bounced off tripe and onions. 'It's typical North Country fare.'

That evening Mulgrew and I went 'dancing' at the Tower Ballroom to Sid Dean and his band with Reg Dixon at the giant organ. The entrance fee was three and six.

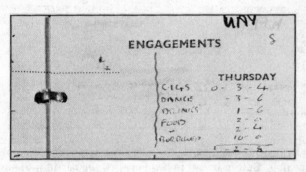

I found a pretty dark-haired girl with a rose in her hair; as we terpsichored around I spoke lines like: 'Nice band,' yes, nice band, 'Nice rose,' yes, nice rose. Reg Dixon was very good, 'Yes, very good, do you come here often? [my God, I actually said it]'. No, she didn't come here often – 'Oh, was this her first time?' Yes, this was her first time, 'Can't we go outside for a walk in the pouring rain?' I bought her a lemonade and a cake. I saw her home, her mother saw me off. I wondered what else she would saw off. 'What time you call this, get inside – as for you – get off.'

Mulgrew didn't get it either, 'She lived bloody miles away.'

# This New Act Has A Big Future

Introducing . . .
The Bill Hall Trio

Here is the "Sporting Review's" first 1947 tip for future variety stardom—the Bill Hall Trio! An entire Spike Jones aggregation in miniature, these zany musicians really can play their instruments. Comedy and hot, pulsating rhythm goes hand in hand. The trio is led by—and christened by—Bill Hall, on violin. A pre-war single act, combining hot violinistics with dry humour, he met abroad Johnny Mulgrew, bass player of such bands as Stephan Grappelly's and the Ambrose Octette, and Spike Milligan, guitarist extraordinary. They grouped themselves together and became the sensational variety act of the Central Mediterranean Force abroad.

By a coincidence, they were featured in the same shows, as another "Sporting Review" discovery now on the road to fame, Harry Secombe, who is one of their greatest "fans."

Currently playing the best night spots in Town, the Bill Hall Trio is a "natural" for our "new act" starved variety world.

In the exclusive pictures above, bass player Johnny Mulgrew is on the left, Spike Milligan strumming his guitar with Bill Hall listening in (centre), and on the right is "Maestro" Bill Hall himself, enthralling himself with his violin virtuosity (fiddling, to you!)

Hall had got it, we thought it was the old dear who pushed the wheelchair. Before I went to bed I crossed the corridor to have a bath, it took me half an hour to clean it, four people were stuck to the side. Not bad for £2.10.0 a week? I'd kill him.

Next morning we lugged our props to the theatre. Band call. Any mail at the stage door? No, says all-smiling stage door man. 'No,' he smiles happily, 'no mail for you.' We lay our worn band parts on the stage, the conductor asks what they are. As usual, I take the call; the trombone keeps missing an important cue – altercation.

'Look, chum.'

'Don't chum me – *son*.'

'Look, *sir* . . .'

'And don't take the piss.'

'Look, you're missing the cue.'

He stood up in the pit looking like Old Bill. 'Listen,' he said, 'I don't have to do this. I'm a fully paid-up joiner.'

'Well, go and join the army,' I said.

On the Monday night the dancers hadn't shown up so we were put on first, the worst place on the bill. 'I wouldn't give this spot to a bloody leopard,' moaned Hall. We did very well for a Monday, we actually got an encore. There was an acrobatic act on the bill – Avis and Zelda Marvi. We all try and chat them up, the Wretch Hall fails to attract them, we all give up, they're both married, so back to the digs, and Cold Collation. "Ot stuff goes off at 9.30,' she says. Where's Hazel? 'Oh, she's gone to the pictures, it's summat with Robert Do-nat, she loves Robert Do-nat.' So beddy-byes, Mulgrew has got a bottle of sweet sherry, we lie in bed talking.

'I'm surprised she likes Robert Donat – I thought she liked Robert Taylor and I was in with a chance.'

'You've drunk half the bloody bottle,' said Mulgrew, holding up the bottle.

'Not the bottle, just the sherry, I know a good shery when I see one,' I said.

'Well, you can't see any of it now,' he said.

'I'm what they call a savant,' I said.

'You're what I call a piss artist.'

Well, we all have our opinions. Smoking, we douse the light, I hear Mulgrew gurgling the last of the sherry. 'Half the bloody bottle,' he said in the dark. So I was in Blackpool, we'd been a success on stage, and I had had a good half hour's groping and half a bottle of sherry, never do things by halves they say, why not, I had. Next day, rain stopped, sun came out and the people – 'It's fun time on the golden mile,' says a loud-hailer from an open-top tram. Mulgrew goes to the Gypsy Madame La Zabilone, 'He's going on a long journey [Notting Hill Gate], he will meet a dark woman [Margo], he will come into money [week's wages].'

'She's amazing,' says Mulgrew, so I go in. She is amazing. I too will go to Notting Hill Gate, meet Margo . . . a variation! 'She will take all your wealth from you' – the rent!

'Why are we wasting our money like idiots?' I said.

'Because we are,' said Mulgrew.

What's wrong with people, they're *all* happy, chewing rock, candy floss, ice cream, funny hats, we even see the old man in the wheelchair. 'It's day – you hear me, you fool, it's day.' There was a Punch and Judy. I'd never seen one, there were never any in India nor at Monte Cassino, just when you needed one. Now none, or not many people, know what a swazzle is. Neither did I, it's what the man uses to make the sound of Punch. I found it hysterical, I went and asked him where I could get one, 'You can't – we make 'em.' So he gave me one that I still have and use sometimes to get my children away from that high-stepping fool, Michael Jackson.

Lots of girls sunbathing, we were admiring them from the prom, when an elderly gentleman said to us, 'It's a nice day – gentlemen.'

My God, he meant us. 'Yes sir, it is a nice day.'

'Colonel Stanley Rowlands – ex-Indian Army – how do you do?'

We shook hands.

'You both look very serious – been to see the Gypsy?' He spoke with a rich voice – with a hint of the con man, this was the nearest I was ever to get to Major Bloodnock. A girl in the skimpiest of bikinis, shuddering with hot young flesh drew the remark, 'Gad, what a trim ankle. You lads, you lads,' he looked at his watch; 'fancy a drink?'

Splendid.

'The Tudor Rose me local.' 'White wine for you and red for you, blow me!' It was the oldest trick. 'Forgotten me wallet,' he knew we knew he was lying; what a wealth of stories. 'Ex-Bengal Lancers,' he backed it up with old photographs (where's me old photographs?).

We told him we were ex-soldiers. 'I was at Cassino,' I said with a note of pride. Which one? Monte Carlo or Nice? He had been in one of the world's last cavalry charges in Waziristan – he showed an old yellow *Times of India* cutting. Did he live here? 'No!' horror in his voice. 'No, I live,' a note of emotion in his voice, 'I live in . . . Bournemouth.' I immediately applauded and nudged Mulgrew to do the same. 'I'm glad you appreciate it.' We walked and talked and 'lent' him a pound, 'Never trust the Gypsy,' he said and was lost in the candy floss.

The week went by, on the Saturday between shows the Colonel visited us, had we a spare ticket for tonight's? No, not on a Saturday, but he could watch from the wings. He was smelling of brandy, when our act started he shouted from the wings, 'Bravo! Bravo! These boys were at Cassino.' The stage manager tried to remonstrate, but failed, his remarks from the wings brought roars of laughter – finally, we dragged him on to take a final bow, which he took in his stride. I kept in touch with him till he died in 1958 – he left behind a mountain of debts, 'never believe in the Gypsy'. We caught the night milk train back to London, which got us in at dawn. At Euston a sleepy taxi driver took our fare, he told us an incredible story, during the terrible fog of 1935 – he was on the verge of trying to get home when a drunken Irishman appeared and said, 'Drive me to King's Cross.' The driver said the fog was, like him, too thick. 'It's life and death I catch the 9.55 to Glasgow.' They argued, finally the Irishman produced a torch, 'Look I'll walk in front till the fog gets thinner – then you can drive me there.' So the wretch staggering in front, finally reaching King's Cross. 'Right,' he said, 'how much will dat be?'

## 13 LINDEN GARDENS

Arriving at 13 Linden Gardens as the milkman was delivering. 'You dirty stop-outs,' he said, 'you won't half get it when you get in.' What was he talking about, we'd spent all week trying to get it. I flopped on my bed and tried to sleep, no, boiled a kettle for tea, flopped on the bed, couldn't sleep. It was Sunday morning, silent – that was 1947, you don't get that any more. I was thinking, I was *always* bloody thinking, what was going to happen, the Bill Hall Trio were never going to be more than what we were now unless we got in a big Show, or Film or Something – here I was, young, full of ideas and energy and all hidden behind a garish make-up and a guitar, still £25 a week, that's more than I ever dreamed of, so I saved it in Notting Hill Gate Post Office, it would all add up, right now it added up to £18, no, I couldn't ever marry Toni on that, not for long anyhow. A letter from her has arrived.

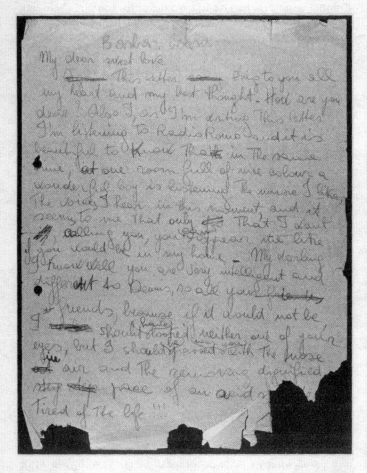

Inside me I suppose I was a mess of confusions – I loved Toni, but being away a gap was appearing. I was still heartbroken over Lily Dunford but was recovering. For a long, long time I believed that I would return to Toni, and then, well, something would happen, for a start, we could do it. I still remembered how, only the equipment needed a little refurbishing using 3-in-One Oil. Ah Capri! Capri! Dreams, dreams. I had stopped playing my trumpet mainly because I'd sold it to buy a new guitar for the act, the old guitar belonged to the CPA, but I still longed to play the trumpet, there is the greatest feeling of euphoria and innocence in playing an improvised chorus based on a beautiful tune.

These days I was hearing new music, Bop, and I found it wonderful, Charlie Parker, Clifford Brown and the Cool School, Gerry Mulligan, Stan Getz, Chet Baker; whereas I was a good swing trumpeter, I was being left behind, behind a guitar with no Toni, no Lily. Wait! There was still Blanche! Arrogh!

We have a week out. 'Sorry boys,' said Leslie MacDonnell, 'but after this there's several solid bookings. Moss Empires like your work, especially Cissy Williams*, you'll never be a top of the bill, you must know that, but you'll work steady.' Thanks, he's just spelled out the future and I don't like it, there must be something else, like relief massage. Meantime, I write new visual gags for the act; for the 'Flight of the Bumblebee', we manage to affix a dummy bee on a very fine hair-thin sprung wire, it is fixed behind the scroll of the Double Bass, it can be released at a flick of a small catch, the effect is in the climax of the number, the bee suddenly appears above Mulgrew's head, it appears to be attacking him, finally catching in his hat as the number ends. Another effect was to sprinkle my head with talcum powder, then sneeze showering me in a white cloud. 'Dandruff!' I scream. It means washing my hair every night. *Ars gratia artis*. The best one was the finale. Special trousers were made for Bill Hall, to pull them off Mulgrew had a hook attached to his bow – one quick pull and Hall's trousers were off, in falling Hall grabbed my trousers, they came off, as Mulgrew walked off carrying his bass his trousers fell down, it was all the stuff of variety and we enjoyed it. So, during this week off, I contacted Reg Bennett, an old army chum. I'd heard that a very avant-garde band, wild in fact, were doing a

*Booking Manager for Moss Empires.

gig in Charing Cross Road. The band was Tony Samson, only aficionados attended, the band had Stan Kenton in mind. Reg and I sat drinking scrumpy – Reg recalls the occasion:

'It must have been some time in 1947 (possibly May). I arrived home from the Queen's Ice Club where I had spent a great deal of time; I was given a message by my mother to say that a Spike Milligan had phoned – she described him as "an excitable young man" – and would I phone back as he had left his number. Unbelievable!! I immediately returned his call, not realising he was living right on my doorstep. When asked where he was living, he replied that he had Neville Heath's old room at a bedsitter establishment in Linden Gardens, Notting Hill, and would I pop round to see him! It did not take me long to make that journey!

When I eventually arrived and was shown up to his bedroom I thought I had arrived on some film set for a Western. There was Spike standing wearing a bright red checked shirt, green corduroy trousers, brown boots, a cowboy hat! (Sadly, no gun holster, or spurs!) He told me we were going to a farewell party given for a band going on tour at a club in Charing Cross Road, so off we went. One must realise that sort of attire in early 1947 was really something! When we got on the bus I could see the horrified expression of the conductor wondering whether a horse was going to get on the bus too!

I can well remember the band playing non-stop at this "jam session" until 4 a.m. During that time we were drinking "rough" cider. We left at 4 a.m. As we walked down Charing Cross Road Spike asked whether I had a "fag" on me. Upon giving him a reply in the negative he suddenly bent down and picked up a stub end off the pavement and asked me if I had a match. This time I was able to oblige!! We finished up having breakfast at Coventry Street. Spike had the poor waitress not knowing whether she was "punched, bored or countersigned"!

After that episode, trying hard to make a living, we sadly lost contact with one another and several years passed by. I had left London to take up hotel management in south-west England. It was some time in the Sixties when I had left hotel management and taken up another position travelling the entire country that I found myself once again "connecting" with Spike, which has *lasted to this present time. Every big city I visited, Spike seemed to be there with his one man show. Many times we met up in various cities, one in particular I will always remember, which took place in a theatre in Leeds where he was performing. After the show Spike suggested that we might have a short musical intermission ourselves, I on the piano, Spike on the drums. Neither of us realised that the party he was with had already left a message saying that they had all gone to a restaurant called "The Get Stuffed" but had left no instructions how to get there! Spike had a Mini at that time and in all my driving experience never have I been down so many one way systems!! I thought I had been scared stiff at Cassino!! How we ever found the restaurant I just don't know to this day. Well, many other instances have taken place, far too many to record, all of which have been a laugh a minute. I finish by saying that it has been a privilege knowing him and he is still featuring in my old age — never a dull moment!!"*

I slept that day till nightfall. Another party! the disc jockey from Midnight in Munich, Muffit Moffat, was being fêted at a party in Soho. It was full of 'in' people and me, even though I wasn't an in person I went in. I didn't know anybody, I knew Mrs Hicks, but she wasn't there. Then, as I sipped a Spanish white wine called 'Olé Corrida!' or It's Corrosion, a beautiful Jewess, long curly auburn hair, large blue eyes, and all other parts enlarged – 'And who are you?' she said. She nudged her friend and aside, 'Look what I've found.'

I said, 'I am an out-of-season Martian, grateful to any bodies that come this way.' She wore all black.

'Well, don't look any further,' she said, '*this* is your body. No! Don't tell me your name, we can become the world's first anonymous lovers, this is my friend, Leila.'

Hello Leila and clear off.

So the evening ran on, Kenny Baker and a trio are blowing the night away, we gather round the stand, I ask a tall Caesar Romero-type what he plays, he said 'cards' – very, very good attempt at being a prat, his name was Tito Burns. He will have forgotten the occasion, if he reads this he'll try and forget it again.

43

No, Helen cannot come home with me, so I'll go home with her.

'No, no! My parents think I'm respectable, they're Jewish.'

'Don't worry,' I said, 'I've been circumcised. Look.'

'No, not here, privately.' A week later.

Helen is coming to 13 Linden Gardens! By getting an overdraft, I laid on smoked salmon sandwiches, it flattened them, now a bottle of Chianti, a few empty wine bottles with candles. Mulgrew bursts in, had he never heard of one of the finest social graces known to man, the door knock? 'She just phoned, she can't come tonight.' Blast, and me wearing my blue silk, red-spotted dressing gown purchased in Naples.

It broke my heart having to share it all with this hungry Scottish swine, who kept muttering 'poor wee Helen' as he ate my salmon and guzzled my wine by candlelight. 'Saving on the old electricity,' he said.

I suppose murder is sometimes justifiable. Never mind eh? Helen would try again, her hot Judaic blood would seek me out, I still had three half candles. 'Well, thanks for the treat,' said Mulgrew, preparing to depart.

'Any time you're passing.' I patted his shoulder. 'Any time you're passing, keep passing, don't stop, just keep going till you reach Beachy Head – just keep going!'

Yes! Helen phoned, sorry about last time, can she see me soon? So soon then; well, it was a week of going to the pictures, and about two dozen candles, but, 'No Spike, this can't go on.' The trouble is I'm a Yock, her mother wants her to go with David (David, David, aren't there any bloody Jews called Dick? or Tom!).

She's a bit of a drama queen now, 'I shouldn't go on seeing you,' she sobbed as she stripped off.

'Well, don't worry, I'm seeing plenty of you.'

'If only you were Jewish.'

I nearly am. 'Did you tell your mother I was circumcised?'

'Oh no,' she sobbed, 'not that.'

What did she mean? Helen just disappeared, why? The world is full of people who have stopped seeing each other. There's a phone call from Bill Hall, Wretch and violin player. He's at Highbury police station, drunk.

Me in the dressing room at the Chelsea Empire, London, wearing the dressing gown bought in Italy

STATION SERGEANT: We have been given your name and number by Mr William Hall, who is under arrest charged with drunk and disorderly conduct. He is in a cell playing a violin, and wants you to come and stand bail.

ME: How much is it?

STATION SERGEANT: It's £25, sir.

ME: Look, Officer, I have it in a bank but at this late hour, would you take a cheque?

STATION SERGEANT: If you have means of identification, sir.

ME: I'll be about an hour and a half. (Oh, those happy days before cheque cards.)

So, at 11.00 of the night, I start the complex trip to Highbury Clink, by every means except rickshaw. As I enter the night, the sound of Bill's violin fills the place. It's the Max Bruch Violin Concerto, and it is magnificent. 'This place isn't going to be the same without him,' said the Sergeant as I paid the money.

Now the monumental job of getting a stinking, staggering Bill Hall to 6 Legard Road. 'Ish not far,' said Hall, 'I know a schort cut.' Two hours with violin solos and farting must be a record for what was half a mile. He hasn't got a key so while the lunatic saws away at *Molto Perpetuo*, I knock and knock; there's no one at home, I look in his eyes and there's no one there either. It's gone midnight, it starts to rain, I leave him fiddling and farting on the porch, I watch him slowly slump to the floor. Good night, sweet prince.

I'm still smoking, I note the contemporary prices in my diary of the time.

In those days one shilling and eightpence for ten, or three shillings and fourpence for twenty; that was pretty cheap for lung cancer in those days, mind you, Mulgrew smoked his and *my* lung cancer (alas in 1970 it caught up with him). Lily Dunford had come back into my life, I had heard with glee (she wrote to me) her marriage had folded; how *do* you fold a marriage? 'You take that end dear . . .' So, I decided not to

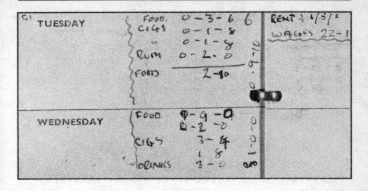

strangle her till her eyes popped, no, I'd do something else that would make her and my eyes pop, so I relit the candles, thirteen candles later she had gone again, though that unforgettable magic of a first love never ever faded. The Wretch Bill Hall phones, 'Is there any news of work?' I say no, is there any news of the £25? He can't remember, it was all a blank to him – good, here's a blank for him, send a cheque, just sign it. How did I get mixed up with these people!!!!

## GLASGOW

Och Aye Och Nose Och Teeth – Glasgow, grotty Glasgow, which someone said belonged to Harry Lauder.

'You'll be playing the Pavilion, Spike,' said Leslie MacDonnell on the phone.

Me playing the Pavilion, me who had no idea how to play one, 'Are you sure it's not the bagpipes, Leslie?'

'Absolutely sure,' said MacDonnell, who was used to me by now. 'It's a good spot: you close the first half.'

'The same money, Leslie?'

'Yes, Spike, Pounds, Shillings and Pence.' He was stealing my jokes! 'Try and speak with a Scots accent – it's safer,' he said.

Mulgrew, the Scottish miser, is stricken. 'Glasgow, man, think of the train fare, man, the train.'

I think of the train fare, it's 17/6d return. Okay, does he want to walk?

Hall is pleased. 'I've never bin to Glassgoad, in Scotland isn't it?'

He was spot on; this was Thursday 8 May, I went shopping for new guitar string and plectrums.

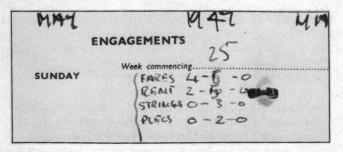

I remember that Sunday train from King's Cross to Glasgow Central, third class, 17/6d, today that's the price of a British Rail sandwich. The carriages are crowded with Scotsmen trying to get to work on Monday or escape paternity cases, they all looked a shattered Tatterdemalion Army, *why* do they come to London? Didn't they learn from Culloden? They slept and farted all the way to Bonnie Scotland; I tell you, there was more smoke, shit and steam in the carriage than in the engine. One drunk kept waking up and saying, 'Where are we, Jimmy?' I called out many stations – among them Falmouth, Bexhill, Rome; he always said, 'Thanks, Jimmy', before dropping off.

My eyes and throat were sore with smoke, Mulgrew loved it, when he wasn't smoking he sucked up what was in the carriage. I went from the crowded compartment to the crowded corridor. 'All tickets please,' the poor collector struggled through the congealed bodies, later a scream came from the next carriage as he clipped someone's finger. 'I hope it's an English finger,' said Mulgrew, with an evil tartan grin.

A visit to the toilet sent me reeling out again, it looked like a Picasso painting in shit, it was everywhere except in the hole. It was dark as the train ironed itself into Glasgow Central, the picture of doors hurling open! This wasn't passengers disembarking, these were victims escaping, it was like Armageddon with the departed rising from the tomb. As usual, the Wretch Hall is missing. Mulgrew and I take our luggage from the guard's van, that is, the Double Bass, my guitar and props basket and on to an antique iron trolley that must have carried claymores for Bannockburn.

'Here-here,' a tartan voice was saying, 'where you going with that, that's mine.' It's a diminutive porter, 'Aye, that's mine.'

'Good,' I said. 'Congratulations to owning up, it must have taken some courage. As you've owned up to the trolley, it's only fair that we should own up to the luggage.'

All this was to a mind that only reacted to Rangers 2 Celtic 0.

'Is it a taxi yer after, there'll be a queue, I'll have tae charge you waiting time.'

Everyone was waiting for Glasgow's three taxis, we paid off the would-be Carnegie. The taxi. '118 Sauchiehall Street,' I said.

'Can you no find anywhere better?' said the scarlet-haired cabbie.

'From what I hear,' said Mulgrew, 'it's the Taj Mahal of Scotland.'

'Oh Christ,' moaned the driver.

No. 118 was Mrs O'Brien's apartments or rather coming apart-ments. We traipsed up a concrete staircase confined by iron railings.

'Ooh – yer early! The others have nae left, can you wait in the hall?' Oh yes, we love that. These apartments are handsome, stone-built, in 1850. We sit and smoke and sit, sometimes we smit and sloke (eh)? We are allocated one bedroom with three single beds. Mrs O'Brien is eighteen stone, her daughter is sixteen stone, her husband is nine stone, six of it is his head and ears.

'You've missed supper,' says eighteen-stone.

We wander a rainy Glasgow and find fish and chips, consumed on the walk, a style highly favoured by people who 'You've missed your supper', which seemed to be half Glasgow with Rangers 3 Celtic 0.

'Oh, fuck this,' said the Wretch Hall, 'let's find a boozer.'

'I'm one,' I said.

We find one named The 45; well, there was more than that inside. When we opened the pub door, twenty fell out. When in Scotland. We all ordered a Scotch, it would be risk of life and limb to order anything else, Hall is nearly killed. 'Can I have some ice?' he said.

At the request, the barman grabbed the edge of the bar to support himself, his eyes rolled like eyes rolling, 'Ice?' he said in a hoarse whisper. 'Ice – in thait?' He pointed to Hall's whisky, 'Mon, did you noo hear what it did tae the *Titanic*?'

Hall insisted, 'I've always 'ad ice in me whisky, it's never sunk me, ha-ha-ha-ha-ha-ha.'

The barman dropped the ice in the whisky, the whole pub went silent at the splash and a low Scottish moan filled the pub. The evening didn't end there, outside we were accosted by a small man in a long ex-army overcoat, 'Here-here-Jamie,' he tugged my sleeve, 'here Jamie –'

I told him he was mistaken, I wasn't Jamie, but I was here.

'Ha yew gat saxpence fer the dancer?'

The dancer? What dancer?

From the back of his overcoat, he took out the top of a Lipton's tea chest, laying it on the pavement he did a convulsed highland fling. 'There,' he said finally, '*that* fucking dancer.'

He was worth it, so I gave him a sixpence.

'Yew mean bastard,' he said. 'As for yew two,' here Hall and Mulgrew got a raspberry and an up yours.

'Look here, Jock,' said soused Mulgrew, 'that's no way for a Glaswegian to behave!'

'Oh? What do you know aboot Glaswegians?' said that fucking dancer.

'Well, I too am a Glaswegian,' said Mulgrew.

'Well, fuck you Jamie – I'm frae Arbroath.'

'Ah well,' said Mulgrew, 'fuck you too.'

We had to separate them, but only after half an hour's intermittent fighting, sometimes Hall and I would hit That Fucking Dancer to help out. 'Rangers 2 Celtic 0,' we shouted.

The fun hasn't started yet, we let ourselves into 118 Sauchie-hall Street by the time-honoured, burglar-proof key on a string through the letter box, we are greeted by an approaching scream, down the passage comes eighteen-stone in hair curlers and a nightdress – following her in the nude and socks is nine-stone husband brandishing an axe. They disappear into a maze of passages reappearing here, disappearing there. We rush to the daughter's bedroom. 'Your father's killing your mother,' we warned.

She smiled. 'Oh, don't bother, he never catches her!'

On our landing we find Jamaican trumpeter Roy Wilkins in his underpants. 'Oh yes, he am nebber catching her, an I bin here de week.' He's off downstairs now, 'To fuck de dorter for de rent.'

And so to bed which left a lot to be desired, like springs; we all slept with our arses touching the floor. All three awake next morning like Le Trio Quasimodo.

'Breakfast is up the ladder on the "next flae," said sixteen-stone and we'd like the rent in advance, no we'd rather pay. Wasn't anyone using money any more?

'Nae more hot water.'

'This is like being back in the bloody army,' said the Wretch Hall, shaving in agony. I don't believe it! The way to our breakfast is up a ladder to a trap door with ill-written words, 'Knock and Wate'. We did so. Above was scraping noises. What was ensuing was thus; directly above the trap door was breakfast table – upon our knocking those at table stopped eating, withdrew their chairs, then moved the breakfast table off the trap door allowing us access to the room. It was an attic room, one side you had to eat crouched. The wall on our side was covered with a floral curtain – with reason, as eighteen-stone placed egg and bacon before me, the wall behind me seemed to be breathing, then grunting; you see, dear reader, behind the curtain in recesses on the wall slept Mr O'Brien and two further lodgers who were nightshift workers. O'Brien wasn't on nightshift, he only got up to get pissed and chase eighteen-stone with an axe before falling into a drunken sleep, from which he was now recovering behind me.

'Molly, whaire ma tea, woman?' he demanded.

'Yer tea's in the pot you lazy bugger, God forgive me,' she replied, crossing herself. 'Get up, it's time fer Holy Mass.'

'Bring ma tea, woman, do you no' hear?' His head is suddenly poked through a divide in the curtain colliding with the back of Hall's neck. 'Who's that?' said O'Brien.

'Look what you've done to the gentleman,' said eighteen-stone.

He looked at what he had done, egg yolk all over the Wretch Bill Hall. 'Awful sorry, laddie,' said the emerged head. Apart from that it was a good breakfast, with us moving the table on and off the trap as and when.

Band call. We are on the bill with an up-and-coming singer, Donald Peers – to me, after hearing Sinatra and Crosby and Vic Damone, this man sounds dreadful, he went on to fame and total obscurity. So much for the sincerity of the public. At the band call he sings 'By A Babbling Brook' and I personally wished he was; he was a nice enough bloke, he just shouldn't sing. There's the Ganjiou Brothers and Juanita, top of the bill, two men with muscles and a girl, an Australian juggler Doig Dowell, these were variety days stretching back to Wilton's Music Hall in 1840, we didn't know within ten years it would be dead. On the first night Donald Peers got, 'Awa hame, yew Sassenach bastard.'

'But I'm not English, I'm Welsh.' The stage manager told him to say so in his act, so he started, 'I'd like to sing songs from my Welsh homeland', which he did and they said, 'Awa hame, ye Welsh bastard.'

We in our rags and lunacy were well received, as we looked like most Glaswegians in the street. 'You poor wee lads,' was a cry from a lady in the gallery. In the week these middle-aged ladies asked to see us. 'We've brought you some claes,' they said and laid two huge brown paper parcels on the flae. 'We saw ye on stage, I'm sure you'll do better wi' these claes.'

We said, 'thank you', I mean what else? They were ladies from the Stage Welfare Services (now defunct); the parcels contained three very good suits, Mulgrew's and mine fit perfectly, the Wretch Hall's was a trifle short. Of course, we had no intention of wearing them, selling them yes. After the Friday show, the two welfare ladies reappeared but gone were the kindly smiles. 'Ye did nae wear the claes,' they said, 'ye must return them.' What a grim silent twenty minutes, save the rustle of brown paper as we rewrapped the suits, with a 'Ye are a disgrace tae the profession going on stage like that.' They were gone, they left the room to our earnest apologies but as the door slammed on them Wretch Hall said, 'Fuck 'em.'

'Off you go then, Bill,' I said.

After the night's show, which came down at 10.45, we would cross the road to hear the band at Green's Playhouse and eye the local talent. The bands were usually so good I just wanted to listen – among them Bill MacGuffy, George Chisholm, Tommy McQuater, Joey Richmond, it was great music, alas it all went unrecorded; it was me, still looking for 1939, me and Lily Dunford at Ladywell Baths in the quickstep contest to the tune of 'I Double Dare You' and Lily's voice in my ear, singing, 'fall in love with you I double dare you.' That's what I was listening for now. 1939 was eight years away and never coming back, but there was Toni – somehow I'd make it back to Toni – and Capri.

As they say in Scotland, there's nothing wrong with Glasgow, there's always the streets with Rangers 2 Celtic 0. We'd try amusement arcades; do you know, dear reader, I actually *believed* that I could manoeuvre the claw crane to pick up those sweets, and was so depressed when I didn't. I'd like to meet the bastard who invented it, I'd have his balls in there with the crane picking 'em up and droppin' 'em all day. We tried mini-golf (6d) and bet in halfpennies, being VAF* members we get into the movies cheap. Scots audiences are great at sending up movies. It was an hilarious afternoon watching Anna Neagle and Michael Wilding in *Spring In Park Lane*. 'Go on give it her, Jamie,' were among the constant cries and, 'She's nae boobies.' 'It's the size of yer pinkie.' And Michael Wilding's wig, it was hypnotic, not once in the movie did he make a move that might threaten it, in fact, the script was written round his wig so as not to disturb it. That mantle now rests with Terry Wogan. What the Wretch Hall did of a day we never knew, he would turn up seconds before we were due on stage, some say he would go in parks and put down a hat and play for money. He denied this, he also denied it when I said

*Variety Artists' Federation.

he had a huge estate to which he retired daily to stalk deer, hurl cabers and shoot lobsters. 'That's a lie,' he said. 'I walk the streets looking like the reincarnation of Paganini hoping someone might recognise me and money.'

On the Saturday night the act went very well. We got three encores, but still the same money. 'You've got an awful guid act there,' said a stagehand. 'You'll go far.' We did, back to London.

The crits from the *Glasgow Herald* had been good, so we decided to put it as an ad in *The Stage*, which set us back £4; it set Mulgrew back ten years. Rangers 2 Celtic 0.

---

## Bill Hall Trio wow Glasgow audiences

Wearing rags but playing first-class music with clowning and jokes, this trio of recently demobbed boys have a promising future. Also on the bill was a Welsh Crooner Donald Peers.

---

Here, for all to see, what my week's finances were in Glasgow.

```
GLASGOW PAVILION,
   MONDAY          ORCHESTRATION.  0 - 12 - 0
                   GIGS            0 - 3 - 8
                   PLECS           0 - 2 - 9
                   STRING          0 - 2 - 0
                   TEA             0 - 0 - 9
                   DRINKS          0 - 1 - 6
                   GOLF            0   0   6
```

We return to London for another week's rest but no! We've been booked across the Irish Sea, one step nearer New York! And Hollywood!

## DUBLIN

'Boys, there's a week for you at the Royal Theatre, Dublin.' We stand dutifully in front of Leslie MacDonnell's desk.

'Well, that's great,' I said. 'I'm Irish, I've never been to Ireland.'

'Neither have half the Irish,' said Hall, 'they're all over here.'

'It's a very nice theatre, cinema and stage show,' says MacDonnell.

'Oh, we could see the picture free,' says Mulgrew, his wallet full of strips of the *Daily Mirror*.

Flying? You bloody mad, Hall? Flying would cost us our wages, no Air Linctus for us, it was the grim train to Fishguard. The night ferry to Dún Laoghaire. A crappy black ship called the *Blessed Virgin* or one of those. It started to rain and us deck passengers. 'Ah, look at the seagulls,' said some mindless twit, so they looked at them, and the seagulls looked at them – bird and man eye-to-eye!!! World-shaking. The cranes are loading lumps of timber on the rear deck – in no special order, it's like a wooden Hampton Court maze – I lost the Wretch Hall and the Tartan one.

The ship sets off. What gloom! Who in their right mind would go to Fishguard – an above ground cemetery – the only thing there is to leave it. A mournful low hoot from the black smokestack. 'Look at der seagulls,' say the voices. We shelter under an overhang. The night is chill. Daumier would have loved this, grim, grey, black, unspeaking lone passengers.

'If you ever go across the sea to Ireland you really must be off your fucking head,' so I sang in a soft voice to Mulgrew.

'Hall's gone for a walk,' said Mulgrew, 'over the side, I think.'

Dear reader, all night standing or squatting, even trying to kip on the timber, I borrowed the top hat prop to keep off the rain, looking like a travelling undertaker. When the Wretch Hall returned he looked cheerful, he'd had a sleep in the karzi.

The mildew dawn haunted us into Dún Laoghaire. 'Dún Layoghairy, that's the proper pronunciation, none of that Gaelic crap,' said Hall. We dock and seek transport.

'Dese are cheaper dorn taxis,' said the driver of a horse-drawn Victoria – so we pile in. 'And,' says the driver, ''tis more romantic.' Yes, the rain poured romantically down.

'The Royalty is it?' he said.

'It is,' I said.

'Oh, 'tis a powerful good theatre – but I tink dere pulling it down.'

'Can you get us there before then?' we cry. It is a fine neo-Grecian fronted affair – we all go through the stage door.

The doorman, Mr Fillan – ah – 'Der Halls of Trio – your dressing room No. 2 – next to der girls. Now dere's a list of digs. Der best for you would be Mrs Morris, 11 Belvedere Road.'

The back stage is as big as the Palladium, fifteen girls are rehearsing to a good orchestra. We phone Mrs Morris. 'Oh yez,' she sez – 'one single and two doubles. Tirty-tree shilling the tree.' Okay – we'll be round for supper at four. Mr George Puttock, the stage manager, in a green velvet jacket and gypsy shirt, he's terribly show business darling – 'Now darling, your act, it's comedy, is it not, is it *not*?'

Yes, it *is* – darling! We ogle the girls – all Catholics, virgins and draped with holy medals – then we practise with the band. They've made an incredible scene for us, it's the banks of the Shannon with a wobbly lamp post. So off to Mrs Morris in a run-down Georgian square, with kids everywhere. 'You know,' said Hall, 'in between Mass they must fuck like rabbits.'

'Come in,' she says. We go down to a basement with a hundred kids.

Our room is quite big if you breathe out. Three beds, washstand, a cupboard, a gas lamp, a smell of cats' piss – and a skylight to the street. Her little daughter, Maureen, is carrying a kitten by the 'troat'; oh, she won't hurt it with her soft little hands, but the kitten's eyes are popping! 'Me husband, the swine, left me with six kids, so I makes do wid der lodgers.'

'Hey mister, is you me new father?' said one of the children; 'we had a new one last week.'

'Shh! you,' said Mrs Morris, 'or I'll kill ye.' Home sweet home.

So Mrs Morris must put it about, and it would be the Wretch Hall who found out. It was he who was getting tea in bed and laundry done – this was all an experience of old Dublin before the Dublin Council got to work on its destruction. I'd sit on the steps of an evening listening to the children's tales, 'And me father when he was on his way home from the pub – he seed a ball of fire and he knew it was the devil and he hid in the pub till the devil was gone.' The innocence of those children in 1947, I'll never forget, there was no swearing or fighting. Often they would ask me for a 'Ponney, mister'.

I visited all of Dublin. The Museum. The Art Gallery – a matinée at the Abbey – *Book of Kells* – Wilde's House, 12 Westlan Row. Seamus the taxi-driver, 'De yer want to see der home he was born in or the one dey *say* he was born in – 33 Synge Street – some say No. 3.' The talk, I had never heard the like since my father, they *all* talked like him – and the drama. On the Wednesday I asked a taxi to take me to the hurley match. He grabbed my shoulder, 'Oh, the hurley match it is. 'Twill be Blackrock dat'll win you see,' then released me.

All the way there he gave a commentary as the game should go, but by the time his clapped-out taxi got there it was nearly over. Best of all were the Georgian squares – Merrion – it was Greek perfect. We went for a walk along the Grand Canal, we'd had a few jars at the Sheeloone, then Bill Hall did a magnificent thing, he fell in; 'My violin! My violin! Save my violin!' Alas, we saved him as well, we took him for a brandy at Murphys, and he there enthralled us all with Irish jigs. 'Can you come tonight, mister?' said Murphy. We'd see.

Walked to Kilmainham Jail; Mr Brennan the caretaker told me a tale: 'Dominic Behan was a prisoner in Mountjoy. Brendan awaited the release of his brother Dominic. When he appears Brendan said, "Have you any money?" "No," says Dominic. "But," said Brendan, "you get paid as a prisoner." "No!" says Dominic. "I was a political prisoner – so I didn't have to work." "Oh," says Brendan, "so for the likes of your principles we've all got to fuckin' starve!".' We drank everywhere. O'Briens, Donigans, Flanagans, Black Bull; it's a wonder we ever got to the theatre. Oh! the star of the show was Cavan O'Connor, 'I'm Only A Strolling Vagabond', getting on a bit but part of the colour of Dublin – it was a city like it was 1909, with beautiful tinker mothers and children begging. I was walking down Grafton Street and heard the most wonderful lady harpist; she whispered to me, 'I'm here every Thursday.' I could have stayed for ever, everyone talked, everyone had a story, like when the last Prince of Wales stayed at the Gresham – he asked the porter to leave him a late supper in his rooms, 'Just a prawn salad and a bottle of hock'; well, the supper arrived but to the Prince's surprise there were two suppers and four bottles of wine. 'I'm sorry, sorr, I tort der was two of youse.' The Prince of Wales said, how would you like to join me at supper, and so he did, during which the porter drank a bottle of wine. When it was over the porter removed the supper, saying, 'You know, I'ha'tort a man wid your money could have afforded a better bloody dinner dan dis.'

We saw where the 1916 Rebels were shot and their graves at Arbour Hill. I suddenly felt tears well up. The act was a howling success. It was all over in a week and I was back in Linden Gardens. I had been to my own country for the first time and had the pleasure of calling wretched Hall and Mulgrew bloody foreigners!

## GOLDERS GREEN

'Ah, a Rose Red city half as Golders Green. Indeed, it needs passports – we're playing Golders Green Hippodrome.'

Mulgrew comes hotfoot from the phone – 'Who's top of the bill – Len Camber, Geraldo's recently discarded South African vocalist.'

'Well, it's a *London* date,' I stressed; 'no bloody train travel and home early.' It was a good date, good audiences, and all the agents went there, even Dick Barton.

Monday band call, very good. Good dressing rooms, the doors all silver and gilt. We're No. 3, a move up the ladder, No. 2 is Cherry Weiner, a lesbian jazz organist. Len Camber is very nice and as personable as a flour sack; he's got a phoney mid-Atlantic accent, about Rockall. 'He's Jewish, I tell you,' says Bill.

'He's not, he's South African.'

'Yes, South African Jewish.'

To settle it they bet five shillings. 'Here, are you Jewish?' says Bill.

'No,' says Len.

'I don't believe you,' says the Scot, stewing over the five shillings.

'All right,' says Len Camber. Geraldo's vocalist outs with his willy, which has a six-inch foreskin.

'Cor,' said Mulgrew.

'That's what they call Apartheid,' I said.

During the week Secombe and I hang around Alan's Club and go to news theatres to see cartoons – we see the newsreel of a shark, its mouth held open. When it's dropped it looks like an idiot. We went into hysterics and stayed to see it round a second and third time.

We are the hit of the bill – Harry Foster and Leslie MacDonnell see us second house Saturday. 'We're very pleased, boys, we're managing to up your money to £100 a week.'

I phone my father at work and tell him. 'I'll come home right away,' he said.

I rode all the way to 3 Leathwell Road and told my mother, I stayed the night and slept in the room where the trains shunted. I still let jazz music run through my head – always had, always will. I turned on my little green Bakelite radio, it's Billy Ternant and his tinkly-poo band – no jazz, but what the hell, this is Deptford not Birdland.

> Dizzy live at 3 Leathwell! Wow! Sing Dizzy, blues.
> Hey there Dizzy playing at Leathwell Road!
> Hey there Dizzy playing at Leathwell Road!
> You play that music
> A knighthood will be bestowed . . . oh, yeah!

I was listening to radio. *Men At Work* was one that grabbed me. It's forgotten now, but it was what put *The Goon Show* on the road. *Men At Work** were ignoring logic and for me it worked, but nobody seemed to notice it. I laughed at Derek Roy, a bit at ITMA, but things that really made me laugh were Groucho Marx, W.C. Fields, Beachcomber, Sid Fields – so there! I was writing things on paper with no object in mind; I'd

*Written by Max Kester.

joke a lot with Secombe, but with variety work, neither Bentine nor Sellers got together much – it was to come. Only when we had a week out or a weak heart (eh?) did we meet. I met Sellers at Hackney Empire where Secombe was appearing. Bentine introduced him to me in the bar; he was 'spraunced' up, felt trilby, gloves, Dick Barton collar-up mackintosh. As usual, Mike did most of the talking. That's all I remember of the occasion.

Inside me I had no idea where I wanted to go. I'd stopped playing trumpet. Big bands were going out, *radio* was the thing, how could I get in? I had no confidence as a solo performer, and never had until Oblomov, so I was a maelstrom of complexities. I certainly admired Secombe, Sellers and Bentine – I'd hang around them.

A week out! The first week we're promised £100, we're out – don't worry boys, it's Bolton next week. Bolton – the Angel of Mons, Manna from Heaven. Bolton, the Promised Land. Bolton, an anagram of Notlob! Yes, Notlob, there was lots to do in Notlob – the pubs, the pictures – wait, it's been cancelled. Sod. Everything comes to he who waits, even unemployment.

## ALLY PALLY

Incredible! We've been booked for the modern wonder, Television! At Alexandra Palace. So important is the occasion that Leslie MacDonnell has summoned us to his office to tell. 'Yes, boys, a Mr Richard Afton of the BBC.' The BBC, the words send the blood swirling in the swonnicles, the BBC. 'Yes,' says MacDonnell, 'the BBC;' he stands to say the majestic words, 'BBC - Tele-e-vision.' He could be Lincoln before Gettysburg, Antony at Actium! TELEVISION!

Hall the Wretch explained the wonder. 'Television!' he said ecstatically. 'It will bring us into people's homes.'

Our parents had already warned me they would never have him in their homes, 'We don't want to catch it.'

The show was called *Rooftop Rendezvous*, the producer Richard Afton, like BBC producers, had delusions of grandeur; he had his name changed by deed poll to Lord Afton, oh yes, dear reader, there are plenty like him in the BBC, those who want weddings at dawn on Navaho Indian mountain tops. The fee! Leslie, the fee! 'Well boys, it's £150 before commission.'

My God, that would leave us each with £40.

'I'll nae ha to cut strips of *Daily Mirror* any mair,' said Mulgrew. At 13 Linden Gardens we informed flatmates Reg O'List, the singer from the Windmill, his girlfriend Jennifer with a forty-two inch bust (the unflattest flatmate).

'Let's have a party,' I said.

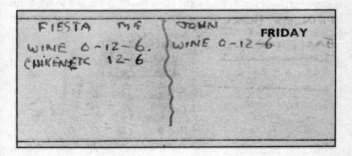

A fiesta, okay. That night we sat on beds eating chicken and drinking Chianti – memories of Italy were still strong. Reg O'List entertained with his guitar. He, Gracie Fields and Donald Peers should never have sung, but, there is Reg now, 'Over the plains, now I hear the Russian horsemen riddinggg.' Please God they're coming for him. I got very squiffy and sang Boo-Boo – 'Body And Soul'.

I woke up next morning with Blanche and her kipper at the door, 'God, I must hurry Blanche – I'm on television tonight.'

'Oo-er,' she said. Yes, that's what people say when you become famous. 'Oo-er.' Mulgrew has already had his kipper and oo-er. We are lumbered with the props. Hall will meet us at Ally Pally. We get a taxi to the gig: Alexandra Palace is a warren of signs and BBC men with hats on who mindlessly point the way, 'Der lift to der turd floor,' said an Irish one. 'Oh yes,' said a clipboard girl, who had as much feel for showbiz as

Mrs Higgs had for hunting basking sharks. 'I'm Penelope Mutts, I'm the floor manager.' Who manages the ceiling? 'You are the . . .' she consults her board, 'Marty Midge and Naylor.'

We are shown into a dressing room with several other performers; some are dressed as cowboys, they are Big Bill Campbell and his Bunkhouse group, all done up in stetsons and a Red Indian chief – all from East Acton. They were practising, 'There's an old covered wagon for sale.'

'If it goes, they'll have to walk back,' said Mulgrew.

A gay floor manager calls us for rehearsal with Eric Robinson and the Orchestra. 'Is this all you got?' he said, looking at our meagre band parts.

'Yes, just play them loud,' I said.

The orchestra applauded our rehearsal.

'Can I have your agent's number?' said Robinson.

'You gonna kill him?' I say.

'No, I might be able to use you, have you got a card?'

'No, just this bit of paper.'

'Make-up?' says a girl.

'Is that what you're wearing?'

'No, the make-up you have to wear is green,' she said. 'It comes off with water.'

Hall has arrived, I knew he comes off with water. I've got good news, he said; it *was* good news, he'd turned up. He'd got a gig immediately after the show at the Domino, a nightclub in Balham, the arsehole of London. The wretched appearance of Hall disturbs the make-up girl. 'I don't think you need any,' she says, backing away. The show centres on the Television Toppers, fifteen rather lovely girls, Argggghhh. Fifteen Arghhhs! The TV show is all very interesting, being live, it's split-second timing.

The set is a Parisian Cabaret with a maître d', an old broken actor with an awful French accent; he announced us, 'End nous, from ze Coco-nut Grover-er, Le Beel Hall Trio.' There's no real audience so a planted one acts insane with artificial applause. Our problem is we have no time afterwards to remove the green make-up, so that's how we appear at the Domino, green.

# IF LOVE COULD FIND A WAY

NO! NO! NOT! a freak show, not beautiful me or mongrel Mulgrew – no, it's Bill Hall, that's it! They've seen Bill Hall and he's a freak. We are seated before the proprietor, Will Collins. He's sending a company to Zurich, would we like that? Well, yes. A pretty smart answer. He was a thirty-three-year-old hyperactive balding man who was in show business on the bottom rung. If his bottom rung, I wouldn't answer it. 'It's a very good show boys, we're to be the main entertainment at the Zuka Exposition on the Zurich See. We have animal acts, performing pigs, the only ones in the world.' His phone went. 'Yes, I'm sure they will,' he puts his hand over the mouthpiece. 'You wouldn't mind assisting in another act?'

'Well, as long as we cop extra lob,' said Wretch Hall; another smart answer.

'I'll see you all right after the show.'

Yes, but would we see him? Other acts were a xylophone man, a mystery act, mother and daughter, there was no mystery who gets the mother. Now our xylophone man has got special bumps on his head, 'Would one of you be able to help playing a tune with xylophone mallets – it's a short piece or he goes unconscious – it's a bit of the William Tell Overture.' So on and on, Avis Dawnton, an acrobat and there's Turto a man who whistles on points and smashes tea trays on his head. They have fixed digs in advance – Mr and Mrs Hitz, 3 Stocherstrasse, Zurich, *Gut*.

While we were waiting for departure day, my musical urge rose to the surface – I wanted to write a musical. I had read the story of Ann Bonney, a woman pirate who had sailed the piratical seas never revealing her womanhood; they must have been a dull lot of sailors – that or she wore a dildo of such proportions it frightened them. I mean she might have flashed it on the *Marie Celeste* and the crew all jumped overboard. Mystery solved.

So I found an old pedal pump harmonium – £5. 'A bargain,' said the man. For him yes. Margo wouldn't allow it at 13 Linden, so 3 Leathwell. I got Sellers to help transport it.

Moans from Mrs Higgs. 'Oh dear,' when she saw it. Finally, we got it to my tiny rear window room.

I thank Peter and promise him a part in my masterpiece. I had alerted my brother in Australia to prepare some costume sketches. The whole musical was influenced by *Oklahoma*!

'Oh what a wonderful morning.' *I* wrote, 'Oh, what a day for living.'

*The opening chorus:*

> ME: I'll pay 10,000 dollars
> For any man collers
> Calico Jack.
>
> *Chorus:* Calico Jack!!!

All through the train-shunting nights I worked on it. My brother's costume designs arrived. One night Jimmy Grafton was taken by one of the tunes (where to?) – he and Jack Jordan got it published.

Jimmy showed an interest in the musical – yes, I'd show Oscar and Hammerstein; at the pub I was showing Secombe, Jimmy Grafton, Charlie the barman, his Dog Kiwi and a regular crone on gin, 'Fuckin' lovely tune!' From the toilets below wafted urinated metholated spirits, that's who. Some Yahoos, Hooray Henrys came in. 'Come on, let's get cracking on some Hutch*.'

'I don't know any.'

'Of course you do, it goes, "When dey begin de beguine".' Before I'd finished, he said, 'Play some boogie – you know.' He pranced round the piano going cha-cha-cha – a real swine, he's possibly the Managing Director of Lloyds by now. Oh God, how every musician hates, 'I say, can you play . . .' and as you do, they walk away. Alan Clare, a friend, superb ballad player, told me a story. A Sloane Ranger and her micromind came in and said, 'Oh dear, ha ha ha, I thought you were a recording, ha-ho-he-ha.' Alan said, 'Ha ha ha – that's funny, I thought you were one too, can they switch you off?' Another

---

*Leslie Hutchinson, coloured entertainer of the Thirties.

(OPPOSITE) My first published song. A total failure

jolly chap said, 'I say pi-ano, do you play this thing?' Alan said, 'Yes.' 'Oh – do you play requests?' Alan says, 'Yes, what would you like?' 'Oh, anything.' He's possibly head PR for Harrods.

Alas – Ann Bonney never saw the light of day, never even saw it at night, but youth, belief, some of the songs were very good. Playing my masterpieces at the Grafton after hours, I ignored everyone else, and they ignored me. I like making sounds; my life was shattered by bone and spoon players, they didn't have a clue what you were playing and didn't care; that terrible clattering of some dead cow's ribs.

Of course, with Secombe and Bentine, they would play the idiot along – 'Were you taught, chum?'

'No, it's just natural like.'

'Yes, seems natural like.'

'Do you read music?'

'No need to, any tune comes easy.'

'Do you know Beethoven's Fifth?'

'Oh yer.' He bursts into the opening Victory Vs of the introduction – on and on he rattled, off his elbows, off his knees, his arse (very funny). Finally, with a furious rattle he stopped.

'Was that it?'

'Yer.'

'Amazing.'

'Yer, I keep it all in my head.'

'That was a very short version of the Fifth.'

'Ah well, I go fast and I leave out bits I don't like.'

I abandon the piano and join in joking and ad-libbing with Secombe and Bentine – with Jimmy adding drinks; he was a shrewd man and he sensed we had something – like rabies.

BENTINE:    I arrest you for nose.

ME:    My nose is innocent – who are you?

SECOMBE:    Just a minute. I'm Inspector Thuds of Scotland Yard.

ME:    This man's nose is on undercover service.

BENTINE:    On or under, make up your mind.

ME:    Then where's its secret cover?

SECOMBE:   He's off duty.

BENTINE:   Not so fast – Secombe.

SECOMBE:    All right, I'll speak slower.

BENTINE:   I happen to be chief nose cover inspector to the Sûreté – *où est cover du nez*?

SECOMBE:   It's in 10 Downing Street – with Mrs Clement Attlee's plumber.

BENTINE:   Her plumber?

SECOMBE:   Who would look for it there?

ME:   Narkington Quench Esq.

BENTINE:   Then all is lost – the only escape is in this matchbox. Etc, etc.

*We pulled a lot of grimaces during our clowning.*

ME:   Sir, this finger will never make it on its own.

SECOMBE:   Hold it on your other hand and purse your lips.

This was all after hours, with just a few late drinkers. One man said, 'Two years in the army would do you wastrels good.'

'We've just done five,' we said.

'Then do five more, you're not better yet.'

It was the late Kenneth More who was fascinated by our humour, as were Norman Castle, Michael Howard, Dick Scrongle, Tim Gritts, Len Trock, and many other people with names.

One night Sellers said: 'I have just eaten the Elfin Oak.'

ME:   Did anybody see you?

SELLERS:   Yes.

ME:   Then you're a marked man.

SELLERS:   I haven't got any mark, only a brown spot on my knee – it's a birthmark.

ME:   How long have you had that?

There were miles of that.

So the week prior to Zurich, I spent the days hanging around with Bentine, Secombe, for ever watching newsreels, cartoons, ribald laughter, mad ideas. In the *Telegraph* it says an atomic paper had gone missing. Bentine and I spent the night drawing up a bogus formula; he knew all the mathematics I just went along for the ride. It ended by scraping the luminous dials off our watches, which contain radium; we leave it all in a phone box, it all looked very authentic – it had taken all night. We kept watch on the booth. Someone threw it on the floor.

There was our salute at the opticians' inaugural dinner. 'Be upstanding, the toast is the Society of Opticians.' We raised our glasses, then used the glass like an eyewash. After hours, Secombe and I would put on masks and say, 'Imagine we are burglars, and we demand £1.' Then there was the argument over the money. 'This pound note is out of date, it's last year's.' The after hours games were endless; for example, who had the ability to survive in the desert? Bentine could, he'd lie on the floor gasping, 'Water, water' – in a flash we'd put a glass by him – he'd drink it. 'There, you see it's all relative.' Secombe can do better. He too is cast in the desert; he crawls the bar floor, calling 'Brandy! Brandy!!' Having got one, 'Hey hoopla,' he leaps to his feet, another desert survivor. 'You see, gentlemen,' says Bentine, 'with close co-operation it is possible to survive desert conditions, provided they're right.'

Then there was the theory by Professor Bentine that during the war it was *impossible*, you hear, impossible for Hitler to have crossed the Channel. The argument raged. What's to stop him? 'What? Psychology, it's never been done since the Normans – the Spaniards, Napoleon, Marcel Proust (a failed Channel swimmer) all failed that strip of water.' Bentine is frothing at the mouth. 'How can he get a hundred thousand men and tanks across?'

'Boats,' said Secombe.

'Ah, well, of course, boats,' said Bentine.

'I tell you how they stopped 'em,' said Milligan. 'For months the RAF dropped hundreds of photos of English landladies. What finally stopped 'em was records of Gracie Fields. I tell you it stopped the tanks at Dunkirk; some Panzer men wrote to English soldiers commiserating with them.'

## ZURICH

But now away to Zurich. The night before, Mulgrew slept on the couch normally reserved for my ageing grandmother, Margaret Kettleband. Dawn broke on 3 Leathwell – I shake Mulgrew, Rangers 2 etc. And my grandmother nearly dead with sitting up all night. How I love her.

My mother, Florence, and my grandmother, Margaret Kettleband, at 3 Leathwell Road, Deptford

*My diary – 23 August 1947*
*At the non-existent hour of six Johnny and I were aroused by my*
*dear mother (slightly less dear due to the early hour). I washed –*
*or something like that – and ate my breakfast. I felt good inside at*
*the thought of working in Switzerland – last-minute preparations*
*and then the taxi arrived at 7.00 sharp (7.14). Piled in the*
*luggage and a last glimpse of mother waving, as we turned the*
*corner of Leathwell Road. We breezed through Lewisham – Old*
*Kent Road – and watched the thousands going to work in the City*
*(what a maddening thought!).*

Arriving at Victoria Station we watch as six farm pigs are
loaded in a goods van. Quite a crowd collected. There were six
large and two young ones, it was a case of railway men and Will
Collins against the Porkers. There were squeals, snorting,
scampering, shit and steam with bales of straw bumping about.
Pigs are not stupid, many railway men are – the men spent
more time in the cage than the pigs. There's a limit on how to
transfer pigs from a cage to a railway wagon. 'Wave yer arms!'
When they did the pigs ran underneath, some pigs ran between
the railway men's legs and stayed there. There were brief bouts
of ride-em-cowboy, there was a period where the back legs
were grabbed and with them going like windmills the pigs were
forced forward, then all four legs were held – making the
restrainers look like vibrating rubber dolls. They hung on but
they were jerked around like dummies. They got one in and
tied his legs – this was how they all ended up, but the RSPCA
inspector said they could only tether two legs and, that way,
they all came out again. Instead of tethering one and two, they
tethered one and three. It took a good hour, followed by
applause, before the goods door shut, even then the pigs stood
on hind legs looking through the slats.

We got our props in the goods wagon, full of Miss Fifi
Franz's footballing dogs, all unusually quiet. 'I give zem ze
tablet,' she winked through three layers of make-up with
eyelashes like black barbed wire. No doubt this would be the
one Bill Hall would be giving it to.

'The Magic Lady'* and her daughter Mavis complain pigs

*This was her stage name.

shouldn't be treated like that, as they sat in the restaurant car eating eggs and bacon. Mulgrew and I sat opposite – taking the same breakfast. Mavis is lovely – they are mother (The Magic Lady) and daughter, but easily mistaken for father and daughter. 'This is our first time abroad,' said lovely Mavis in a North Country accent. 'Mother's been, haven't you, Mother?'

'Oh, aye, circus in Berlin and Vienna before the woer, we got out just in time, Germans took the elephant but let me go.'

A wise choice. Her husband Bert 'Tarzan' Ladlie was mauled by one of his lions, 'Simba' his favourite, suddenly on the motorbike pillion he bit his head, he had twenty-eight stitches and wore a wig. He was dead now, buried with his wig. 'Me, I'm doing well with Mavis.'

We are all sharing the same carriage. Mavis is next to me and my plans. We cross into France, by night we are whipping through the French countryside – I smoke in between dozing, Mavis asleep on my shoulder (how did she get up there?), I'll just put my arm around her blonde body. Dreamily, she opens her eyes and smiles; poor old Lily, Toni and Capri. 'You don't mind,' she smiles. No, my dear, rest your head on my Cecil Gee Camel Hair £5 coat, shapeless enough to look like a camel. We shudder and thunder through the night.

Zurich! Immediately sky, mountains, water, cigar smoke. We all disembark to a prearranged PR group, among them Fräulein Linder Ublatz; she's the interpreter. First, she'll have to interpret her name. We are all given the address of digs. We must also report to the Zuka exhibition concert hall 'tomirrow, *ja*'. Linder is thirty-nine, like a plumper Veronica Lake, then there's her assistant, Frau Bleeker, fifty-seven; another for Bill Hall? She is to accompany us to our digs. We have a supply of Swiss francs, we get a taxi. 'Well, apart from that fucking awful journey,' says Wretch Hall, 'I like the place; the atmosphere is dead right.' One of his dew drops is dangling on the end of his nose; the morning sun is streaming through it making it a crystal jewel – oh! it's gone along his sleeve. Our address, 3 Stocherstrasse. Herr and Frau Hitz; big apartments; we ring a doorbell. Hitler in Alpine shorts opens the door; he is as animated as a freshly boiled egg. Frau Bleeker explains we are the new clients. Tightlipped, and with the cheeks of his bum clenched, he shook our hands, hesitating before the Wretch Hall. Standing behind in a housecoat that made her look like a cupboard with the doors ajar, was the weak and timid Frau Hitz; she's like him without the moustache. *Ja, gut!* Hall has a single room, Mulgrew and I a double. We are handed a list of charges, times of meals and front door locked at 0100 unless requested. Here is a sample of the dialogue.

HERR HITZ:   Ve must make zer agreement.
US/ME:   Yes; and added a *ja* to be friendly.
HERR HITZ:   Please no *ja*, I speak English, I go five year to night school etc.
US:   Yes.
HERR HITZ:   I have zis written agreement that every Friday you will pay my wife twenty schillings each.
US:   Yes.
HERR HITZ:   So please sign here – here – and here.
MULGREW:   I'll sign first because I'm Scottish.
HERR HITZ:   Scottish good.

*We all signed the typed document.*

HERR HITZ:   Who will keep zer copy?
ME:   Me – because I'm not Scottish.
HERR HITZ:   Not Scottish good.
BILL [*who was pissed off*]:   I get fuck-all.
HERR HITZ:   Fuck-all?
BILL:   Yes, I get fuck-all.
HERR HITZ:   Fuck-all? You say?
ME:   Thank you.

Our rooms were very neat and tidy with washbasins; toilet in the hall. There is a sign in the slot which says *Aben* – or occupy. His wife looked like a wraith of work, pale, domestic, pigtails – blue eyes – she looked overworked. Oh dear, you can see what that poor girl needs – a good dinner and a fuck.

Whenever her husband was at work she always gave shy smiles, yes, indeed; Bill was right, she needs einer dinner and ein shag. I'm not sure what work he did. He left every morning on a bicycle with a packed lunch – and came back with it intact, was it a reserve? She just washed and dusted all day – the house was clinically spotless. When they discovered that we all smoked, three large ashtrays appeared in our room – mine had a swastika underneath. 'Think he was a Nazi?' said Bill. Then one Sunday breakfast, the fool says, 'We three all Jews – Jews you understand?'

He looked straight back, '*Ach, Juden,*' and told his wife. She didn't seem worried.

'He in concentration camp,' said Hall pointing to our Scot.

'Oh,' said the German, 'that is not good.'

'Yes,' said Hall. 'Three years in Lewisham.'

'Oh,' Herr Hitz repeated. 'Lewisham – *ja* – Lewisham!' and repeated to his wife . . . Lewisham.

'Ach, Lewisham,' said the wife sadly.

Bill didn't like Germans. 'The bastards did my dad in World Woer One, and the bastards got me into the second one, they're all Nazis – did you hear 'is bottle go when I said we were Jews?'

Perhaps there was a mite in it. They weren't a happy lot, clean, polite, rich, even the street sweepers smoked cigars.

'Amazing, a world war,' I said, 'and it didn't touch 'em – all bloody well fed. Good luck to them. I wish to Christ I could have escaped here during the war – oh boy.'

'What would you 'ave done then – got pissed?'

'Got pissed – of course – as a point of Scots honour, I'd have been pissed half the time—'

'The other half in prison – that's the Scots – pissed or prison.' And Rangers 2 Celtic 0.

'It's nae a bad life, but it takes a lot out of the wife and kids.'

'Kids? Scotsmen eat their kids, don't they, Spike?'

'Yes, the first three usually, then they settle down.'

'Aye, well it's an old Scots custom. Sometimes we eat our guests – mind, with your ragbone body you'd be safe.'

So went our conversations. Bill thought the Irish were all: 'Bleedin' thick, good at building – houses – railroads.'

'What about Oscar Wilde and Shaw?'

'Yes, they were good at it too.' Perfect ignorance is unbeatable.

The good life on the Zurich Zee

I took Mavis on the Zurich Zee on a pedalo, just to see her in her costume. ''Aven't you got a costume?' she said.

'Yes, but I haven't got a body, so I'll just watch yours, darling.' I really was skinny.

'If you'd been at Belsen, they'd have thrown you out as too fin,' said Hall, himself six feet two inches – and seven stone with clothes, without clothes he didn't register.

Mavis, her *mother* and I went for a ride on the scenic railway, which took us into the hills around. Quite beautiful. A small country, small population, no bloody immigrants, so no racial tensions, all very acceptable, small is super.

'It reminds me of the Lake District,' said Mavis.

'Yes,' said her mother, 'it's the mountains and the water – they're just the same.'

'No daffodils,' I said.

'It's too late in the season.' Some bloody mothers know everything!

'There's some cows like the Lake District,' I said.

'Mostly sheep there,' said the clever bloody mother.

'Grass,' I said. Yes, grass, never mind, there was lovely Mavis's body to run my mind over, in places she was like the Lake District. 'I do a poem,' I said.

> I wandered lonely as a cloud
> That floats all o'er dale and hills
> When all at once I came upon
> My dog being sick on the daffodils.

'Oh, that's terrible, Mother,' said Mavis. 'I warned you about 'im,' she said with a fairground smile; yes, you had to cover a fair bit of ground to get a smile that size. Mavis and Mum go home to their digs at night; this night they ask me round to dinner after the show. We take a tram along the lakeline, then stop by their flat – it's on to the lake, very nice; it's self-catering. Her mother makes a wonderful roast beef and two veg – after all the sausage and sauerkraut, it was wonderful.

She put on the radiogram (it fitted perfectly) and she said, 'Go on, 'ave a dance,' so Mavis and I did. It was super. Foxtrots, waltzes – tango – wow! if only her mother would fuck off. It was a wonderful imperfect evening. As I get back to the digs, Scottish Mulgrew is being dropped off by taxi by his old dear.

'Nae mind she's an auld dear, I make her happy and she's doing ma laundry.' Wasn't love wonderful. He sings:

> 'I love her, she does my laundry,
> I love her although she's eighty-three.'

The show attracts crowds, it can't fail. The city is crowded for the Exposition, the show runs shorter without the pigs, but there's less shit about; all the fans are free of it.

Now a grotesque romance; Mulgrew chats up Frau Bleeker back and asks for her phone number. I'd have asked for her osteopath. Cut it short he had an affair! When I questioned him why, he would cry with laughter at my bafflement. 'What's she got?'

'Me,' he said through the tears.

To this day I'm baffled! Yes, Bill Hall is after the 'mystery lady', but she doesn't see anything in him to interest her; wait till she sees his x-rays!

The Zuka Exposition is a great commercial fair on the banks of the Zurich Zee. The stage is set in a great restaurant tent, the stage at one end, the other with dining tables, the walk to the middle of the stage takes five minutes. There is no pit band, but a twenty-five piece Italian Orchestra under its dynamic five-feet bald-headed Pippo Barzizza – and very, very good. He knew all the latest and standard tunes, but they just *miss* the point. They play loud, fast, high notes, but they can't swing. At rehearsal they are knocked out by our Trio. One of our acts is already at work. Eyes-o. He sits next to the box office, doesn't move or blink; so that people don't poke things at him, he's in a glass box with no roof, so people toss money. His one curse – he has piles, and sometimes they nearly drive him insane. I would stand and watch his staring, unblinking smile knowing his arse was killing him.

The exposition is alive with people and goods, a country that had never seen a war. The place is alive too with lederhosen oompah-pah bands. On the lake, helmsmen yodel, all another

Mavis on the Zurich Zee with me

world from Glasgow Pavilion with Rangers 2 Celtic 0. The rehearsal went well except the performing pigs were chaos! Three pigs are all put into a little cottage, the whole thing is based upon the wolf and huff and puff – the guy in the wolf skin is an ex-muscle man; he huffs the house down, the house falls on him and the pigs escape, but they couldn't be got off! One pig at stage level crapped on a diner's table; good Germans make mit zer laff ha-ha. One afternoon Mavis and I take a pedalo on the Zurich Zee.

The sun is shining, Mavis goes for a swim – I don't swim; I've got a costume, but I haven't got a body. So we settle to this life. Digs, we come down for a breakfast *en famille* – Herr und Frau Hitz, me and Mulgrew – Hall rarely appears; they say grace, then porridge and boiled eggs. '*Gut*,' he'd say. '*Ja, gut*,' we'd say – he never knew I'd shot his uncle at Cassino.

I have learned to do the announcements in German and

S. Milligan

Herr. Hitz
German
Boarding
House Oberau
Zürich
1949

getting laughs on them. Love! Laura Gugoltz has come into my life. After we'd done our turn, I'd go and sit at one of the tables, and there was Ingrid Bergman! A drink? Lemonade. She speaks English, she's a relief programme seller, oh what a relief; she doesn't recognise me from the act and is saying had I seen it? She didn't believe me when I said I was in it. 'Oh, you are so funny with your violin.'

'No, that's not me, that's the Wretch.' She must never see him, otherwise like the young girl in *Lost Horizon*, she'll age a thousand years. Can I see her sometime?

Yes, in the Park tomorrow. 'First I have appointment with my feet.'

'What?'

Oh, she has a rash on her foot, a foot which looks like it was sculpted by Bernini. Things are happening. An agent from Italy, Ivaldi, has seen us and wants to sign us for an Italian tour – wow, Toni, Capri! It *was* going to happen.

Oh the pigs! They were a disaster and were sold. We saw their sides hung up in the Zuker Butcher's tent. Now, *my* efforts on the xylophone skull man. I was given two ping pong balls on sticks and played the intervals to the tune of 'Nola', while he opened and closed his mouth. Occasionally, a ball would fly off, in which case I had to double my efforts with one. This drew sympathetic applause – everyone has sympathy for a person with only one ball. There was nothing doing with Mavis, or Laura, there was nowhere to go. What a pity 13 Linden Gardens room was going empty, with twelve half-burnt candles and a whiff of Neville Heath. So we did a lot of street cafés – drinking coffee till the bladder burst, the ears sang, and pupils like pinpoints. After the penultimate show, Pippo Barzizza and his wife took me to their hotel room to talk about showbiz in Italy. His wife serves more bladder-bursting coffee. He has a bald head like a bladder being slowly inflated. I can't wait. 'You do very well in Italy now, they like-a Jazz. You see Mussolini no like Jazz, he say Jazz is *decadente* Negro music; he no make Jazz music.' No, he was making Clara Petacci and all *that* Jazz. Pippo Barzizza's daughter is big time in Italy; she's called the Bomba Atomica. He showed me a photo, she had lots of fallout – Argggh!

Before the show closes, we have signed a contract with Ivaldi to open in Rome at the Teatro Belle Arte. We decided to go home first, then come out again. So, railway carriages, dim carriage lights, swaying, snoring, struggling. Opposite me is a priest. I share my bottle of wine with him. He gives me half his cheese – God, it's good to be a Catholic. Mavis is in another carriage. Infidelity; I suppose it's someone else's shoulder, her mother's? What an evil mind I had! How could I suspect her mother's shoulder. I myself have no idea what she saw in my shoulder in the first place, it was a shoulder you could have seen in any cheap jacket with torn armpits.

# HOME AGAIN

We go back to the great shores of Britain; I make for 13 Linden Gardens with Mulgrew and settle in, pretty excited by the promise of the show in Italy, but as we would discover, it won't be all sunshine and wine. At 3 Leathwell I meet my darling grandmother, who has shrunk to two feet – wait, she's kneeling down – one leg is bandaged for varicose veins, she had inflicted a black eye on herself in her sleep, so she looks like one of the defenders of Rourke's Drift, or the Palais Glide; she is dear to my heart, in fact, to all of my organs. She is very dear to my pancreas, I love her from the colon, oh yes, when I love, it's everything.

I tell her the wonders of performing pigs, and how they ended up as bacon; she is an old Victorian lady, has served as an Indian Army wife from 1904–46, but as she said, 'The Wogs have taken over and we left.' She is in transit to a coffee plantation in Kenya where her son-in-law, violent anti-wog, Major Bertram Kent, ex-Rajputana Rifles, thinks he can use the black African slave labour to grow coffee, and keep up production by shooting every third coloured gentleman – it didn't work. But my calm, colonial grandmother spent the time knitting for the poor of London, which happened to be all at 3 Leathwell Road.

Bertram Kent's practice of shooting every third coloured gentleman caused a shortage of farmworkers, so he left the dark continent. My aged grandmama had had enough shooting; she shipped back out to India (at eighty-nine) to stay with a docile Aunty Eileen and her husband, Brian MacIntyre, who decided to stay on in India under wog rule. I think she became a Harijan.

I am trying to finish Ann Bonney and it is finishing me. I write a letter to Toni saying I'm coming – prepare for Capri II! We have to vacate 13 Linden Gardens with Blanche crying, 'I'll miss you, you're very nice, better than Neville Heath, it's a wonder he didn't do me in.' Yes, it was a wonder.

# BACK TO ROME

Now off to the lasagne-caked shores of Italy. More props, suitcases, good suit to meet Toni, portable mattress and hormone tablets. Let's get the journey to Paris over, eh? And the Brenner Pass, eh? The Simplon, eh? And into a sunlit Roma Centro Ferrovia, eh? We have to go to digs with wartime friends Signora Ciampaglia and two ballerina daughters, Marisa and Marcella, on the Via XXI Aprile. We hardly knew them during the war, but we and our money were very welcome. I am keen to see Toni; that will be 'arranged' says Marisa. But first we must get a taxi to the Teatro Belle Arte. It's where all the latest acts are given a break. A charming miniature opera house. Backstage we meet Ivaldi's rep, a fat Egyptian, Arzanofata, a sixty-year-old agent who's seen it all except his own. Top of the bill is Byron Cutler, a gay Negro dancer from the Katherine Dunham Troupe, beautifully made, very sensitive, with BO. Very fine pit orchestra who are amused at our tatty 'Tiger Rag' play-out music. The conductor smiled, 'Is that eet, sir?' I assured him it was. Byron Cutler's dancing is exquisite.

On our bill is a girl singer, god save us from goddesses, she is *beautiful*, a saturnine Medusa without the snakes, eyes the size of lifeboats, coal-black magma intensity; her skin is like Carrara marble and her voice like ice and fire. '*Monastaire de Santa Ciarra*,' she sings. If she'd taken her clothes off, I'd have eaten them. It's a very, very good first night; Toni is with Marcella, but there's something wrong. There's a distance between us – is it the orchestra? We go for dinner afterwards, but Toni is avoiding me; all very jolly, mind you, but it's not

*Left* Johnny Mulgrew with Marcella amid the ruins of Rome, taken by the ruins of Milligan. *Right* Johnny and me indicating each other under the Arch of Constantine, Rome

on. It's painful, but only from the waist down. She looks so petite and stunning.

The Three Nights. We are a big success. We are invited to a jazz club to play but no Toni. Plenty of excitement at the jazz club, wine, a few partisans about, signs, *Partito Comunista* – Good God! a police raid all in the wagons—Perhaps Toni knew something!! We show our British passports and are released, but are warned the club is a Communist recruiting depot.

Rome *was* a beautiful city; there was space, no bottom-

84

pinchers, no crowded pavements, the traffic was light, Tourists 0 Rangers 2. Johnny, Marcella, Toni and I just strolled in the spring sunshine through the ruins of ancient Rome. Toni teases Mulgrew, whom she calls Ginetto, about his drinking and smoking. She is a class above us. I've no idea what's below. Marcella too is good family, quietly dressed, polite; they are both aware of their Roman heritage – and me of my Deptford one. Worlds apart, was that what Toni was realising? I acted polite but crazy, jumping up beside Roman statues, jumping on podiums, a bit of Mussolini impressions. 'Stop it, Terry –

Johnny and Marcella by the Pool of the Vestal Virgins, who were at lunch

*pericoloso così.*' We had tea in the Villa Borghese, then the show. Oh, that girl singer, Mitti Mille, the voice, where did she go? Where did Byron Cutler go? Where did I go?

There's a girl at the digs, a friend Pia. Very pretty, very mischievous, red light. One night, after the show, the girls do Mulgrew and me up as tarts – we went on the streets to see what happened. What happened is the *Carabinieri* ran us in, we had to get the Assistant British Ambassador to fix that we were not gay. It was a bloody-minded *Carabiniere* that ran us in in the first place – I think he fancied us and was stricken in the nethers when he found we were men. Fun while it lasted. Johnny has the girls in hysterics; as pasta was being rolled, he made incredible willies out of them. How can you be jealous of pasta? I was amazed at the variation of willies he had in his repertoire. I think the ladies were disappointed when it had to be made into spaghetti.

Toni is difficult to see. She has many appointments. Pia fancies me. One afternoon I'm in my bedroom in the flat, she sleeks in, locks the door behind her, and without a word, strips off. My God, she's got a beautiful body, so when in Rome . . . On the last night I take Toni to dinner, but she is very distant; is there another man? Well, I know now there wasn't – not even me. Since those days she has told me I seemed too unbalanced, too quixotic, and my life had no centre. I had no regular job, and she thought I would be influenced by the lifestyle of Billiard Johnny, who both drank and smoked too much. You can see by her letter she isolated me from them as a personality.

''Ow you gettin' on with 'er?' said Wretch Hall.

I told him, 'Not too well.'

''Ave you given it to 'er yet?'

No, I had not 'given it' to her.

He's met a bird and, 'She's lovely – she does it slowly.'

Not too slow, Bill, in that condition you can catch cold – no, people who screw slowly should wear thermal underwear and woollen contraceptives – yes, contraceptives should be used on every conceivable occasion. Wow. So that last dinner with Toni.

'I don't understand you, Terry,' she said.

'What don't you understand?'

'You life – you so uncertain – you understand?'

'No, what about my life?'

'For me it is very diffcult, no *stabilità*—'

'No *stabilità* – no stability.'

'Yes, in one year where you are?'

'I don't know, I don't know.'

'You see, I don't think this life very good for you.'

'But I have to make a living, Toni.'

'I know, Terry, but I think some better for you.'

'What?'

'I don't know,' she shrugged. 'I don't know.'

There followed a long traffic-filled silence. My hand was on the table, she reached out and put her hand on mine. 'I love you, Toni.'

She laughed, and it hurt. 'You love me? I don't think so, you love me in good time like Capri, but now I here in Rome, you go away Milan, then where, you go home, no. I think not you love me.'

She was wrong, I did love, it's just that the setting was wrong. I needed a steady job and money enough to marry – buy a house – I wasn't in that league, and it was breaking us up. Money, Fuck Money. Yet she didn't want money, she wanted me but to the beat of a different drum. So I saw her back to her flat at 53 Via Apeninni – and said a sort of goodbye – then back to my flat.

The Ciampaglia family are all waiting for any gossip. Am I going to marry Toni – is she pregnant: my God they're like harpies, Pia among them but simmering with jealousy. Johnny has been home some time and is rightly pissed with Marisa on his lap teasing him. She doesn't know she's sitting on his volatile packed lunch, which if aroused would hurl her to the floor. Senora Ciampaglia had once been the 'girl' friend of Reg O'List. She asks about him. I say he was married now but still sang. She says she's very sorry. He had lived with her, she had cooked and washed for him, he had promised to come back. I said there was time – he was in good condition and could still sing the world's worst version of 'Begin The Beguine'. Ah yes, she remembers him singing, the worst possible memory 'I

Recordo'. How could she forget, how could anybody forget Reg O'List's version of 'Begin The Beguine'. It stayed in the mind like the memory of a terrible accident, which it was.

I off to my room to pack for the journey on the morrow, but wait for Pia. This time she does exactly the same act – door locked, strip off then screwing. She wants to know what that perfume is. I say it's Toni's (days before aftershave). '*Cattivo, te molto Cattivo*.' I'm bad, very bad, but now she seems to be screwing in revenge against Toni – she's beating me on the chest, crying and orgasming and in that order. I lie back and think of England.

Ten o'clock. Rome Station – crowded with people, Toni is not coming, but Pia is there, done up like a dream with black woollen stockings to the knee and cork-soled shoes. She throws her arms around me crying.

"Ow Christ, 'oo's this one?' says Hall.

'We're just good friends,' I said.

'What's she howling for?'

'She has a headache and it's me.'

Pia clings to me even as the train moves away. She walks along the platform, a tearful handkerchief in one hand, waving with the other. Isn't life cruel.

'Did you give it 'er?' said Hall, who is interested in such things.

'No, I didn't give it her – she gave it to me.'

"Ot stuff, eh?' he said.

Yes, she was very hot stuff. We all are stuck in the corridor as the train is packed. One of us takes turns to guard the luggage, while two of us make for the buffet car. Hall and I manage to get a table. 'The smell of bleedin' garlic,' says Wretch. 'Do they carry it in their bleedin' pockets?'

A lady waitress the size of Mount Everest takes our order – '*Due caffè e latte*.' We dunk the pastry into the coffee.

"Ow do you think we did at the Belle Arte then?'

'Well, we did best on the bill with Byron Cutler a close second.'

"Ee was a brown-hatter, wasn't he?'

'Actually, he was a black one.'

"Ave ter watch yer arse with Negros like 'im around.'

'I'd found him very civilised and an excellent piano player.'

'Wot's 'ee doin' over 'ere – I mean there must be more work in America – wonder why he left the Katherine Dunham dancers?'

'Same as us – work – adventure.'

'I wonder what's waitin' for us in Milan. This wog, what's 'is name, Arzanofata?'

'Yes, I wonder if you can trust him. I remember the bleedin' A-rabs in the war – a twistin' lot of bastards.'

'I think Arzanofata is a bit more civilised.'

'I don't know, one minute they're scrubbing camels' arses in the desert, the next they're theatrical agents – I bet he's got desert sores on his legs.'

We must have a look when we see him. Hall relieves Mulgrew.

'He took long enough,' moaned Mulgrew. 'Yes, Johnny, he was talking about sores on Arzanofata's legs.'

'Who's Arzanofata?'

'He's the Egyptian rep. for Ivaldi in Milan.'

'Oh, that bloke.'

'We were discussing the sores on his legs.'

'What, am I hearing proper?'

'Yes.'

'What about the sores on his legs?'

The waitress comes, '*Uno caffè e latte, per favore*.'

'Bill said he wouldn't be surprised if he's got sores on his legs.'

'Oh – so – he's got sores on his legs – so I've got pimples on me bum – but I don't go round discussing them.'

'No, it's just we were talking about his reliability as an agent.'

'What have the sores on his legs got to do with it?'

'Nothing, it was all a joke – forget it.'

Long pause, looking at the landscape.

'I need new strings for my bass.'

'Oh, they'll sell them in Milan.'

'They ought to, that's where the Milan Opera House is.'

'Oh, I've just remembered – I forgot to pay Mrs Ciampaglia the rent.'

'You can post it.'

'Yes, so I can; damn.'

The journey is uneventful, save for us being clambered over in the corridor. I hate perambulating travellers, those idiots who, once aboard a train, walk the corridors till they get to their destination, putting miles on their journey.

# MILAN

Waiting at Milan Central are Mr Ivaldi and Arzanofata and his desert sores. 'Blast, 'ee's wearing trousers, he must be hiding them,' said Wretch.

Oh, what a welcome. Mr̄ Ivaldi, a very good-looking, middle-aged Italian, slightly rotund, with a fine head of wavy oily black hair. 'Wel-a-come to-a-Milan – I have a car-a here to take you to your place—'

Mr Arzanofata adds his welcome, 'Yes – we hear very good from Belle Arte – very, very good.' Mr Ivaldi, in a large expensive Fiat, drives us through the sunlit bustling streets of Milan. At the magnificent Duomo we turn into the Via Agnello, No. 6 – a terraced home. We are let in by type-cast landlady, silver hair in a bun, large dark eyes, bosom, legs, teeth. Signora Castelli – she has a high whining voice – *Si accomode*.

Again Bill Hall has a room of his own. Johnny and I together – nice comfortable rooms with bath and shower. If we'll unpack, Mr Ivaldi will take us to lunch.

A lively restaurant in the giant Galleria – a glass-covered shopping centre with pigeons flying through the rafters. We are to play the Teatro de Milano, starting tomorrow (Monday) for a week, then a tour.

Ivaldi overwhelms us with questions, when did we meet, are we famous in England? Yes, we are famous in Blackpool, Glasgow, Dublin. Was I in the war? – yes. Dare I tell him I shot his uncle? 'I tink you do verra-well in Italia – I not see you like you play like I not see in Italia.'

Really?

He effuses at the table.

'Stick it,' says Hall. 'Ee's paying.'

We will be on the bill with Ugo Tognazzi (now a film star), a 'top Italian comic'.

'He must have taken over from Mussolini,' said Mulgrew.

'No, no. Ivaldi never followed Mussolini. He big fool – he not bad man – he just stupid.'

Amazing how a man can be stupid yet run a country twenty years, who's stupid.

Ivaldi didn't fight. 'No – me hide.'

Why didn't I think of that?

Mr Arzanofata left Egypt after the war, but during, and Bill Hall was interested in this, 'Me work with Montgomery in messenger service.' No, he never got desert sores, why?

'Just asking,' said Bill.

Would we like to visit Ivaldi's office – why not, it's Sunday, all the other offices are closed. It was ideal Sunday viewing, posters of Italian stars, desks, real wooden desks with papers on top and pens and pencils, ink, in inkwells, now filing cabinets, great, ah, 'See *your* poster.' There's our bill and our name in big red letters. '*Famous a de Londra, première volta in Milan.*'

'You lak?' says Ivaldi, holding it up.

He's certainly holding us up. 'Yes, we lak it, we lak it *molto buona.*' Yes, there's something to be said about Sunday visits to offices, fucking boring. He drives us back to our digs, where we settle in. Signora Castelli wants to know would we like some, 'Tay, Tay Inglese?' So we drink our 'Tay' Inglese. It tastes more like the River Tay.

'It's true,' says Mulgrew, 'foreigners can't make tea.'

I tell Mulgrew he's mistaken, this is not tea, but 'Tay Inglese', an entirely different drink made from low grade Mucklebush leaves.

After we put our things away (mine's been put away since Pia) we take a stroll to see the Duomo. It's stunning, like lace made from stone – there's continuous Mass, so Mulgrew and I (Hall's gone) sit in a back pew and listen to the sung Latin Mass – beautiful – candles, incense, chanting; it's nice being a Catholic. 'Do you like all this, Mulgrew?'

'I dig the singing – I don't understand the rest.'

You're not supposed to understand – you just have to believe – that's Catholicism. Mulgrew's natural follow-on to church is a wine bar. We sit outside in the afternoon sun, people go by in their Sunday best.

'It's nice here,' says Mulgrew.

'It's nice anywhere', I said, 'provided you're there. I mean at this moment it must be nice in Monte Carlo, but we're not there, so it's not nice.'

Mulgrew, from his smoke, grinning, looks at me, shakes his head. 'We aren't getting any better are we?' he says.

I will though, when I was in church I had prayed, and crossed myself. Why not, I'd crossed everybody else. In my time I'd even crossed London and Tower Bridges.

'Lots of pretty signorinas,' he observed.

'Yes, all signorinas should be in lots. Lot number twenty, sixty signorinas, what do I hear?'

Isn't the Last Supper painting somewhere around here? Leonardo da Vinci, wasn't it?

Yes, it's at the Carthusian Monastery of Santa Maria, let's go. We don't know the way, but a taxi does. Fancy, the Last Supper by Leonardo. It's closed. It's being renovated. In passing we see a music shop. We know where to buy our strings on the morrow. We have one worry. We don't have much in the way of lire – in fact, there's nothing in the way of lire – it's a clear run, except we don't have much. 'Tomorrow I'm going to ask Ivaldi for an advance,' says Mulgrew.

We go to an Italian cinema and see newsreels of Primo Carnera wrestling in America – cheers go up every time he throws someone out of the ring. Poor devil, one-time heavyweight champion of the world – now a grunt and groan. I'm sitting next to a girl, who in perfect English asks me for a light.

'Are you English?'

No, she's Dutch, she's a ballerina whose company has gone broke – so on and so on and I make a date to see her on the Tuesday for tea at a place she gave me the address of – La Tavernella, off Via Emanuele. 'It's like a little mews.' Like all cat lovers, I adore little mews.

Mulgrew is stunned. 'You've only been here ten hours and you've picked up a chick.'

'This is no chick, Mulgrew, this girl is from The Royal Dutch Touring Ballet who are broke.'

I slept fitfully that night, tossing and turning. I could hear the late trams on the Via Emanuele, perhaps I was excited by all that was happening. I craved audience laughter and applause and couldn't wait for our opening on Monday. The theatre is the Tivoli on the Piazza Fontana, it's a modern one built under planning of a Mussolini consortium of architects. It's very stark, lots of marble. Marble apparently reminded Mussolini of the Roman Empire, the one theatre I'd never played. I played marbles as a child, it never reminded me of the Roman Empire.

The Monday night is a sell-out as Ugo Tognazzi is a big star, he's a young, good-looking, stand-up comic. It's a fine pit orchestra, unlike England, as it consists of full-time musicians and not part-time plumbers and miners. Byron Cutler is on the bill and causes more of a stir than applause, but again we are the hit of the night, and Ivaldi and his friends congratulate us, all very voluble and excited, much to the amusement of Bill Hall, whose only interest is to find out how Arsenal are doing. Ivaldi opens up champagne. Our dressing room is crowded with smart first-nighters, among them Ivaldi's daughter Irena. Oh no, she fancies me too. She doesn't waste time. Am I married? No I'm not married, I'm single man, she just has to count me to find out. Would I like her to show me around Milan – I thought of Johnny Mulgrew left alone with Rangers 2 Celtic 0, so I said, 'Yes, if my friend can come too.' (Come too? He wasn't unconscious.) Okay, she says, but really means 'Sod it'. Ivaldi takes Ugo Tognazzi, Byron Cutler and us to dinner at Guattiero Marchese, a no-nonsense true Italian pasta restaurant. I sit between Ivaldi and Mulgrew.

'I got an advance,' whispered Mulgrew, patting his breast pocket. 'I'll give you yours later, it's an advance of wages.'

Good, I like to see my wages advancing. Opposite me sits Irena.

'You act is wonderful,' she giggles. She's a plain girl, with two plain magnificent boobs that could only improve with massage. She is mad about 'swing music'. 'You like Benny Goodman?' she says.

I say, 'I don't know, I've never met him.' She doesn't understand.

'I have book you for Verona – Torino – Astoria – Savona – Arezzo. You get plenty work, *molto lavoro*,' said Ivaldi. It all sounded good as did the noise he made eating, like a pig.

Miss Ivaldi won't leave me alone. She is very sweet but speaks to me all evening in broken English, until I'm pissed off. 'Would you like me to drive you home?' I wanted to tell her she already was. No thanks. Mulgrew and Hall are getting pissed and staying on, so I walked the still busy night streets. It's a commercial city. It felt like London. I stop at the looming mass of the Church of Sant' Ambrogio. It's open even though it's midnight, a low Mass is being said. It has a lovely, lovely atrium and portico. Carolingian altar is a madness of filigree saints and cherubim; if I remember my history right, Charlemagne, King of the Franks, was crowned somewhere round here, where the King of the Freds and Jims was, I don't know. I walk back past the fairy-tale Duomo; it's a mass of delicate spires, strange how most religions point heavenwards. I'm pointed bedwards.

Soon I'm in bed in No. 6 Via Agnello, street of the lamb, and I sleep as sweetly as one – and always the rumble of the late-night tram. Then there is the rumble of that Scottish swine Mulgrew – crashing into my room waking me up, actually shaking me, as though he was trying to wake the dead. 'Here, wake up,' he was trying to say. I had to translate from 'Hedge, wak upish,' – it's three in the bloody morning and he 'wants a fag [Ishwand da fagh]'.

'Look at the time,' I said. What a silly bloody thing to say. What possible good can it do a drunk to look at the time. I give him the packet.

He drops them in the chamber pot, thank God it's empty, he rolls them all out and tries stuffing them in the packet, breaking half of them. I snatch the remainder away. Now he wants a light. 'Haff youd gorra lide, Jimmy, arrrrg.'

Oh God, he's going to be sick. I leap Superman-like from my bed and stick his head in the washbasin. I won't go into the revolting process, save I slept with the stench in the room. Next morning he has to clear the basin. I can't describe it.

Now, the meeting place of all Italian artists is the Galleria –
or the Piccolo Galleria; they converge on there every morning
at about 11.00. We get the habit and meet all our Italian
contemporaries. Everybody is there, including the Dutch girl
I'd met in the cinema, Jani Rywyck was her name. What was
she doing? Nothing. Looking for work. She is living on her
savings, and is staying at 10 Via Agnello. Apparently, this is a
street of theatrical digs. Would she like to go to the pictures,
she'd love to, so, pictures are on all day in Milan. First we go to
a coffee house; even though it's winter, people sit outside,
some sit inside, which is the same as outside, except it's not.

I take a closer look at Jani. She has a flawless white skin –
very little make-up. 'I can't afford it,' she said. Neither could I.
I had to rely on my natural beauty. She had a ballerina's figure,
walking very upright with her head held proud. Her hair was
dark brown, drawn back in a ponytail. She tells me of the trials
of her ballet company, how the agents had made off with the
money and left them stranded. She was sharing digs with an
Italian ballerina whose mother is the landlady, feeds them and
doesn't charge them rent. She tells me horror stories of
starvation under the Germans. She and her family had actually
reached the stage of starvation and were eating boiled tulip
bulbs, her sister was still in hospital suffering from post-
malnutrition – post-malnutrition – I thought that was a shortage of mail. She warned me about Italian theatrical agents.
On then to the pictures to see *Open City*, with an amazing
performance as a priest by Aldo Fabrizzi – in fact, he was a
well-known comedian. I was very moved by the picture, but
during it we do a lot of snogging, so much a woman behind us
admonishes us with, '*No, no – no buona così.*'

## MILAN TOUR

The week goes by with the Trio being a great success, with full
houses, then Ivaldi says, week out before the tour. Just a bit
suspicious, but he pays us meantime. I'm having a romance
with Jani – we visit all the cultural places, Castello Sforzesco,

Museo della Tecnica, Leonardo da Vinci. There before us are his drawings of aeroplanes, tanks, submarines, if only Henry Ford had been born earlier; we walk in the Monte Stella woods, we get tickets for La Scala reduced in price by Ivaldi – all week we just take in Milan and have it away at night. All the while I'm pestered by Irena – so one night I give it to her, then thank God the tour starts. Now I'm not going to give you chapter and verse on the tour, but the best bits, the big attraction is from South America, is the Edmundo Orifici and his Havana Cuban band, along with a chorus line. Some speciality acts, jugglers, etc. and an act with monkeys. So first stop is Torino, we are all in a huge charabanc – with the monkeys in a trailer. So Pistoia – with its great Piazza del Duomo and Giotto murals. Arezzo, with the home of Guido Aretinus, who revolutionised the old musical system with the tonic sol-fa. The Church of St Francis with murals by Piero della Francesca, the façade of the Church of Santa Maria della Pieve, the Etruscan vases, all too much. Genova, home of Paganini – his actual violin – by some amazing string-pulling, Bill Hall is allowed to play it and amazes the natives. Savona where Bill Hall catches it – it starts with him screaming at dawn when he goes to do a pee.

'I told you you'd get it,' warned the puritan Mulgrew.

'Oh Christ – it's like passing red-hot nails.' Hall finds a doctor and penicillin saves his bacon. (Where do we get these sayings from. Bill Hall hadn't any bacon, just a swollen dick.)

Torino, where there is a *Sveglia*, that is, the city stays up all night, streets are full of people in costumes, we join them in our stage clothes and make-up, so we fit in well. We start playing jazz and are soon surrounded by a crowd of enthusiasts, then a bloke comes out of the crowd, knocks my top hat off, and hits me over the head with a bottle. I went unconscious. I woke up in a hospital waiting room, briefly. I have three stitches in my head. But in my make-up and costume, they treated me like a leper. The end of Torino. But Jani's warning came true – we weren't always being paid by Ivaldi – we got IOUs, but you can't fucking cash IOUs, raged Hall to Arzanofata.

'Eet will be coming – just soon.'

We were into December, we had been out here three months. 'Three months is long enough,' said Wretch Hall.

'Not for a murder,' I said. 'Three months is for feeling little girls' bicycle saddles and stealing outsized bras.'

'Let's stick it out a little longer,' said Mulgrew.

Well, I didn't want to stick mine out any longer, I preferred it covered up.

'You know,' said Wretch Hall, 'that bloke whatsitsname, Anyfarter, first time I met him I had a feeling.'

'Oh, did he like it, I've never felt an agent with Anyfarter.'

'Let's spend Christmas here,' said Mulgrew.

'Spend Christmas,' I said. We had bugger-all to spend.

Hall is washing his socks. 'I'm bloody skint,' he said.

'I'll try and get a sub,' said Mulgrew.

'Yes, a sub – then we can go home underwater and miss customs,' I said.

'You're fucking useless in a-a-a—'

Crisis?

'Yes, in a fucking crisis.'

No, I wasn't! What about the Munich crisis? I didn't panic – I went on working as a semi-skilled fitter at Woolwich Arsenal. And the crisis when Hitler attacked Poland – I was eating a kipper for breakfast when the news came through on an Ekco radio they were crossing the frontier into Poland and bombing Warsaw – you know what, I went on eating that kipper and I even drank a second cup of tea. So don't talk to me about a crisis – I remember that distant February in North Africa, 1943. The Germans had almost surrounded our gun position – did I panic? No, I fucked off.

'Those two bastards Ivaldi and Azanofarter, wait till I catch them together.'

'Bill, be careful, it's very painful when you catch them together.'

'Oh, bollocks.'

'O'Bollocks,' I said, 'that's Irish for testicles.'

Hall is washing a second sock – the whole of his great mind is concentrated on that sock, what a humble social article is a sock! He holds the sock open under the tap and lets the water run through to rinse it.

'It's coming out the toe, Bill! That sock isn't waterproof – I should refrain from wearing that in rainstorms, if you did, you would leak – it would be terrible at a party to find you were leaking on the Vicar's carpet.'

'I 'ave ter wash 'em every night, I suffer from smelly feet.'

I said I suffered from smelly feet – his.

'Well, hard bloody luck – just think how lucky you are you haven't got mine.'

So I thought how lucky I was not having his.

'I haven't heard,' said Mulgrew. 'I have nae heard a word from my folks.'

'Well,' I said, 'it's very hard to hear Scotland from Milan, you need good hearing.'

Mulgrew is wreathed in smoke, 'I recall how they killed a young Prince in Berkeley Castle in 1200.'

Then he went silent and Hall and I stood like nanas awaiting the information. 'Well,' said Hall. 'How – er how?'

Mulgrew blew smoke in the air. 'He had,' he laughed, 'he had a red hot poker up his arse.'

'Thank you, Johnny Mulgrew, we learn something new every day,' I said.

'I was thinking,' said Mulgrew, 'it might help you to have a poker up your one.'

Oh, so? While we're on about it, does he know the Irish long-jump record? It's from the top of Beachy Head to the bottom, and was only done once.

'This is very bad drying weather,' said Hall, hanging his socks on the back of a chair.

It was, in fact, Sunday in Torino, we have visited Hall this evening after we had been out with some of the Havana band; we had taken our instruments into a trattoria and had a busk – one was a trumpeter, Chico O'Higgins, he plays great with Bill and the diners loved it. We drifted home via the wine bars in the Corso Vittorio Emanuele – tomorrow morning early the coach takes us back, all except the two monkeys who've been sold to the Torino Zoo. After three months, our clothing was getting a bit shabby, creases in trousers were a forgotten memory. There's a lot of asking the chorus girls to sew buttons, they are very willing. Bill Hall is having an affair with an old

The Bill Hall Trio on stage

boiler; she was the wardrobe mistress, now she's his as well. He must be doing a good job. He's got creases in his trousers. So we return to Milan for another week's variety, but still only the promise of money. Signora Castelli, our landlady, is patient about the rent, we tell her our situation, she understands, which is more than we do.

We all go to the Ivaldi office and demand money. Signor Ivaldi shakes his head and waves his hands in the air; it's not good enough, we need money. He explains that the theatres are slow in paying, he says they are three weeks behind, but '*Speriamo*', perhaps today – he has put a call through for them – and if the money doesn't arrive today, he will go to the bank. What with, a gun? He opens a small cash box and from it gives us five thousand lire – it's very little.

'If we don't get more money soon,' I said to Johnny, 'I'll fuck his daughter again.'

Mulgrew said, 'I'd go further – I'd fuck him.'

With our meagre wage we went back and paid the rent.

This part of the story shows how skint we became – in anticipation of returning home, I had bought my parents some crystallised fruit in a gilt and wood box, while Johnny had bought a boxed bottle of Asti Spumante. We awoke on Christmas Eve morning – we had no money, we could not afford the customary *caffè latte*, so I opened the box of crystallised fruit and Mulgrew opened the wine – we lay abed, eating and smoking.

'Merry Christmas,' I said.

'Sod Christmas,' he said. 'I hope I nae have another like this.' The chances were remote.

'Put it down to experience,' I said.

'No,' he said, sat up and put on a silly, silly grin. 'Let's put it down to poverty.'

We drank a toast to that. I leave you, dear reader, to guess what a breakfast of crystallised fruit and Asti Spumante tastes like. Of course! There was Irena. I phoned her. Could she lend me some money? Yes, yes, but she must 'see' me – so she comes round with twenty-thousand lire! Mulgrew goes for a freezing walk, 'I've done some things in ma time,' he said as he went out into the cold like Captain Oates. As he said he'd done some things in his time, I was doing things in my time. Irena gets it from me and I get the money. This is how business *should* be done, but she doesn't want to leave, yet Mulgrew has had enough of frozen balls. He comes back and I gently ease Irena out, she says her father will kill her if he finds out about the money. Good. Oh my God, at last money!

Signora Castelli has invited us to have Christmas lunch with her, she has no family, her three sons were killed in the war, one must have been an uncle, they never married, of course not, who wants to marry the dead soldiers. She asks do we have anyone we'd like to invite, of course Jani! So Christmas lunch laid for eight; she has three friends, one is a priest and two are fellow landladies. It's a great piece of roast beef with

Chianti wine. The priest speaks English: are we three all 'eathens – no only me, I'm all Catholic the others are barbarians. I noticed when the priest was saying grace Hall and Mulgrew looked embarrassed, Mulgrew wanted to laugh.

This will be my last Christmas in Italy and I will be leaving the country where I had met, up to then, the love of my life, Toni. Now we have one more week's variety in Milan. The Havana Cuban band have gone and it's Ugo Tognazzi topping. Jani suddenly disappears, so for the time it has to be Irena. I still feel guilty about the twenty-thousand lire, I never paid it back, well not in cash, I think she got good value for money, I gave her my all and she gave me thrush, or spotted dick. I told her, she took me to her doctor who, shall we say, knocked spots off me. Spotted dick eh? It could have been worse, she could have given me Treacle Duff. Argggg.

Ivaldi isn't coming up with any work, we are pretty down and out. The New Year, no work and we are skint again and, I might add, hungry. Then Wretch and Belsen-lookalike, Bill Hall makes an astonishing discovery. 'Follow me – and don't ask any questions.'

So we follow him and don't ask questions. 'This must be something special, Bill,' I said, because it wasn't a question.

'Yes, it is, you'll be surprised.'

'There's no doubt, Bill, I'll be surprised,' I said. 'That's not a question is it, Bill?'

He looked sideways at me, because that's where I was; in doing so he collided with a pedestrian. '*Mi scusi,*' said the victim.

Mulgrew says, 'Ha' you got a fag?' Now that was a question but not to Bill Hall.

I told him, 'Don't worry, he was talking to me,' but where is he taking us? We've been walking half an hour without asking him any questions, through the old marketplace, Piazza Mercanti, alive with fish, meat, vegetables, chickens and ducks. Hall stops to look.

'Is this it?' I said.

He fixes me with knitted brows but some stitches have slipped. 'Are you asking me?' he said.

'No, no, I was asking me, I often ask me, is this it, and

usually it is, Bill. Like I once went to Regent's Park Zoo to see a rare white tiger, when I got to the cage I said to myself, is this it? And it was. No, Billy, you said you didn't want any questions, I respect a man's right to privacy.'

The noise of the market is deafening.

'Could you kill a chicken?' said Mulgrew. We were walking Hall's coat-tails again.

'Yes, if I had to, if it was a matter of life or death, my life, the chicken's death,' I told him. 'I'd wait.'

'What?' he said. 'Wait for what?'

'Wait for it to die – I mean, it's got to go sometime.'

Hall has come to a halt in a maze of small alleys. 'It's round here somewhere,' he mutters.

God help me, I'm going to ask him. 'Look, mate,' I said, 'we've been walking for nearly an hour, where the fuck are you taking us. Dover?'

He gave a wink. Silly sod, what good is a bloody wink? That's what they thought Nelson was doing when they shot him. I was getting cold, they were all shrivelled up.

At last, he stops in a narrow alley, above a door is the sign, *Partito Comunista de Italia*.

'This is it,' he said, knocking.

'We're not Communists,' said Mulgrew.

'No, but you're going to be,' said Hall.

The door is opened by a man in a red Garibaldi shirt. 'Ah, Meester Bill,' he said.

I recognise him from the jazz club, all is about to be made clear. From a small hall we go into a large room like a Public Kitchen, it's full of people – some eating, some just chatting, lots of cigarette smoke. At the far end there are cooks preparing meals. 'This is Guido,' said Bill. We shake hands. Guido leads us to a desk in a corner, Guido sits down, hands us three forms to sign. What's going on? We are joining the Communist Party; as soon as we do we get a free meal of pasta. I had to hand it to Wretch Hall, this was a masterstroke. So I ate my first spaghetti meal as a Communist! In the weeks that follow, we try to join again, but we get recognised.

Hooray, we got some back wages from Ivaldi, now was the time to quit, now read on.

# TRIESTE – YUGOSLAVIA

After one of our shows on the Ugo Tognazzi bill in Milan, Ugo introduced me to Jean Rocca, a tall blonde girl with large brown luminous eyes and a maternal smile; she worked in the rag trade in Milan, what was surprising was she spoke English with a Roedean accent; her mother was English and father Italian, she loved our act and asked the Trio out to dinner.

'She must have bleedin' money,' said Wretch Hall.

'Well, I'm bloody hungry,' said Mulgrew, 'and this is our chance to eat, man, free dinner,' he said, feeling for his knife, fork and spoon. We had dinner at the Tavernella, off the Corso Venezia.

'Yes,' said Jean, 'I'm in the material business, you know, suit lengths and such.'

I told her I didn't know any suit lengths and such. Her grandfather, Poppa Rocca, had a villa in Cannero on Lago Maggiore; as she spoke her eyes widened and closed, it was almost hypnotic.

'Wot your grandad do?' said Wretch Hall.

'He's retired,' said Jean with those eyes going. 'He used to be a restaurateur in London, but he got into trouble with the police.'

Oh, this was interesting, so I said, 'Oh, this is interesting.'

'Oh, indeed it is,' said Jean craning forward with a wicked smile. 'He owned a restaurant with "rooms",' she repeated, '"rooms" above and he let them out to, shall we say, ladies *de la nuit*.'

'Wot's that mean?' says Wretch.

'Tarts,' said Mulgrew, 'you ignorant git, ladies of the *nuit* – the night.'

'All right,' says Hall, 'all right.'

'He', went on Jean, cutting into a Pollo Supreme, 'used to bribe a Police Constable Goddard to turn a blind eye.'

Oh, amazing, I never knew they took men in the force with a blind eye.

'It became a big scandal.' Jean was enjoying telling all this, her eyes opening wide enough to pop. 'Many big names were involved, but they bribed Goddard to take the blame, and he retired with what was a secret golden handshake. My grandfather was deported.'

'Was he ruined?' I said.

'Only his reputation,' giggled Jean. 'He sold up and bought the villa in Cannero, of course he misses the life.'

'It's a wonder he didn't get life,' says Hall, 'dealing with tart of the *nuit*.'

I know Jean is favouring me during the conversation. Mulgrew and Hall are silenced as they devour mounds of spaghetti, never knowing when it would happen again. Hall is polishing his plate with bread. Yes, Jean, we would like to take up the offer of the villa, so with a smile, a lingering handshake and a phone number. God, how is it the giving of a phone number can be so sensuous? *Addio Jean. Speriamo*!

We had done a week at the Teatro Odeon and were going down well; on the Tuesday a group of students from Milan University came backstage to talk about the 'Jizz Music'. They were from some Jazz Club. Could we come along Sunday and play for them? Hall is starting to talk '*quando soldi*'. For Christ's sake Hall, these are students, they haven't got any money.

'Neither 'ave we, I thought I'd start askin' them before they start askin' us.'

*Si si*, we'll play for them. The University bus will pick us up outside the Galleria. Sunday morning, the bells of the Duomo are ringing out their iron prayers as a busful of excited students arrives and collects us. They all talk to us at once, are we famous, some girls ask are we married, I was famous in 3

Leathwell Road, no, none of us are married, but we all practise. When they discover Mulgrew is Scots, they ask, 'Is anything worn under the kilt?' He say, '*Niente, tutti in lavorare ordine.*' At the Jazz Club we meet two Italian musicians who play piano, tenor. We have a great session, so much so we get a write-up in the *Corriere della Sera*. At the weekend Mr Ivaldi tells us there's no work next week except the British Officers' Club in Naples, and a US frontier post on the Yugoslav border, but we'd have to make our own way there – he couldn't afford the fare.

By the time the gig arrived we were skint, so what, my watch, that would have to go. In the Galleria, on the *Borsa Nera*, I sold it for seven-thousand lire. We book the night train to Trieste, Hall doesn't turn up in time, and we watch our train depart while we plead with the ticket inspector, '*Non-poss-costa piu di me lavoro.*' So now, the bus, the coach, we struggle to the coach station, Mulgrew watches, in tartan trepidation, as his double bass is loaded atop the crowded coach that leaves at midnight. Mulgrew and I sit next to a huge woman with a moustache and ten bosoms. In Italy, even on a short journey, relatives come to cry and say goodbye – the huge woman has a tiny smiling man waving goodbye. She reaches out of the window to shake his hand; while it's down the others shake it as well just in case they're related. It's a wonder the coach doesn't explode with people.

Finally, with weeping and moaning the coach pulls away, I fall into a deep upright sleep, even though I'm in tourist class I try hard to sleep first class – it's one way to beat poverty. We – and by we I mean mostly me – awake to cold but sunlit day. On our left we are passing an incredibly blue lake backed by snow-dusted mountains. That lake has haunted me. I've never, despite poring over maps, never been able to find its name or location, the nearest was Lake Garda, but I don't think it was, but it was a lake, I could tell by the water, but alas you can't tell the name by the water but if you know the name you can tell the water, if it's Coniston, you can taste it and say this is Coniston, mind you you don't *have* to say it, you can say this water tastes like Lake Como, but that would be foolish, especially in the Lake District.

'Where are we?' says an awakening Mulgrew.

'Italy,' I say.

Bill Hall looms, looking wretched after a night's sleep in the Quasimodo position. 'Have you got a fag?'

I told him I had, why?

Can he have one – 'It's to kill the hunger,' he said.

All around us the seasoned Italian travellers are slicing French bread and eating garlic sausage. We British have a smoke for breakfast. The lady with the moustache offered me some salami. '*Mangiare – mangiare*,' she said. '*Io fatto questo.*' She says she made this, I explained to my comrades.

'*Molto buona*,' said the Wretch Hall, smiling at our donor. Well, she must have sensed we were starving, as the salami vanished at speed of light down our throats, she fed us the lot like a farmer's wife with chickens. '*Molto buona*,' said Hall again.

I added, '*Grazie.*'

'Yes, *grazie*,' said Wretch Hall, returning to his seat with yet another of my precious cigarettes.

I offered our benefactress one. 'Oh no,' she said almost in horror. '*Mai fumare.*'

Mulgrew grunted under his breath, would she like a fuck?

So, in a loud voice I said, 'Excuse me madame, my Scottish friend says would you like a fuck?'

She smiled back, '*Non comprendere.*'

I told Mulgrew, 'She doesn't understand.'

Mulgrew was doubled up in evil laughter. 'I can't imagine her on the job,' he was crying, 'that moustache!!!'

The lady was now aware, I think, we were taking the piss.

'*Perchè lui ridere?*'

I explain that it was a joke I told him; she nodded, but the supply of garlic sausage ceased.

We arrive in cold dusty Trieste; we know where the British Officers' Club is, but first some coffee. We stack our instruments at an outdoor café, next to a bullet-pocked wall hung with dead flowers and guttered candles, site of partisan executions by Germans. We sat at our outdoor table huddled in our overcoats (lies, all I had was a mackintosh [see pictures]). A waiter appears. He looks like Charlie Chaplin, without a bowler, but if he had a bowler none of us had a cricket bat ha! ha! (still there reader?) he showed his displeasure at having to come outside. '*Tre caffè latte, per favore.*'

'*Tre caffè latte, pronto,*' he snarled back and gobbed in the gutter.

'Perhaps that's what he came out for,' said the Mulgrew, 'we're lucky he wanted to gob, or we might never have seen him.'

I watch hypnotised as a dew drop runs along Bill Hall's nose, reaches the end, then commits suicide. I watch it fall almost in slow motion to land on his boot. The waiter delivers our coffee and another gob in the street where it is flattened by a passing taxi. The hot coffee and the sweet rolls are like manna – in a manna of speaking. I am the keeper of the privy purse, I pay the bill to a non-gobbing waiter, he smiles, '*Inglese?*'

'*Si-si,*' I said, '*Inglese.*' I point to Hall then, 'Scottish,' to Mulgrew, '*Ma Io – Irlandese – Cattalico,*' so that filled him in. The gobbing waiter comes out and lets another one go. We have sufficient money for a taxi but I advise walking for economy's sake.

'For Christ's sake,' says Mulgrew, he of the short legs and long willy, in the army he'd been excused shorts and in Scotland excused the kilt.

What a strange sight we made on the dusty streets of Trieste, I could but keep hearing the hymn, 'We Three Kings of Orient are, bearing gifts a-travelling far.' Finally, we arrived bearing our own gifts at the entrance to the OFFICERS' CLUB CMF. A sergeant at the door checks us, "Oo?'

'The Bill Hall Trio,' I said.

'Oh, what do you want?

We don't want anything, sergeant, we've been booked here to appear in cabaret.

'Cabaret?' the word was new to him and news. 'I don't know nuffink abaht it, I call the horderly hoffice.'

Ah yes, the orderly officer, Lieutenant Johnny Smart; he remembers us from our army days. 'Yes, I caught the act in Milan, no idea you were back in the country, so it was I who booked you.' He looked at the lean, long, lank Wretch Bill Hall. 'Have you had lunch?' he said.

'Three days ago,' said Hall.

'Oh, come on,' said Lieutenant Smart, who could tell malnutrition when he saw it.

No, we were too scruffy to dine in the Officers' Mess so we dined in a room adjacent to the cookhouse, a nice room with golf clubs, cricket bats and polo sticks – such unique decor, I'd never seen the like. We are waited on by a lame Corporal Wells of the Grenadier Guards.

'He'll look after you,' said Smart getting out of the room before he caught it.

We told the lame Corporal we were ex-serving soldiers.

'Oh – what happened?'

It was strange for him, three rather scruffy civilians who turn out to be British. 'We liked it in Italy, so we came back.'

The Corporal is, 'hinterested, was we ever in action?'

Oh yes.

Where?

I reeled off North Africa, Salerno, Cassino, from then on his demeanour changed from treating us like wogs. A splendid lunch, *Fritto di Mare* and *Sole Bonne Femme*.

'Doesn't that mean "good woman"?' said Wretch Hall.

'Of course, it does,' said Mulgrew. 'Sole good woman.'

Hall sips a glass of gratuitous wine. 'Why don't they say it on the menu. "Sole good woman"?'

Mulgrew pauses his chewing, 'It's more mysterious in French, you say it Sole Bonne Femme.'

'Yes, Johnny's right. Sole Bonne Femme. Like Scots Salmon in Scottish is Le Salmon Ecosse.'

'Get away,' said Hall.

Get away, that's all he thought of was getting away. Hall was never satisfied wherever he was, all that was keeping him with us was the food, and the money to come from the gig.

'We got a selection of desserts,' said the Corporal.

'Oh good, we'll 'ave them,' said Hall. It was three of the clock, our gig wasn't till nine-thirty. 'I'm going for a walk,' said Hall; of course, a walk, that's all he could afford.

I daren't take a walk as I had holes in both my shoes; however, Johnny and I, the Celtic part of the Trio, were allowed into the billiard room, where the lighting made our

Pose showing hole in shoe

unkempt appearance less discernible. But officers kept calling us waiter and ordering drinks. So passed the afternoon to the clicking of balls, not always on the table.

Lieutenant Smart popped in. 'The dance starts in a minute, you'll be on in the interval,' he looked at his watch; 'that'll be about nine-thirty, you can change, you don't mind changing in the gents' toilet, it's the only place we've got.'

What if Noël Coward were appearing? Of course, we don't mind changing in the gents' toilets, we love it, amid the smell of piss and shit, that's what show business is all about. But where is the Wretch Bill Hall? Well, he's found a floosie and had it away. We are fascinated! *How did he pay*?

'I didn't, before she could get her clothes on I did a runner.'

'Oh dear,' said Mulgrew, shaking his head. 'That poor girl giving her all, for fuck-all.'

'Yes,' I said, 'that's what I'll call you from now on "Fuck Hall".'

So we change in the toilet, no one has informed anyone that we were in there, many strange looks and remarks and getting pissed on. So there we all stood in our stage rags; of course, getting tired we occasionally sat on the toilet. One of the officers must have reported us as a Sergeant of the Military Police came in. Thank God, Lieutenant Smart, embarrassed as he was, explained our presence. Still we waited.

'Sorry, we're overrunning,' said Smart. 'Five minutes.'

In that five minutes a drunken officer staggered in and was sick on Mulgrew's bass. With the assistance of a bucket of water, we managed to clean it in time for the cabaret, but it stank of vomit, which had got inside the 'F' holes.

'Ladies and gentlemen, direct from the Coconut Grove, London — the Bill Hall Trio.' The Italian band for some unexplainable reason played us on with God Save the King. The act went down a bomb, hoots of more! MORE! As we struggled through the crowd for our exit, there she was — Jani Rywyck! But oh! the difference! She was smothered in make-up, a black satin body-clinging dress.

'Jani,' I said; 'it is Jani isn't it?' I still wasn't sure.

'Yes,' she said, 'it's me.' Her voice was nervous, 'See me when you've changed.'

Who did she think I was, Dr Jekyll? Thank God for showers, which we all took.

'Do join us when you're ready,' said Smart.

Of course, there was so little difference between our stage and street clothes that when we reappeared they thought we'd come back for an encore. Jani was waiting, she took me to an unbusy part of the club. She had become involved in the underworld and was now the girlfriend of an Italian gangster involved in the black market. She had become involved and now was too frightened to get away. Never mind that, any chance of a fuck? No, no, no! – he's away at the moment. Can she put us up for the night, we're homeless; no, but she knows a 'safe house'. *Safe house*? Has it a guarantee against wood-worm? The house is in Via Delphi – an upper-class brothel, we are given two rooms at the back of the house, all smelling of cheap perfume. They are luxurious by our standards, over-looking the harbour and the rent. They are Mussolini modern interiors, stark, with Cubist paintings and prints, and of all things, a bidet in the room that we used as an ashtray. Jani sees us in, she will see me in the morning. Can she bring cigarettes, yes, yes, yes.

Her gone, we divide up our cabaret earnings, thirty-thousand lire, sounds a lot but with the lira at twelve hundred to the pound it's about ten quid each, but then living in Italy is cheap. We had with us two bottles of Chianti so we smoked and drank ourselves to sleep.

'Where did you meet this bird?' says Hall.

I told him all.

''Ave you 'ad it away wiv 'er?'

'Yes, at home and away.'

'Cor, you lucky sod.'

I am not lucky, I just am blessed with good looks, and could sing like Bing Crosby. Our next gig is tomorrow at a place on the Yugoslav border called Isonzo.

'What the Americans doing there?' says Mulgrew, now enveloped in smoke.

'They're waiting for us to do our act,' I said.

'I fink,' says Wretch, 'I fink we need a new agent, I mean back in London, does Leslie MacDonnell know we're appear-ing in a bleedin' place called, wots it, Izonko? No! We ought to be closing the first half at the Palladium!! Not appearing in bloody Izonko.'

'What date is it – I know the year,' says Mulgrew in smoke.

'It's the 26th of January,' I said, 'and it's time we went home.'

On this we decided it was time, we'd had plenty of

adventure, made money and blown it, so after this, home and beauty – well, home. We are kept awake by moans, screams and the cracking of whips as the clients below us were catered for. 'Lucky bastards,' said Hall. 'Just what I could do wiv, a good shag and a whipping,' and he cackled with laughter. Oh, the thought of Bill Hall in fishnet stockings being whipped with pink ribbons. It was like something on a motorway, a turn-off.

We are awakened by Jani, with a tray of coffee and rolls. 'Good morning,' she smiled. God she looked beautiful, beautifully sun-bronzed, in a tight white dress, down boy!

'Did you sleep well, boys?' (Boys?)

Yes, we were rocked to sleep by the sound of the sea, Jani. 'And whips,' I said.

'You have to be out of here by one o'clock.' That's when her Mafia lover is back. I can see she is not happy, she wants out. 'But I don't know how, I'm trapped here.'

I advise her to go to her consul. She'll think about it. She leaves us, we use the luxury bathroom to the limit, she kisses me goodbye with a look of fear. Any chance of a quickie? No, No, No – he is coming back. So that was the last I saw of Jani – did she ever get back to the ballet? We get a broken-down taxi, who will take us to Isonzo if he can find it. '*Sono cinque chilometri* [It's five kilometres].' It will cost, '*Tre mille lire, signori.*'

'We've no bloody choice,' says Hall. 'What did we fight the fucking war for, this isn't democracy – this is fucking fascism.' He then shouts at the baffled driver, 'Mussolini – No, Bon – fucking fascist. Three thousand lira! *No bona fascist!*'

The driver, in distress, suddenly raised his hat and said, '*Viva Churchill, Viva soldato.*'

Calm restored. We strap the double bass on the roof, the taxi being black as was the double bass cover, many people crossed themselves as we passed 'That's all we bloody needed,' said Hall laughing, 'to be mistaken for a bloody funeral.' We thread our way out of town, twice we are stopped by *Carabinieri* at various checkpoints near the Yugoslav frontier, each time they check the bass for smuggled goods. They soon back off at the smell of vomit. Mulgrew holds our only official document; it's our contract to play for US Forces at Isonzo, stamped by the American Consul in Milan, it gets us through all the checkpoints.

At the British one, Hall recognises a Sergeant Reg Owen.

'Cor Blimey, Bill, wot you doin' 'ere?'

'We was in the same battery,' explains Hall. No wonder we took so long to win. Via Sergeant Owen we scrounge tea and sandwiches.

'I thought you'd gone 'ome,' said Owen.

'I tried,' said Hall, 'but I couldn't remember where it was.'

Owen knows where Isonzo is. 'It's a dodgy area! There's shooting up there! It's a disputed area, didn't they tell you that?'

No, none of our contracts mention shooting.

'Don't worry, the American post is under cover. It's a mile up this track, tell him [the driver] to take it easy.'

'Wot you mean, take it easy,' laughed Mulgrew. 'He's been takin' it easy since we started.'

The driver is moaning about the road ahead.

'He wants another thousand lire,' I explained.

'He wants a kick up the arse,' said Hall.

We give him both. Off we set, it's a rising mountain road with spectacular views, a thousand feet below. The driver grumbles all the way. Suddenly a white-helmeted US police-man fronts us, 'Who you guys?'

We produce our contract.

'Ah, jeez yes, pull in here, we bin expecting you, you were supposed to be here yesterday.'

The taxi pulls into a lay-by, we go through a canvas door into dug-outs in the mountain. We finally arrive at a canteen – several GIs drinking, smoking. 'Fellas,' says the policeman taking off his white helmet to reveal a GI haircut, 'these are the Limeys who've come to entertain us.' There was absolutely no reaction – these guys were bored out of their skulls.

- The policeman took us to meet Major Evelyn White. 'Ah gentlemen.' A tall grey-haired man, blue eyes with myriad blood vessels, a kindly man with a Colt .45 at his hip. 'Follow me.' He led us to a bell tent with electric light and a glowing stove. The excitement. 'This is our R & R room, make yourselves comfortable.'

How?

'I'll send you in some refreshments.'

Indeed, hot coffee and doughnuts. 'Where you guys from?' said the GI who serves us.

Deptford? Highbury?

'Never heard of them places,' he said. 'I'm from Brownsville.'

Wow, Brownsville, oh wow.

He spoke with an elastic drawl. 'Brownsville, Texas,' he added. 'Oh wow, Brownsville, Texas,' really? Did he really live there?

'Sure due – ma familey are orl theire. Now, yew gat averything yew want?' Cigarettes, sho, he cud gait some – no, no charge, compliments of Uncle Sam. Major White says the boys are ready for the show when we are.

'We'll change, be ready in five,' I said. Dressed like tramps, we are led into a small dug-out with four men peering through slits at Yugoslav territory.

'Boys,' says Major White, 'here's the Trio to entertain you.' So in a space six feet by eight we did our act, four men clapping was our reward, was this the end? The money? Not yet, we are led to three more front-line dug-outs, where we perform for parties of two to five men. Was Val Parnell right? Showbiz! Help! Then, giving us a good meal they sent us on our way on to the now dark road. We pocket our earnings: fifty thousand lire. Destination Milan, where we hope to collect our belongings and then Villa Jean. The taxi driver moans about the dark, I tell him it's not our fault, it happens every night in Italy. 'Oh Christ, he wants another thousand lire.'

Hall explodes. 'Mussolini no bon – fascist – one thousand no bon.'

Taxi driver agrees, but it's still a thousand lire and a kick up the arse. We rumble down the mountain road all clutching the ropes that hold the bass on the roof. After an hour we arrive at Trieste Central, we catch the 10.00 and are in Milan by 01.00, Bill hives off while Mulgrew and I return to No. 6 Agnello Street and straight to bed.

# VERONA

The morning we are awakened by our landlady calling, *'Sciopero! Sciopero!'* Ah, the trams and buses are on strike, lying in bed we feel the full impact. *'Disgrazia,'* she says, *'sempre, sempre sciopero quando Mussolini viva – non posso sciopero.'* She goes away crying over lost trams and buses, and saying the rosary; it is heart-breaking. Well, we've got lire, let's to the Galleria! It's a cold day but the Galleria is dry and alive with fellow artists, we order two *caffè latte*; I better explain *caffè latte* is a bowl of milky coffee you dip a rum baba into. We are joined by two showgirls, Christina and Mia, unattractive, which is why they're out of work. 'O 'ello Spak-ello Jo-nee – where you been, we no see you this time.' They're skint so we buy them *caffè lattes*. They give us the news, Ivaldi has booked us with Angelini and his orchestra for Verona. It was true, Verona!! Romeo and Juliet, a glove upon your hand!

We all travel on the orchestra bus, lots of showgirls, lots of chatting up, like 'were I a glove upon your hand'. 'See this lot,' said Bill Hall. 'They're all lining each other up for a shag.' No, not me, I still had Toni on my mind. We pull into Verona at night and are put up at a large old-fashioned boarding house in the Via Safi. We are shown our rooms; I'm on my own, lovely!

We eat *en famille* in a big ground-floor dining room, I'm being fussed over by a buxom dark-haired waitress, she wants to know my name. 'Teree.' I always give that name to girls, it sounds more romantic, because an Italian girl saying 'Spak' (Spike) is like a custard hitting the wall. This girl Gina is Sicilian and tells me, *'Tutti Siciliani molto passionato.'* Okay, well, I'm lying in bed reading, a tap at the door and in comes Gina, and so a glove upon her hand and district. Indeed City of Romeo and Juliet. *Amore. Amore.* 'You very hot like Sicilian,' she said; it was very nice to get these little unsolicited testimonials.

At breakfast next morning, I didn't know what to say, Good morning? Sleep well? We are all rushed off to the Roman Amphitheatre, the site of our next performance – a stage has been set up with mikes and speakers. The amphitheatre was beautiful, apart from being stripped of its marble it was almost intact. It looked a bit out of place with twelve chorus girls singing 'I Can't Give You Anything But Love, Baby' in Italian. I make friends with Carlo Santamaria, the guitarist, and we spend time at the hotel playing duets. When I wasn't there he did them on his own.

'I been and seen it,' says Hall.

Seen what?

'The balcony, didn't I, where Romeo and Juliet were. Yer.'

It would be criminal to miss it, so I take Gina, and I do the 'oh, that I were a glove upon your hand,' silly sod, but I was young. Saw Juliet's sarcophagus, but it's empty! Quick, call the police, Juliet's escaped – *sfuggiere*!!! Gina has to get back to work, so I wander the Montague and Capulet streets, and imagine, she will see me tonight with her testimonials. On a cold day like this Juliet would have worn woolly knickers and Romeo thermal long johns.

The show that night went well, but the amphitheatre only a third full, bookings are poor – oh no! they're going to cancel! One more time with Gina and *addio*! Milan, here we come again. On the coach we agree the tour is over. We've had enough. Johnny and I are going for a freeby at the Villa Jean, does Wretch want to come?

'Villa Jean me arse,' says Hall, 'wot you want there?'

'It's a holiday.'

'Not me, it's been one long 'oliday, don't you want to go 'ome, I do.'

'Of course, we long for those traffic-laden foggy streets, for British Bronchitis and St George. No, we got a chance, don't you understand you cockney gronk, to live in an Iti villa on a lake!!! You must be barmy to turn it down,' I told him complete with gestures, and imitation trumpet calls.


# VILLA JEAN


Back at 6 Agnello I phone Jean Rocca, that evening I take Johnny and her to dinner at the Tavernella. 'It's very quiet,' Jean says, those enormous eyes widening and closing. 'There's nothing much to do but walks or boating.' Walking and boating, the finest exercise known to man and sailors, you rarely see a sick walker or sailor unless they're ill, even then you can be buried by the roadside or at sea. Who could ask for anything more, it all sounded ideal. So we have to take the coach to Novara then a boat to Cannero, she will 'drop in' to see us occasionally; we store our instruments at her flat in Via San Paulo behind us; we make a final visit to Signor Ivaldi to collect our Verona money.

'I very sorry show not go – time very bad in business, oh so bad, not so bad soon again I write Foster in Londra – my daughter and I say good you luck you all time.'

Yes, the daughter was there and cried, she wrote her home address on a card, all that and twenty thousand lire.

We pay our outstanding rent, which is outstanding – a total of six thousand. So off now, lugging our cases carrying a mess of clothes worth up to £1. The coach is half empty, it's Sunday, that's why, half of Italy are on their knees, we're on our bottoms in the coach, the ticket collector speaks English. 'You go Novara,' he clips our tickets, yes we have to, that's where the coach goes. 'Very nice, Novara.' Yes. 'We catch boat to Cannero, we go walking and boating *vacanza*.' He was so interested, especially when I told him walkers and sailors rarely fell ill. He said his father was a sailor in the Italian Navy, he died at the Battle of Mataplan, bronchitis. So there. At Novara a small crowd of rosy-faced plump peasants await the boat. They all talk excitedly, they are going to a funeral of a relative at Cannero, possibly a sailor or a walker.

If we hurry we might be in time for the roadside or sea

Poppa Rocca outside the Villa Jean

burial. The boat, a quiet little steamer, chugs gently across the
millpond surface of Lago Maggiore to the little pier. PORTO
CANNERO – we follow Jean's instructions, five hundred
yards up Via Roma, Villa Jean is on the left. We knock on the
door, an ample black-haired Italian Mamma greets us, this is
Gladys Rocca, Jean's aunt and Harpy.

'Ah, welcome. [She speaks with a Cockney accent!] You
must be Johnny and Spike.'

Blast, he's got top billing.

'Come in, come in.'

It was a large rambling villa built into the hillside – the
sloping, stepped gardens a mass of semi-tropical plants.
Coming down the stairs was Poppa Rocca, an angular man in
his seventies with a bald head. This was the man who had made
headlines in the 1930s . . .

Johnny and me by the Lago Maggiore

'Ah, please,' he gestured us in; for us the right direction. 'Gladys, this my sister, she show you to your room.'

It was indeed a rambling house that needed attention, or better still, stand at ease. The room was at the top, two single beds, a wardrobe, dresser, all the necessaries. Through the window the magnificent Lago Maggiore. We have lovely old-fashioned down mattresses and pillows.

'When you've settled in we've got tea for you,' said Gladys. Now Gladys was ugly but one of those who radiates goodness. Her story; she was living in London married to a Dennis Jones, a Welsh lad. The war came, he was called up, wounded in the lungs at Dunkirk, became an invalid. After the war her brother, Poppa Rocca, now exiled, was living on his own in Cannero. Dennis Jones was told he should go and live in a warm climate, got it? Yes, Gladys came and did housekeeping for Poppa while Dennis, now on a pension, became an odd-jobman in the village. When we arrived he was chopping wood (what's odd about that, did he do it with scissors?) for one of the better-heeled villagers. It seemed a role reversal, here an ex-British soldier working for ex-enemies. We all sat down for tea, bread, butter and jam. It didn't take long to realise the Roccas were having a struggle to live, so we chipped in with the shopping. A lot of the time we played cards, dominoes or Bocci, a sort of Italian bowls. At night we got stewed on Rocca's homemade grappa.

'Those bloody police in London – *bastardi* – look, every hotel in Soho have room for *prostituto*, but they catch me. You know why, I no pay protection money.' Poppa Rocca ran his thumb back and forth on his forefinger – he was lying, it was he who bribed Constable Goddard to look the other way, towards Catford. It's dark, cold, we sit around a wood stove.

We meet Dennis, he's just up from the village with a sack of logs, he's a small, slim man, blue eyes and lank brown hair, he's very emaciated, and most certainly has consumption – an exhausting cough. He joins us, yes, he was a gunner at Dunkirk. 'Oh boyo, what a cock-up – everyone without a clue, I was lying on the sand when this Junkers bombs us, I got it in the back.' He stands up, raises his shirt to show us a ghastly scar.

Should I show him my appendicitis? I couldn't see Dennis lasting long.

'He's only got a 60 per cent pension,' said Gladys, refilling our glasses. God! Grappa was like drinking raw spirit, felt good, I sang a few songs – 'Blue Birds Over The White Cliffs Of Dover', Dennis and Gladys join in – we all stare into the fire, little else to do in Cannero of a night.

Poppa sings an Italian song. 'I sing song about Florence,' not Nightingale? no, Firenze – Firenze. '*Sul Arno Argento*,' he sings. He has a strong wobbly voice that sounds as though he's got a rat trap on his balls. Dennis puts some logs on the fire.

'You two married?' says Gladys.

'No, we are not married—' I said. 'I proposed to him but he turned me down.'

Dennis laughed and coughed. Thank heaven, he didn't bring it up, we'd have drowned. It wasn't late but we all turned in. I lay in bed enjoying the absolute silence – a silence I'm sure no longer lingers over Cannero.


Jean Rocca has arrived, unannounced; a young female on the premises and I hadn't shaved. 'Don't worry, Spike, it gives you a vagabond appearance.' She's over for two days and intends to show us over the Castello Malpaga. 'It's very interesting,' she says with those hypnotic eyes. We all retire for coffee.

'We love it here, Jean, but we'll have to leave soon before our money runs out.'

'Yours runs?' she giggles, 'mine gallops.' She looks in her handbag, fiddles about. 'Oh, thank God! I thought I'd lost my return ticket.'

Please God, let her lose it.

'What have you two been up to?'

I told her we'd been up to the bedroom and down. What no walks. Walks? Hasn't she seen the graves by the roadsides?

'Walks,' says Mulgrew through smoke. 'That's for people with legs.'

'You've got legs,' says Jean.

Mulgrew rolled his trouser legs up. 'Call these legs, they're only supports.' They look like pickaxe handles with hair on.

That morning, Mulgrew and I sunbathe, it's warm by day but

cold at night, perfect. 'I wonder what my mother and father would say if they saw me now.'

'They'd say there he is in Cannero.'

'When I was born,' said Mulgrew, 'my father sued the doctor, he said I contravened the Trade Descriptions Act.'

'You still do, that's why I'm so kind to you crossing the road. I mean without your double bass, what are you?'

'Five feet, seven and a half,' he said, 'and packed with talent.'

'But very badly packed, look at the lumps.'

Jean leans out a top window. 'Lovely day.'

'Yes, Jean and what a pair.'

'I'm helping Gladys get lunch,' she says.

I say we'd like to give Gladys ten thousand lire for our keep.

She says, so would Gladys. So far we've done it in dribs and drabs, Johnny gives her dribs and I the drabs. I get up and run up to the bedroom, I meet Jean on the stairs, it was meant to happen, I kissed her and wow she kissed me.

'It's this mountain air, Spike,' she said, descending the stairs.

I collected the ten thousand lire and gave it to Gladys, she burst into floods of tears. I look for a life belt. Money, the blessing, the curse. I blessed having it and cursed having to give it to her.

'Oh, thank you, Spike,' she said. Don't thank me, you old cow, give it back where it belongs.

'It's nothing,' I said, wishing it were.

'I'll make a special dinner.' Collecting her shopping bag she went off. Bang! Was she doing a runner? You never know with Ities.

'Ten thousand lire.' Mulgrew makes a heart attack. 'If only my poor parents *heard* that amount, ten thousand,' he wailed. 'All is lost!!! and the pension fifty years away!'

I convince him we're getting value – value for spaghetti – because that was the main meal. We talk about what to expect when we return home.

'I don't know – it'll be wait and see,' he says. This must be the waiting bit.

Johnny at the Villa Jean, early morning

The sun streams in, awakening Johnny and me.

'Bloody hell, that sun's hot,' said Mulgrew.

'Then we mustn't touch it. Today is adventure day, Johnny.'

'Oh, hurray, Milligan the Master Manager,' says Mulgrew of the addled Scottish mind. Who in their right mind would invent the bagpipe? To an already depressed race, and haggis to a nation that put salt – yes, SALT – on their porridge, and what lunatic invented a kilt in a country of high winds and thistles! No Mulgrew – today we visit the Castello Malpaga – 'What in the world', says Mulgrew, arising and scratching, 'is Castello Malpaga?' I explain it means Castle of Bad Payments – sort of final rates demand.

Gladys has made us an English breakfast. Egg and bacon. 'Only one egg each I'm afraid,' she says. 'Chickens don't like cold weather.'

'Yes, I suppose the wind gets up the back,' says Mulgrew.

Jean giggles. 'That's rude, Johnny.'

Johnny Mulgrew shows his appreciation of culinary arts by smoking and eating, sort of barbarian dexterity. Breakfast over, Jean leads us to our appointment on Castello Malpaga. But there's a ritual – Jean, beautiful Jean, takes us down to a waterfront house to borrow a boat from Signor Marcini, on board we then row to Signor Cerruti, who has the key to the castle. The thing is huge, about seven inches long on an iron ring; he warns us to be careful with it as it's the only one left. Why does anybody want to lock up a ruined castle in the middle of the lake? The Prudential. Signor Marcini guides us to the water gate and, using the key, rows in. We tie up and explore the castle. In the fifteenth century the Brothers Mazzarditi used the castle as a base for pirate raids, we see the stone gallows where they hanged their victims.

'I wonder what it's like to be hanged,' said Mulgrew.

'Wait here, I'll get a rope.'

Mulgrew deposits his cigarette in the lake.

'Isn't this a wonderful place?' says Jean, leaning over the rampart on tiptoe.

'Yes, it is a wonderful position, Jean, don't move!'

Signor Marcini shows us the dungeons below water level.

'You see,' I said, 'one day they'll be letting them to Pakistani Patels.'

Signor Marcini has never heard of Pakistani Patels, of course not, Pakistanis were in India, very hard to hear them from Italy. Protruding from the walls are dozens of gibbets for decapitated heads.

Jean shakes her head. 'Can you imagine anything so cruel,' she says.

I try hard to think of anything so cruel, many things passed my mind but nothing so terrible, landladies' Cold Collation, that or cats with their bums on fire going up the A1 Yeowwwwwwwwww . . .

We return by our rowing boat with Mulgrew doing us proud and himself and anyway – In, out – in – out – I shout like a cox.

'Make up your mind, do you want me in or out of this boat!'

Ahhh! He has given himself blisters! Good job we're not working*. 'For someone who's never rowed you were superb, you sure you've never rowed before?'

* Meaning he wouldn't be able to play the Double Bass.

Johnny mastering oarsmanship. My curls in the top right of the picture

'No, never.'

'Then you're a natural bad oarsman. The shortest distance between A and B, are you listening, Johnny, is a straight line, you believe it's circular.'

'Aw, give over, if you don't like it, swim.'

We dock safely. I help Jean out of the boat, she nearly falls in but *I*, you hear me, *I* save her. I throw my arms around her.

'Oh God,' says Jean, 'and I can't swim.'

She doesn't have to, she's on dry land.

As we reach the front door of the villa she says, 'It's all right, Spike, you can let go now.'

Blast, never mind, night and Mulgrew are falling.

'That rowing really took it out of me.' I told him I never saw it come out of him, it must have been quick. Mulgrew is used to my insane patter, but Jean isn't.

'I don't know where you get it from,' she says with those eyes, which are now flashing invitations.

'I don't know where I get it from, Jean, it arrives once a month by boat from Scandinavia, I just glue it together on the Monday.'

'Gladys has made a special dinner for-er tonight,' says Poppa Rocca; he is holding a wine bottle. 'This wine very old, Bardolino 1939.' I remembered the date as the start of the war, where was that bottle when I needed it?

'I must freshen up,' says Jean, ascending the stairs; oh that wobble!

It was a momentous dinner – minestrone soup, then chicken liver risotto – then – oh no – bread and butter pudding. The Bardolino is a let-down – 'It's corked,' said Mulgrew. Of course, you ignorant fool, all wine bottles are corked, that's what keeps the wine in – but wait, Poppa Rocca says it's corked – so do Jean and Gladys, so I learn something. I drink my corked wine and say it tastes fine. Ignorance is bliss and pissed. We all get very mellow – 'Mussolini – not bad man like people say,' says Poppa Rocca. 'He make many good things – like Hitler he make country strong,' he goes on and we start to disagree.

'I think he ruined Italy – and he made me spend five years in the army,' said Mulgrew.

From left to right: Jean, Gladys, Poppa Rocca and Johnny, checking he has money

Poppa Rocca paused, 'So what? now all finish – he dead – Clara Petacci dead – all dead . . .' He raised his glass. 'Here – good friends,' he said and drank.

Gladys is going to bed, and Poppa and all of us. Goodnights, one special one. 'Goodnight – Spike,' says Jean. All right, you've guessed. I slept with Jean Rocca, what do I mean slept, I was awake half the night, and she was awake the other half – we took turns, folks! Next morning no one suspected, except Mulgrew, who knew.

'I thought,' he said through smoke, 'you were carrying the torch for Toni.'

'I am, but sometimes it goes out,' I said. Jean has to return to Milan for business reasons, having finished her business here. I take a last group photo.

'Sorry to go,' she said, as the steamer sailed, its mournful
hooter echoing round the mountains. What are we made of?
Last night we seized upon each other like life committal and
here am I waving goodbye to her, never to see her again ever.
Someone explain life to me.

'I'll explain,' said Mulgrew as we walked back to the villa.
'You are a dirty little devil, it's a wonder you don't catch
something.'

The only thing I was going to catch was the train home. On
our last night we supplied the wine and gave Gladys another
ten thousand lire. We had to be careful now as we had just
enough to get back.

'We'll miss you,' said Gladys, 'won't we, Poppa?'

He smiled. '*Si*, you lucky – I love London, I miss you very
much.'

'Apparently, from what I've heard, you didn't miss much
when you were there.'

He laughed and slapped his thigh, then winced because it
hurt. '*Mamma mia*,' he said in fluent Italian, 'I'm getting old.'

Yes, when you get old, certain parts mustn't be hit. But *how*
do you get old, you can't send somebody out shopping and say
' . . . and while you're out, get old.'


Now you know I said I would never see Jean Rocca again, well
I didn't until we returned to her flat to collect our instruments,
she put us up for the night and yes I did, with the girl I would
never see again, I think she was suffering from some form of
sleeplessness and it was me. Oh Jean, those long legs, and two
of them, just the right amount. She took us in a taxi to Milan
Station and again waving me goodbye for ever – only this time
for ever. Johnny and I get two corner seats.

# HOME AGAIN

Before departure the carriage fills, among them a priest and two nuns. It's the right train for Calais and soon we are dozing to the clickety-click of the rails.

'*Bigletti – bigletti*.' The ticket collector arouses us and off we loll again. I slept until sunlight and Mulgrew jogged me. We are halted at Domodossola. 'Piss Pots – Customs, Piss Pots pliss.' We show our piss pots, they match the photos to our faces – and pass down the carriage. There's a chance of food from platform vendors, bread, cheese, salami – a quick cup of coffee and a bottle of wine. The train pulls away as we munch our food.

'I wonder where Bill is now,' mused Mulgrew.

Indeed, where – weirdo, who could, when pushed play like Paganini, but you can't go around pushing people to play like Paganini. I got in conversation with the priest who is Irish and there's us been swearing in English.

'Oh, I should have told you earlier,' he said, 'I was just fascinated by, shall we say, the poetry of your language.' He's a Franciscan on his way back to Ireland, he's been in Rome on a sabbatical.

'What exactly did you do?' I said.

'It's a very good excuse for a holiday, with a lot of praying in between.'

I tell him I'm a Catholic, but I don't believe in God. 'Ever since the war I can't believe, I believe in Jesus, but I prefer Buddha, whereas Jesus seemed only interested in saving man, Buddha saw every living thing as sacred.'

'Oh yes, he was a good man, that I'll say.' He wouldn't be drawn.

Johnny; taken at a railway halt, Northern Italy

'You believe what you believe – and I believe.'

Would he like a swig of our wine?

He believed he would, and in full view of the two nuns he swigged a bit. The nuns, in fact the whole carriage, smiled at the impudence.

No, he wouldn't want to argue about God. 'Can you see the wind?' he said, that was supposed to be a show stopper.

'No, I can't see the wind,' I said.

'Think about it,' he said.

Now, I didn't want to sit there thinking about the wind, it was bad enough having it. Was Buddha's God the same as

Jesus's? No, no, no, but he'll have another swig of wine, would he bless the wine, he looks a bit embarrassed, so I didn't push him – but it would have been a great moment if he had.

'Don't let him drive you mad, Father,' said Mulgrew through smoke.

'Don't talk to him, Father,' I said, 'he's a barbarian Protestant.'

'Oh, there are good and bad,' said the priest smiling.

The nuns are talking in French and eating sandwiches from a little wicker basket.

The Father addresses them in French – whatever it was, they smile. 'I was telling them we're arguing about God,' he said.

'Ah, Father, you don't get this on English trains.'

The French countryside flashes past, partly snow-covered. I drift off to sleep, drift, drift – zzzzz, I go. Through half-closed eyes I see Mulgrew relighting a dog-end.

It's Calais in winter, it has all the charisma of a clogged toilet. French stevedores are shouting and jostling us as we board the *Invicta* – the grey channels from Calais lead to a mist-laden sea, fog horns are sounding, but as the morning proceeds this mist lifts and we see the English Channel in all its pristine brown. The ferry is almost empty, it's cold, we sit in the second-class lounge and have tea and toast.

'Well, chum,' says Mulgrew, 'it's all over – yes.' He paused, drew on a cigarette, exhaled – 'It's all over.'

I told him, 'Don't you remember you said that just before you inhaled, your mind's going, the long journey has got to you. You must hurry to a brain surgeon, I've noticed you going downhill for a month and I've been waiting at the bottom.'

'Och, will you hear this looney,' he said, with calm eyes of a sage. We went on the after deck and took photos.

Ah, the cliffs, the white cliffs, look what those seagulls have done.

'Listen Johnny,' I looked deep into his eyes, took one of his hands in mine, and at the ship's rail sang, 'There'll Be Blue Birds Over The White Cliffs Of Dover.'

'Oh fuck off,' he laughed, pulling his hand away. 'I'll be all right, it's travel sickness, I'm sick of bloody travelling.'

Returning from Calais on the *Invicta* after the tour of Italy

My father, Leo, on his way to work in Fetter Lane, London

The train also almost empty, we find an empty smoker. As the train draws away we both stretch out for a sleep.

'Please take your feet off the seats, gentlemen.' Ah, the conductor. He clips our tickets and we go back to sleep but—

'Gentlemen, I asked you not to put your feet on the seats.'

The bastard, the horrible swine bastard.

'What you gonnerdo?' says smoked Mulgrew.

'I'm going home to Mum and Dad, I've hardly written to them, they might think I'm dead.'

'*Think*,' said Mulgrew, '*Hope*, mate.'

I took the tube from Victoria to London Bridge – amazing how there *is* a different atmosphere from the Continent – it doesn't feel so exciting; no, standing here on a cold platform at London Bridge, suitcase and guitar, there is a distinct lack of excitement. 'Is this train for St John's?' I said to a miserable bloody British Rail porter.

'Dunno,' said the miserable bloody British Rail porter.

Yes, the guard knows, the miserable bloody guard knows. I sit in a third-class carriage and a young man gets in – 'Is this train going to Beckenham?'

'I dunno,' said miserable bloody Milligan. Ah yes, Beckenham, he comes back this young man.

'Yes, it is going to Beckenham,' says the miserable bloody passenger. He then sits in a corner and, hand in pocket, starts to *play* with himself, giving himself an erection, which seems the size of a cucumber – I was in a non-smoking compartment, but it appeared that wanking on BR was permissible. I just wanted to get off before he tried to fuck me. He was still wanking away when I got off at St John's, as the train pulled away I shouted through the window. 'Don't forget – stop at Beckenham.'

No taxis, here, I lug my suit and guitar case, desperate for a bath. Mum greets me at the door, 'Oh my son, my son, how lovely to see you.' We exchange standard clichés, 'Why didn't you tell me?' – surprise – 'you must be hungry' – yes – 'tired' – yes. Bath, well it's a zinc one in front of the stove – boil a pail of water – well I've bathed in some luxury bathrooms, nothing beats one in front of a stove, plus tea and toast. I give my mother a present of a rosary – always safe with Catholics even though she's got a dozen. 'Oh, it's lovely, son.' Lovely? It's awful, appalling imitation purple pearls, arrrrrgh. She loves it, but then my mother thinks Lewisham is beautiful and a painting by El Greco 'very nice'. I up to my bed and give my mother her second present, my laundry, six months' worth with skid marks galore. 'I'll soon have this lot drying in the garden,' she says. Aren't mothers wonderful – this one is. I go up to my little back bedroom and sleep the day. Home. I awake in time for my father's return from the Associated Press where he works in Fetter Lane, a good name as he is fettered there from nine till six. He hated it. 'You know why the British have wars? To get them out of this bloody awful climate.'

He shakes my hand warmly, actually it was quite cold, but that's what he meant. 'So, back from foreign climes.'

What are climes, I don't remember seeing a climes in Italy or Switzerland, and I'd never heard English climes mentioned. I related our success.

'So the tour was a success,' he slumped into the blue moquette armchair with a cup of tea. 'Made some money, eh, son?'

'No, Dad – we had villains who sometimes didn't pay us, or did a runner.'

'Oh, didn't you report them to the police?'

The *police*? Half of them had to be bribed, no, I had no money left, so could I borrow a fiver?

'Welcome home, son.'

In my luggage I had brought a bottle of Tokay – so we stoked the fire up and I recounted my travels.

'Well, son,' said my father, 'you are seeing the world, so what next?'

The next world. 'I'm thinking of leaving the Trio and going solo, it's the Amy Johnson in me.'

# GERMANY I

Sure enough, there is no work, we all have phoned Leslie MacDonnell. All he has for us is an Army Welfare Troop show tour. Oh Christ, back to that. I move back to Linden Gardens, same room. The Trio have to decide, a troop tour of Germany or bugger-all, we all think bugger-all a bad thing – in fact, none of us thinks much of bugger-all – so it's to be a series of one-nighters in the Fatherland.

So here we are on an RAF converted Wellington Bomber being flown to Berlin from Northolt. It's a small company: Benn Futz, a Polish juggler/acrobat; Vico Wilson, a Liverpudlian comic; Eric Prills, a pianist; Dennis Max-Holm, a comic; and Avis Trenchard, a singer. All about thirty and all about broke, but all very nice people and grateful for the work. Our tour manager is an old Queen, William Hodges. 'Now,' he said, as he came along the plane bench seats, 'we're all going to get on, or maybe some of you will get off. Mind if I sit here?'

The pilot shouts, 'No smoking please, till I do!'

'Nothing makes you need a fag more,' says Mulgrew. The plane's engines drown out conversation.

Airborne, the navigator comes round with a large coffee flask with plastic cups. 'You can smoke now,' he says.

'Ta,' says Mulgrew, who already is.

'You're a naughty boy,' says the navigator.

'No sir, he's actually a naughty girl but he had the operation,' I said.

Navigator laughs, spills coffee on Mulgrew. 'So sorry.'

After a deafening flight we land at Tempelhof – on the tarmac, all waiting an AWS coach on to which a Sergeant directs us. Berlin looks grey, the centre is war-torn, great chunks out of the Brandenburg Gate – we are driven to the Schoenbraun Hotel – or rather Hostel. Endless traffic of civilians and soldiers, each one seems due for an important critical meeting at which they will be killed.

A jolly officer of forty summers meets us. He is the living image of Neville Chamberlain, an artillery major, Tom Wells. 'Well, you're all very welcome – you'll all have separate rooms, but I'm afraid the bathrooms are communal. This is Corporal Harris, if you follow him,'

'Ba – ba – ba,' I go as we climb the stairs.

'I'm sorry the lift's not working – it was damaged in the war – RAF bombing.'

'You mean that lift was put out of order by us and that's why we're forced to use the stairs?'

The Corporal laughed. 'You can put it that way.'

I can and I have – fancy the RAF targeting lifts. All our rooms are nice, clean, stark, but for the bed there is no furniture, a wall cupboard and a sink.

Hall comes in, 'Handy, the sink, I've just done me socks.' He, this Wretch, seemed in a constant battle with his socks and underwear, night after night he'd wash one or the other – there are times when he only washed one sock, yes, *one sock*, and when asked why, he'd say almost with dignity, 'The other one doesn't need doing.'

We are gathered again by a Corporal, Collins by name, and taken to lunch in a private room. We are waited on by ex-POWs in white jackets and very good they are.

'I don't know,' I said to Hall, 'I think I shot his uncle, and by the way he served food, I wish I had.' I discovered my Kraut was at Cassino – so was I! We involuntarily shake hands, he speaks a smattering of Italian so the conversation is:

'*Me combattere in Cassino. Seben maise. Cassino molto nix good – boom – boom.*'

'*Ich in Royal Artillery – grossen Kanonen.*'

'*Grossen nix gut.*'

I say, '*Grossen Kanon molto bono per you.*'

'*Me ich beinen paratruppen.*'

So he was one of the bastards that held us up for sixteen months.

'*Me*,' he went on, '*combattere in Castelforte*.'

Castelforte—? My God, we must have killed dozens of his uncles. My heavy battery rained shells on that village for two days. '*Mein Kanon, boom, boom, Castelforte zwei tag*–!'

'*Oh, molto morto, mi amico*.'

'*Mi dispiace – ma c'est la guerre*!'

'What you want ter talk ter these bastards for?' said Hall. 'Two years ago the bastard would have killed you.'

Agreed, but now he's serving me at table and I got him running around me, getting me seconds, he never dreamed from his little funkhole in Cassino, that one day he'd be serving me apple pie mit der kustard! Anyway, despite trying to kill me in Italy, he wants to know if he can take us to the nightspots. Well, for my nightspots I use Germolene, but we'll see. His name is Ernst Bohem, he 'knows' places.

The evening we are driven to do a concert in a drill hall for REME, there's no stage – we perform at floor level, only the front row see, except for the acrobats. It's a full-blooded soldier reaction – with cries of 'get your knickers down, darling' for our singer Miss Trenchard. She came off to cheers in tears, 'I've never been so humiliated in my life. I want to go home.'

Now for the nightlife of Berlin, city of sausage, sin and Sally Bowles. So Ernst takes me to the Blaue Himmel, a cellar, but what a cellar, just table, chairs and a stage, the demimonde are here, men done up as women, women done up as men, waitresses in short skirts with no knickers. We were the only normal ones there.

'*Vobisdu*,' says a ravishing waitress, white-faced, kohl eyes, red lips and bare bum.

A pot of tea for two please.

Tea nix!

'Okay. A bottle of Moselle.'

'*Ja, darlink, une Moselle*—'

'You like,' said Ernst.

'*Molto bono, ja*!'

'*Ja*,' he said, frothing at the mouth. He leered at everything that went past, there's a drag queen on the stage with ridiculous act, with a whip, some soppy 'aporth from the audience is standing on stage while she sings, '*Ich slagger*

139

*barnhoff*' and cuts the buttons off the silly bugger till his clothes fall off – the audience are at that drunken animal stage when anything is suggestive – uproarious laughter for things totally unfunny, every joke was below the waist. 'Oh, *wunderbar*,' says the paratrooper from Cassino. Mind you, it's all a wondrous experience – I mean – Hitler didn't need to shoot himself to avoid the Russians. Believe me, if Hitler had seen this mess he would have committed suicide long before.

Now the main act, a busty, frowsy, over-made-up tart prances on and does a dance, she strips off then a man with white make-up and a long black mac does a sort of dance to piano and violin accompaniment, then whoosh – off flies the black mac with a dramatic chord from the piano. I cried with laughter – then to the signature tune of Laurel and Hardy, he screws, complete with cymbal smashes. All through there are cries of encouragement in German. There were cries of encore, even Heil Hitler, so the male participant tried again, also with the ridiculous Laurel and Hardy tune – not before he took a sip of water from a glass set on a table.

'A lot of fucking good that will do him,' said Wretch Hall. 'What he needs is Guinness and oysters.'

I was by now unfit to talk, I thought it all too funny for words, then no, no, no! As the bloke starts to screw her again – there is an introduction on the piano and she starts to sing, 'Wien Rose', her voice shuddering on each thrust.

'No wonder they lost the war,' said Hall. 'They was all fucked.'

Well, we saw the night out – there were more songs by homos and lesbians made up in fantastic make-up – forget Liza Minnelli in *Cabaret*.

We took a taxi back to the digs and an old German Porter let us in with enough grovelling to demand a tip. '*Danke schön! Mein Herren – Ich nix Nazi – Ich bin ein Democrat*.'

'Lying bastard,' said Bill, 'they were all fucking Nazis otherwise they couldn't have kept going so long.'

We walk the stairs, 'Bloody RAF,' said Mulgrew – so a night's sleep. The noticeboard on our door – Breakfast from 7.30 – 9.00. So at five to nine we'll be there.

Five to Nine queue for breakfast, yes Hall slept well and his socks were dry by the morning. Major Wells moves among us, 'Jolly good show last night, well "we" catch a plane to Hanover this afternoon, do a show at the Opera House and fly back.'

'Not much time to see much,' said Hall.

Well, I told him there wasn't much to see, it's like the Russians left it.

'I'd like to see Hitler's Bunker,' said Mulgrew.

'She's dead,' I said. 'Anyway, it's in the Russian zone so forget it. It was unbelievable that a man would let a city be razed before shooting himself – had he shot himself a month earlier we'd possibly be staying at a hotel. Oh here we go.

'All on the coach, please answer your names,' says a nameless Sergeant.

Next, the Dakota with bucket seats. 'Seatbelts,' shouts the pilot and we are away over the ruined city, somewhere below us is the male water-supping actor, resting.

Miss Avis Trenchard has not left us, she quite properly dried her tears and said, 'I'm not gwoing to be put orf by some wude soldiers.' She is a darling nineteen-year-old girl, opera-trained, 'dwaddy' is in the Foreign Office, the girl is innocence itself and seems to 'twust' me. 'You'll look after me, won't you, Spywke?' Of course, of course, I'll look after her and fuck her, of course. Our Polish juggler, Benn Futz, is air sick. William Hodges has given him a nylon sock as a sick bag. I watch hypnotically as the sock becomes the shape of a foot. Looking out the window, I am almost stunned at the bomb-damaged landscape. How did they hold out so long, where did they go? There wasn't a building standing.

'Where did they make the Tiger Tanks, there's not a factory in sight,' said smoke-shrouded Mulgrew.

'I've got it,' I said, 'they made them in inch squares and posted them to the front.'

'Fuckin' rubbish,' says Hall.

'Shh Bill,' I whisper, 'not in front of Miss Trenchard.'

'I don't understand,' says Wretch Hall.

'You can say kill out loud but not fuck. I mean, she'd rather be fucked than killed wouldn't she?'

Above the drone of the engines I don't think Miss Trenchard can hear us.

'Seat belts,' shouts the pilot, 'and fags out.'

We come down slowly.

'Oh, we're not going to cwash are we, Spywke?' Miss Trenchard clutches my arm.

'No, we're as safe as houses,' looking at the bombing below, there wasn't a house in sight. I told her flying wasn't dangerous, *crashing* was dangerous. A very smooth landing, we all applaud.

'Thanks,' says the pilot, 'but I'm taking you back, by which time – ha, ha, ha,' he twirled his whacko moustache, 'I'll have had a few.'

Someone is saying, 'Anyone want to buy one nylon sock.'

Off the plane, no coach but an army three-tonner is waiting. 'It's gettin' rougher all the time,' I say as Schnozzle Durante, 'if tings get woise – I'm complainin' to Winston K. Churchill, ha, ha, ha.'

'I give up,' says Mulgrew. 'Let me guess . . . W.C. Fields.'

'You don't know a good impressionist when you see one.'

Mulgrew giggles, 'Er – the Ritz Brothers?'

A new Sergeant appears. 'I'm Sergeant Watson. I'll be looking after you, if you just answer your names,' he smiles. 'Sorry about this.'

As we answer our names we clamber on the three-tonner, helping hands pull Miss Trenchard aboard. She lets out a little squeal of delight or was that me pushing her bottom. Sergeant Watson bolts up the tail board, across the tarmac.

'Hanover is the seat of the Hanoverian kings,' I tell Miss Trenchard.

'Oh weally – I believe we're appwearing in the Opwa House.'

And what a magnificent one, pure Baroque, the interior's like a palace.

'Now if you'd all like to leave your props in your dressing rooms, just choose one,' and laughed. 'There's forty to choose from.'

'I'll take five,' I said, slouching off like Groucho Marx.

'You see my dressing room,' says Hall, who's chosen No. 1. 'Come and 'ave a look.'

Well folks, the room was like a miniature ballroom – so on

The Bill Hall Trio in action

the polished marble surface Hall deposits his carrier bag of props and 'Is that all?' giggles Hodges, our 'queen'.

'There's one still in the laundry,' says Hall.

'Come on, they're waiting to take us to ...' Hodges paused, struck a gay pose, 'The Hotel,' he mouthed. 'Hotel Grand Holstein.'

Another Baroque but worn-down building equally lavish in rooms, Mulgrew and I share. I avoid billeting with Wretch Hall, as I'm convinced every night after sock washing he becomes a werewolf. Ah! but we don't eat here – we go to the sergeants' mess for lunch. Oh, now a coach mit zer German driver.

'I'll be leaving you here,' says Sergeant Watson and Adolf here will take over. Adolf is a compressed midget all of five feet five inches. He sits on a high cushion to drive and disappears behind the dashboard when he declutches; as he disappears we all shout, '*Auf Wiedersehen*, Adolf'. He keeps

grim-faced and pours with sweat. No. 34 REME Workshops –
a sentry halts and checks Adolf's documents; we give the
sentry a cheer as we go in.

Yet another i/c party, 'Corporal Allan, follow me, folks.'

I ask Mulgrew, 'Did you know you were a folk?'

'Aw, awa boil yer heed,' he grinned.

'Where's the ladies?' Miss Trenchard is nigh to.

Corporal Allen takes her to ATS toilets. She comes out
blushing. Soon we are ushered into a dining room where lunch
is being served to eight tables of NCOs. 'You have to help
yourself here,' said Corporal Allan. So trays, knives, forks,
spoon, cup, steak and kidney, apple pie etc.

'You see,' said Hall the Wretch, 'they'll be askin' us to
fuckin' sign on again.'

Mulgrew tells him as things are back home it might not be a
bad thing. While we're seated another jolly decent officer
appears. They're all between forty and sixty; you can't but feel
they haven't been in action, haven't heard a gun go bang, and
possibly caught it once.

This herbert is tall, thin, grey-haired and grey-faced. His
sunken eyes appear to be touching the back of his skull; he has
of all things an Adolf Hitler moustache; it badly needs
trimming as it hangs well down over his bottom lip. This is
Captain Nuttall.

''Ee looks like fuck-all,' says Bill Hall.

'Ow do everyone, [God, he's North Country] 'ope yer all
been tooken care of – I'm 'ere to see you're arl reet, yes.' He
then buggered off to the bar, of which he reeked, possibly.

'The fingerprints on his glass were still warm by the time he
got back,' I said – mind you I said it to Benn Futz our Polish
juggler, and I shouldn't have because a) he had no sense of
humour and b) he didn't speak English. But he gave me a
sickly grin, some left over from the flight.

'You know,' said Miss Trenchard, 'I've nwever been away
from hwome before, Spywke.' It was nice of her to confide in
me – me who wanted to screw her away from home, where
Mommy an' Poppa couldn't see. But no Milligan, she was too
nice, damn it.

144

We are told the show starts at 6.45, curtain down 9.15, flight 9.30 approx. 'Hear that, Mulgrew and smoke, we're going on an approx. flight possibly on the same approx. DC9 that brought us approx.'

Half the audience at the Opera House are local civilians. It is a special occasion. This is the first time they've been allowed into their *own* bloody theatre since the armistice. There's a full German orchestra in the pit in full evening dress. Likewise lots of top brass and local dignitaries in the boxes and front row. Of all people, Brigadier Sir John Holmwood and Mr Adenauer are in the Royal Hanoverian box.

'If I'd known this I'd have washed my socks,' said the Wretch, lying back in the velvet-buttoned splendour of his diva's dressing room.

'There are bloody speeches first,' said smoked Mulgrew.

The Town Mayor – 'A great pleasure to welcome the people of Hanover to our concert tonight. This is the first time . . .' Etc. etc. (I won't bore.) The show was a roaring success – but we 'brought the house down'. (What an idiotic cliché, who wants to bring a house down, think of the people upstairs asleep, eh?) The Germans didn't understand Dennis Max-Holm, nor Vico Wilson our Liverpudlian, but we, who did music and mime, tore 'em up, paralysed them. 'They should never have lost the war,' I shouted over the applause. The cast were introduced to Mr Adenauer, who should never have lost the war, and if it hadn't been for all the Krauts we killed we'd have had a bigger audience.

Sir John Holmwood thought our act awfully good and were we professionals? I heard myself saying, 'No, sir, we are bricklayers by trade on a working holiday.' Thank God, he laughed, with relief as he left us to meet beautiful Miss Trenchard. A complete change of demeanour. He loved her act and he loved her voice and he'd love to fuck her, he has wafted her away to a clique of brass hats, all red tabs and whisky fumes. Ah, he's edged her towards a table of champagne – we are still at the lager table – ah, here comes Willy Hodges, still with make-up traces of his drag act and in a Hello Sailor mood. He's already in the I'm anybody's mood, so unlike you and I who wake up with sore heads, *he* wakes up with a sore arse, and believe me there's a lot of them about. We disengage after the drinkie-poos. There are lots of stunning fräuleins in 1930s dresses. One realised how hard up and under pressure they were for everyday goods.

'It's their bleedin' fault for losin' the war, mate,' Hall insists. 'We've had it bleedin' hard, we risked our lives, oh, look at the tits on that bird, and they got what they were askin' for – I wonder if she's askin' for it.'

Smoke-ridden Mulgrew says, 'Jimmy – you can fuck any of these for a bar of chocolate.'

Fool, fool that I am, I've eaten *all* my ration. There should be a warning on every packet: a Warning – Eating this chocolate can lose you a fuck.

I chat to one gorgeous Marlene, 'I learn English speak – I listen BBC and I write down – now I go English school – and I pass my class.' She's sixteen and never knew anything but war and build-up to it. 'I belong to Hitler *jungen fräulein*, but I no like, my father soldier, he die in Africa.' Oh Christ. She is a divine spirit. She had suffered her father's death, and non-stop air raids. She now works in the NAAFI. 'You know NAAFI?' she said. 'I get chocolate free.' There is no justice. But it was wonderful seeing this blonde, blue-eyed stunner, with no rancour – didn't say she was never a Nazi, never mentioned politics, didn't *hate* anyone – it sort of blew a fresh breeze through a jaded personality. I hated leaving her, she was too innocent, too young, and, she had CHOCOLATE!

Back to our Hotel Grand Holstein.

'I could have got off with a dozen birds,' said Hall, as we ascended the stairs.

'This must be the only bloody lift not bombed by the RAF that doesn't work,' said Mulgrew.

Hall, lucky sod, is on the first floor. 'Come in, come in, let's ring for some beer, it's not late.' His room is like a palace, a satin-hung four-poster with two-headed-eagle bedhead.

An old waiter answers the bell.

'Three,' Hall holds up three fingers, so he got it right. 'Three bottle beer.'

'*Ja – gut, drei bottle beer*,' he writes *slowly* on his card.

'You can remember that,' says Hall impatiently.

'*Ja*, I remember,' he said slowly.

'You like bottle open mit glasses?'

'Yes, but not slowly.' Hall takes off his desperate eight button, five still on, overcoat. Slowly and even more desperate, he lies back in splendour. 'Why is this all so temporary – why do I have to go back to Legard bleedin' Road, eh, answer me that.'

I held my hand up. 'I can answer that, my lord – you have to go back because you live in Legard bleedin' Road and you live there, my lord, because you are bleedin' skint.'

Ah, the beer. The slow waiter comes slowly across, places the tray slowly on the table, slowly he starts to open a bottle; in one tigerish bound Hall snatched the opener and in a trice opened – even while he opened the third his other hand had transported a bottle to his fragrant nicotine-stained teeth through which it gurgled like the sewer sluices at Battersea.

'Dat is two marks, sir,' said the slow waiter.

Then the evil Hall in slow motion went through his pockets looking for the money. 'There, my man, one . . . two . . .'

The waiter smiled and left.

'It's Minden tomorrow, in'it?' said Wretch as he walks across the room to check if a pair of woollen socks hanging on the back of a tapestried chair are dry.

'Yes, Minden,' I said. 'Famous battle there.'

'Wot?'

'What do you mean, wot?'

'Well, wot was famous about it?'

'Well we won and on Minden Day those regiments taking part are allowed to put a rose in the cap.'

'Oh, that's marvellous, isn't it – I was in a battle in Norf Africa, I got fuck-all to put in me hat, only me bloody head.'

As he makes off to wash his socks, we leave. I fall asleep with the face of that divine German girl.

I don't know how one has dreams like me, but I dream I'm standing at Oxford Circus, and I am dressed as a traffic warden – but on my hat is written the words KNICKER WARDEN. I have a long stick – on the end is a mirror. My job is to check women's knickers and if they are not up to standard – they are given a fine.

My God – this is travel. On the tarmac waiting for us is a helicopter. (Did she get away? No, by hell, he copped her.) The pilot, like all pilots, was a Battle of Britain type; all had DFCs, wore scarves, and had moustaches peculiar to the RAF. To my question he said, 'There's no landing strip at Minden.' It explained all. Poor old Benn Futz is looking grim and holds a sickbag. I'm holding Miss Trenchard, or she's holding my arm. The noise is terrific; we are on bench seats with over-the-shoulder safety harness. Before take-off (or I've just remembered), the second pilot told me the pilot had been a glider pilot at Arnhem, so we're in the hands of heroes. Futz travels with his sickbag in front of him but in twenty minutes we are putting down at Minden in the grounds of HQ BAOR – a man with two ping pong bats directs us down. Down the narrow ladder I hear Bill Hall telling Hodges that: 'a famous battle took place here . . . rose in their caps.'

Another reception party. Captain Norman Levy and ATS Sergeant Joan Page (from Scotland). We are introduced by Willy Hodges. Needless to say, Norman Levy spoke with a strong Jewish accent. 'I'm entertainments officer for the Minden area – so, well, any complaints come to me.'

'Does that include lurgi?'

He smiled, 'Lurgi, that's a new one on me.'

I assured him to avoid catching it one stood on one leg in a bowl of custard and barked.

'Very interesting, Mr Milligan – exactly what is it?'

'Lurgi, Captain, are little tiny spots of shit on the liver, brought about by long service in desert stations where the higher the fewer, and one must avoid muffed squalikons unless approached naked downwind with a squalikon emulsifier, unless of course you can grab a sensitive area and crack them together.'

All this got laughter from the party but a strange bemused look on the face of Sergeant Joan Page; as we walked to the waiting coach she said, in a broad Scots accent, 'Awa wi' ye – you're just making this up, yew must be the comic.' Now let's describe this ATS lass; she has a figure like an hour-glass, red hair, green eyes and a face like Greer Garson.

'No, I'm just a musician. Vico's the comic.'

She doesn't want to know. 'Och, I love music – do you like jazz?'

I get on very well with her. I want to get on better.

'Sergeant Page will accompany you to your billets, it used to be a hotel, but I think you'll find it comfortable,' Levy gives us a polite little salute.

Sergeant Page has seated herself next to me. 'Was I married? Did I have a girlfriend?' she presses me.

'No, I'm as free as the wind.'

She tells me she is just getting over a broken love affair.

'Don't worry my dear, I'll be the glue to those pieces, I'll kiss it better.'

'Have ye a fag?' Mulgrew has run out.

'When I die, Mulgrew, I've left instructions that I'm to be cremated and I want you to inhale the smoke.'

'Oh, come on,' he wails, the nicotine craving from his balls to his throat.

'Och – here, have one of mine,' says Sergeant Page, producing a silver cigarette case from her bag. 'Can't see a fellow Scot go without.'

'Oo ta,' says Mulgrew. 'Which part you from?'

I know where all her parts are from – Scotland. I am automatically extending my lighter to the fuming Scot.

Sergeant Page offers the case to me. 'You smoke?'

Ta. She snaps the case shut; now admit, reader, that snap is a very satisfying sound. On the case is engraved a heart and 'With love'. 'Was that him?' I said.

'Naw,' she smiled. 'He was the one before.'

'Oh,' I said, 'can I be the one after?'

'No,' she laughed, ' you can be during.'

Oh, how I suddenly loved the army.

'Spywke, where are you, are you neglecting me?' Miss Trenchard has stumbled down the coach. 'It's my birthday today.'

'Oh, happy birthday,' I interject.

'And I'm inviting you to my party tonight where that's gwoing to be.'

'A party. Great, can Sergeant Page come?'

Yes, everybody – 'Ewerybwody.'

The hotel has been converted into barracks barely worse than being converted to devil worship. I have a single door with an adjoining room (eh – quick Nurse, the tablets). It is stark and looks more like a ward or a prison cell. I'm not there a moment when a tap on the door – it's Sergeant Page. She comes in, closes the door by flattening herself against it. I flattened myself against her, this making her a part wood, part me sandwich. I kissed her as though, well, that's how. 'No,' she said. 'Not now, tonight.' That explosion over, she says, 'They're serving lunch.' She looked at her watch, ran over to the wall mirror, checked her hair and make-up. 'Tonight,' and she left. The space she left was like a vacuum. I was nearly sucked out the door with her – wow. Tonight wow II.

Lunch in a canteen, but served by ATS girls.

'This is the sergeants' mess, but they had theirs early so we could use the hall, very nice of the dear ATS. I've got such a headache.'

Who was it, Mulgrew? No, he's worried about forgetting his make-up. He thinks he's left it behind in Hanover. 'What a lovely song that would be, 'I Left My Make-up Behind In Hanover.' He needn't worry, Sergeant Page has 'a bag full of it'. If only she knew, so did I. The lunch is the same one we had yesterday.

'Steak and kidney pud, only eaten once,' says Wretch Hall.

'Yes, dear, they fly the stuff ahead for us,' says our queen. 'Nothing too good for old queens like me.' He does pretend tears.

'Don't cry, dear,' I say, patting his hand. 'There's a hosepipe ban in the area.'

He giggles, throws back his head and in pantomime tones says, 'I assure you nothing is banned in my area, duckie.' General laughter; we are all comfortable in each other's company now. We all know each other. One thing unrevealed to the company is the ritual of Bill Hall's laundry. The show is in the Garrison Theatre, a nice garrison, fuck-all theatre. A replica of the interior of a local drill hall. This time it's a military audience, and the show goes like a house on fire; stop, who invented these clichés, our show *didn't* go like a house afire; we'd all have been burnt to bloody death. No, the show

150

got tumultuous applause, especially Miss Trenchard, whose birthday was announced from the stage. Cries of Good Luck Girl, and time she 'ad it. The romantic fools.

Yes, there is a party in the ATS Restroom organised by Sergeant Page, no less. There's a radiogram with lots of Benny Goodman records, so there's lots of jitterbugging. There's a great spread of sandwiches and beer. God knows who's paying, but there it is.

'They dwid it all fwor me,' said rosy-cheek Miss Trenchard. 'Oh, come on Spywke, let's dance.' Well, it was something. She couldn't – neither could I. We looked like two suet puddings stuck together. 'Oh, you dwo dwance jolly well,' said the little idiot. She was acting a bit strange; then I heard she's been plied with sherry. Then she starts to fall over, then she wants to be sick, then she wants to dance on a table and falls off. Then it's time for bed. We all drink too much.

It's gone two by the time Sergeant Page crept into my bed; an hour later we too were gone two. She keeps waking me up to do it. I need rest, I tell her; no, she's never felt like this before with anybody; yes, darling, but twenty times, I've been coasting the last ten. I think she flew out the window, or was it me?

I awake with knocking on the door, a face appears, it's, it's, it's, *it's*, that's who it is, it's *it's*. 'Wake up,' says Mulgrew. 'It's bloody midday [so that's who it is].'

We fly back, at Chinese dentist (two-thirty), what's the matter? Why won't I speak? If I can just get my tongue unstuck from the roof of my mouth.

'Do you need a spoon?' said Mulgrew.

'No, no, why did you wake me, I am to be Queen of the May.' I don't feel well. It's that nasty feeling I get sometimes, same as in the war. My head is burning; no, don't pull the blind. The MO and Sergeant Page come to see me. I tell him I'm an anxiety-state manic depressive. He gives me some white tablets, they just make me feel dopey. 'Am I fit to travel?' Am I fuck, somehow I make the plane to Hanover and we fly straight home for Northolt. I sleep all the while with strange abstract dreams. Two that keep recurring. A lion on a ward-robe about to spring on me, and a ceiling with revolving half coat hangers.

# HOME

I get home to 3 Leathwell Road and go to bed. It's almost the
end of the Bill Hall Trio – though we don't know it. My mum is
worried; I've been in bed five days, unshaven. 'Get up, son,
have a wash and a shave, you'll feel better.' Perhaps. I try a hot
bath in front of the fire. Mum adds another bucket of hot
water. Had I caught something when I was in Germany, did I
sit on any dirty lavatory seats, or eat any German food? No, I
didn't eat any lavatories or sit on dirty food. The doctor comes
(yes, in those days). He wants to know when I was in
Germany, etc. No, he says I haven't got German measles or
rabies. My temperature is normal, my pulse rate is fast. He
writes a prescription. My dear mother goes out in the rain to
the local chemist. 'It's a good tonic,' he tells my mother. My
mother tells me, 'It's a good tonic.' It gives me the shits.

I went to tell Bill and Johnny I wanted to finish with the
Trio; Bill took it badly. 'You'll never work again, you bastard,'
were his parting words. The Trio went on with a new guitarist,
Bart Norman, once of the Three Admirals. The Trio went on
working for another thirty years doing the same act. When
Johnny died six years ago, it finally stopped.

## ANN LENNER TRIO

The Bill Hall Trio was not the last trio I would appear in. No,
Jimmy Grafton has found me work – Ann Lenner, one-time

lead vocalist with Carol Gibbons at The Savoy, wants to break away. So she wants to form a trio but finds it hard on her own. I am introduced to her at the Grafton Arms, which is becoming for me what Berlin was for Isherwood. Ann is a petite lady in her late thirties. 'Hello, pleased to meet you, Miss Lenner – I hope I'm suitable.'

She smiles. 'Well, you look suitable.'

We are joined by the third member of the Trio, my old friend Reg O'List, late of the Windmill Revue. 'Super, super,' he said, so now, the act.

'Mostly vocal with a little light comedy,' says Ann.

Jimmy Grafton is to write the act for us, Reg and I will accompany Ann on guitars. Reg has a straight, shivery, light baritone, Ann is a soprano with a very good range, I'm – well, light Bing Crosby baritone. So, the act is on. Our first job is in an Army Welfare Show, Swinging Along, with the comic Eddy

The Ann Lenner Trio. From left to right: me, Ann Lenner and Reg O'List

Publicity shot for the Ann Lenner Trio

Molloy. He's never made the big time, he's a summer season or pantomime comic – in America called a second banana. I can't imagine what a fourteenth banana's act must be – it must be so bad you're not allowed on. We rehearse the show over the Irish Club in Eaton Square. My God, the fug that arose from the bar below! You got pissed inhaling it.

The Ann Lenner Trio goes like this: I spring from the side of the stage singing 'Flat Foot Floogie' with the Floy Floy. To cut me off, Reg O'List comes from the other side singing 'The Cossack Patrol' – then Ann Lenner enters centre singing 'I'll Capture Your Heart Singing'. Light patter – who do you think you are? I think I'm me, who did you think I was? Etc. Then 'A Quiet Town In Crossbone County', made popular by Danny Kaye; during the number I clowned a lot, and I became aware during rehearsals people in the cast were laughing out loud, the best way – I can't remember all that act but we ended on a sing-along – your favourite tune, but not mine. For a briefing on the show, the whole cast assemble at the·rehearsals on the Friday before we leave, and, wow, there's eight girl dancers. Captain Richard Leche tells us we will play Hamburg, Munich, Lüneburg and Vienna. I spot one of the chorus girls, Dorita Smith, another redhead with green eyes. She is Head Girl. We do a complete run-through of the show – I have to appear in some of the Eddy Molloy sketches, which I think are as funny as a baby with cancer, but it's work, money and, perhaps, fame.

'Well, looking forward to the trip?' says Reg.

'Yes, it would be silly to look backward to it, even sideways at it – no, it's best to look forward, it's a jolly good direction. In the dictionary it says, Forward: at or near the forepart of anything. Well, that's where I wanted to be, Reg – at or near the forepart of anything. How proud my mother would be when she saw me on stage. "That boy there near the forepart of anything is my son."'

Poor Reg got three weeks of this. 'Spike, my boy, I will do my best to understand you, I am older than you in years (even minutes!) so I'm a patient man.'

'Yes, Reg, with your complexion, you look like a patient, if you lie on the floor I'll call the ambulance.'

Reg smiles. He hasn't got the mind that can handle my ravings. Reg is just lovely, kind, solid but square. Reg and I compare wages, well rather *I* compare wages. I say, I'm on £30 a week, anyone want to swop? 'No, Spike, I too am on that princely sum; it'll suffice, it'll be hard to save, I tell 'ee lad.'

No, I said, if he didn't save it, the sum would stay at £30, no matter what. You could transfer it from your back to your breast pocket provided, in between, you didn't spend any, it would end up £30. I didn't have £30 at the time, I only had one, and I showed Reg how I transferred it from my back to my breast pocket, then slowly I returned it to my back pocket, then I triumphantly showed the pound safe and sound.

'Very good, Spike, very impressive, as soon as I get my £30, I'll sit up nights practising that very valuable financial move.'

I said, 'I must warn you, in time the money will start to fray, and that's when to spend.'

'Yes, that's enough for today,' says Reg, 'I'm wearing thin.'

'Are you all packed?' says Ann – all this while the chorus are going through the routines.

'Yes, I'm all packed, Ann, and most of it is in this suit – well, half of my underwear is; I always travel light, that's why I leave my mother and father behind.'

'You won't bugger the act, will you Spike?' she said.

'You'll see, I'm a good pro., as good as £30 can make.'

In the rehearsal break, I go down to the Irish bar for some cigarettes. 'Twenty Players, please.'

'Oh no, sir,' says the Irish barman. ''Tis only Sweet Afton we have.'

What in God's name was Sweet Afton?

''Tis an Irish cigarette.'

*Irish* cigarettes? Like saying Irish bananas. So I smoke Sweet Afton; where, when and how in Ireland were they growing tobacco? I felt so proud, yes, I felt my knee, elbow and wrists and they all felt proud. I wondered where the tobacco plantations were.

As she danced, all flashing, cherubic limbs, I watched Dorita Smith. God, she was luscious – but I was luscious too, me and my nine-stone Belsen body.

Here I was, really standing still; I was in a Trio that was

Dorita Smith (centre) in Hamburg with fellow dancers

mediocre compared with the Bill Hall Trio, so where was I headed? I could clown, tell jokes, sing, play the guitar and it was in the style of Danny Kaye who was now wowing audiences. I'd done all the continental touring I wanted; I needed another tour of Germany like a drowning man needed a piano. Somehow, there just might have been a drowning man who needed a piano – take the *Titanic*: the lifeboats were full, those drowning would have been very grateful for a piano floating by. There is a story of the *Titanic*'s band, a quartet; as the ship sank they played on, the violin leader said 'Keep playing', but as the ship tilted, the drummer slid away, then the piano, next the cello – to avoid the water, the leader stood on a chair – finally, he too slid into the Atlantic with a cry of 'Fuck show business'.

# GERMANY II

Saturday, we all assemble at Liverpool Street Station – all in clusters – the musicians together, the girls in another group. I stand smoking Sweet Afton with Reg O'List, he doesn't smoke. 'Never have, Spike, how did you start?'

'A man with a pistol said, on your marks, ready, steady, go.'

O'List bemused. 'Seen Ann yet?'

'Yes, I saw her yesterday—', when is he talking about? Ah, here she comes, all done up to the nines. I'm done up to about three.

'Couldn't get a bloody taxi,' she says.

Major R. Leslie will come along with the show as manager, voyeur and bore. By good fortune, in the carriage dead opposite me sits Dorita! Why did I say she was dead opposite me, they wouldn't have dead dancers in the chorus, would they? 'It's a non-smoker.' That's what she said when I lit up my Sweet Afton. Thanks to bloody cigarettes, I spent a long time in the corridor or the toilet. Dorita is sorry about it, so is her friend Pat. 'It's just that we don't like cigarettes,' they say. Oh, they don't know what they are missing, bronchitis and about £500 a year, silly little fools.

Here we are, Harwich – springboard for Holland – all confusion, steam, shouting, jostling; I and my suitcase remained calm amid it all.

'Are you a good sea traveller?' says Reg.

Yes, I am, provided it's calm, no, I've never been seasick, I know people who live at Bournemouth who are seasick, they're sick of the sight of it. We're all shuffling up a gangplank on the *Harwich Queen* – we have our own Queen, Billy Dunlop, who is really second banana to Eddy Molloy. He is, like most gays, a most agreeable person. Billy is Scots from Glasgow. 'Oh, my father used to beat my mother,' he said, 'beat her.'

Oh, what was it, the hundred yards?

'I think that's what turned me – I don't know – people say it's an illness, well I feel perfectly normal.'

Yes, he felt normal, and stop that. What's this? Dorita has a boyfriend, Joe, how dare she? I've only known her a week and already she's had a boyfriend for a year – you can't trust men – so who can you trust? Elephants, you can trust elephants, you can rely on elephants – elephants are reliable – if you can see an elephant, you *know* he's there – there he is, reliable, so for me to trust Dorita she'd have to become an elephant, but, how do you go to the pictures with an elephant? 'One adult and one elephant, please.'

Ah, but, 'I'm not really going steady with him, in fact, in truth, it's over but I haven't told him.'

Well, that's better, no, not better, she wants to be seasick and we're nowhere near Bournemouth. It's a very rough crossing with everyone down with *mal de mer* and seasickness. I wonder if elephants ever get seasick. I'm sure Bournemouth is safe from them, I mean, imagine elephants being seasick in Bournemouth with the highest rates in the country. The Hook of Holland; arrived in Van Gogh's motherland and not a one-eared person in sight, and no sight of a hook either – weak from the voyage, the cast of Swinging Along came ashore.

The *Harwich Queen*? They are saying it should be called the Sick Bucket. Janet Orwell, one of the girls, needs medical attention, a blue-uniformed first-aid man takes her to the Port Doctor, who gives her some tablets and smelling salts – plus a nip of brandy. The train for Hamburg is waiting, so, shakily, we get Janet into the carriage, the girls fuss around. 'She shouldn't be travelling, really,' says Dorita, who seems to have taken charge – 'Oh, there is a restaurant car on, good!' So Boy Scout O'List comes back with a tray of tea, poor Janet Orwell sips it like Extreme Unction.

'Oh, thank God for tea,' she said almost in ecstasy – then gently fainted. Everyone becomes Florence Nightingale, the lady with the lamp – or was it Florence Nightingale, the lady with the lump? The instructions are limitless. 'Lie her down, head between her knees – rub her wrists - rub her knees' – the train has suddenly started and sent us in a heap on top of poor Janet, a second jerk drops a suitcase from the rack on to Reg O'List's head.

'Bloody hell!' He and I struggle it back on the rack.

'Ah Watson,' I say, 'that is one of the strangest cases I've worked on.'

The flat countryside of Holland is flashing past, windmills and tulip fields being planted. We all seem to have settled, I'm sitting next to Janet Orwell. 'How's it now?'

She's still: 'not 100 per cent, but I feel better.'

The bar is open now, so I loaf off to bring her back a Cognac – no, no, no, she couldn't drink it, so I showed her how I could. Ah, that's better, she looks much better now.

'So do you,' giggled Reg O'List. Oh yes, there was nothing like a brandy to make someone else look much better.

Major Leslie, holding a shaky gin and tonic, is visiting his charges. He too is looking much better. 'It won't be long now,' he said, and departed, sipping his wobbly gin. What won't be long? What was he talking about, was he referring to his poor, long-unused willy, how can he go around commenting on how long things won't be?

'He means the journey, you silly sod,' said Reg, who really enjoys my verbal extravagances.

'I've never been to Germany before,' said Billy Dunlop.

'You'll find the old place changed,' I said. 'The RAF have bombed all the lifts and you can get anything for a bar of chocolate.'

'I will use mine prudently,' said Billy. 'I might find someone nice,' he said with a saucy grin, 'you never know.'

I told him straight, I never know anything – go on, ask me the date of the Trojan Wars, go on!

No one was willing to speak. Brave Reg spoke. 'Okay, I'll be the fall guy. When were the Trojan Wars?'

'June the 3rd, 1936.'

There was a giggle-filled silence.

'You see,' I said, 'I don't know anything except ha ha! Except there are no dry cleaners in Peru.'

All the carriage are amused at my rantings. 'Girls,' said Dorita, 'I think Spike Milligan is on drugs.'

'Yes, I admit it, it's called – wait for it – Sweet Afton,' I said, pulling one from the packet and lighting it.

'No smoking,' chorused the carriage – so there I was in a cold corridor, sucking on Irish tobacco.

It's starting to rain, it lashes the countryside in great scythes as we cross the border into the Fatherland – we see the remains of the Siegfried line. God, we were travelling over pain-impregnated, blood-soaked land, was it only three years and forty million dead ago, those people out there were all haunted by it, no one had gone untouched. I was very touched by it; people said I looked touched.

Reg sticks his head into the corridor. 'When you've finished your lung cancer lesson, we've got some fresh tea!' How did they get past me in the corridor with fresh tea? Lies, there is no fresh tea but I'm given the order for some. As I stagger down the corridor I meet the pianist, Jack Jordan. 'Ah the maestro – give us a tune,' I say.

'Oh Christ, Spike, this bloody drummer! Oh hell, he gets faster and faster – he's got a hot arm.'

'He gets faster,' I said; 'that's wonderful news, it means we'll get home earlier every night.'

'Silly bugger – you didn't bring your trumpet, did you?'

'No – I had to put it down – it had— [Here I clutched my head in a sob] rabies – my little trumpet had rabies.'

Jack looked long at me, drew on his cigarette. 'I'm leaving you before I catch it,' he said.

I get to the tea bar; a mixture of nationalities; there was a time in Europe when people who were displaced in the war were crisscrossing the world, trying to find their roots again – my roots were in my head so I knew exactly where we were. Comes my turn.

'Pless?' says the Van Gogher.

'Eight teas, pless,' I say.

'You wid der Concerter party, yes?'

Yes.

'Oh, lot nice girls I see, lot nice.'

Of course, lot nice. There's an Ahhh! of appreciation as I

swing into our carriage. 'Girls, the tea barman says you are lot nice girls – what have you to say to this accusation?'

Pat Joyce, a tall, dark Irish girl with a tremendous accent, says, 'Oh Jasus, I know girls a lot nicer dan dis lot, Holy Mary!'

'Ah, so there's Holy Mary,' I said.

'Now den,' says Pat, no doubt a devout Catholic when she was not at it. 'Don't blaspheme about our Dear Lady.'

I'm passing around the tea. 'Don't worry, I won't have a word said against the Dear Lady, but I must warn you, the prayer books are full of her – I mean, did you know she had an illegitimate child?'

'Oh, it's a wonder God doesn't strike you dead,' said the shocked Catholic, smiling but holding her hand over her mouth. 'You'll go straight to hell, man!'

Straight to hell – there was no such transport! I'd have to change at Crewe and Slough.

Major Leslie has brought his gin and tonic to visit us again. He looks much better, the gin was working wonders for him. 'How are we all?' he lisped.

Reg, you were a captain in the war, answer him.

Reg shakes his head and smiles. 'All correct and present, sir,' he said.

The train has journeying soldiers on board, who slouch past our carriage. They have spotted our Harem. (A spotted Harem? Must be Measles.) And keep coming back to ogle them – ogling soldiers are not a rarity – in fact, most regiments are ogling ones – the Brigade of Guards are an ogling regiment; in fact, the Earl Ogilvy is the Officer Commanding. You watch the Queen's Birthday Parade. Ogilvy says, 'Eyes right', and the entire Brigade ogle the Queen, but not the horses, they ogle straight ahead.

'Oh, look!' Dorita points out the window, corn stubble is being burnt – it looks as though the countryside's on fire.

'God, it looks out of control,' says Billy Dunlop.

'It's stubble burning,' says Reg. 'They do it every year.'

'So they never learn, do they?' I said. 'Wait a minute,' I said, 'that's no stubble burning.'

'Oh,' said Reg, sitting up like a Headmistress. 'And what, may I ask, is it, Professor?'

'That is an American Army flame-throwing attack on the Siegfried line – you don't believe me, do you – didn't you notice the driver of our train was wearing a smoke mask? This train is running late. [I looked at my watch.] Good God, it's exactly 1944.' We have winged past the burning.

'It appears the battle's over,' said Reg, like a psychiatrist calming a lunatic. 'Now who's taking the cups back before the next attack?'

More ogling soldiers.

Pat Joyce stares back. 'God, de're *so* rude – don't dey know it's rude to stare, where do dey recruit these fellas?'

I said, they go into the forest, shake the trees and they fall out.

'Dey should ha' left dem under the trees,' she said, applying a lipstick, a special demo for the soldiery. She holds up a little hand mirror and applies it distinctly for the soldier yobbos in the corridor, there's three of the dolts. Oh, where were they when the shit was flying – I slide the carriage door ajar. 'It's a pound an hour for staring,' I said in a cheery voice. The dolts look at me thunderstruck. 'If you're going to stare at me, that's two pounds, and—'

'Eh oop,' one of them said and nudged his mates, indicating me as one of the enemy.

'Nout 'arm in looking,' one lout said.

'Yes, but can't you go and stare at the engine driver, he might let you pull the whistle.'

I obviously had offended them – and like true young British lads, had I been in a dark alley, they'd have had me down and kicked me in the balls. They slouch off.

'I was in the army five years, but I never met any as thick as them,' said Reg.

'All right, Miss Joyce, you can stop the demo now,' I said.

'Hamburg – Hamburg!' A Van Gogher ticket inspector is warning us of the forthcoming station.

'Oh,' I said, 'I am disappointed – when I heard him shouting Hamburg, I thought he was selling them.'

'Oh, and perhaps he was,' said Pat, 'and he's sold out.'

Thank God for Pat Joyce, she's witty. 'There's only two Irish people on the train,' I said, 'and they're both us.'

'Both us?' It was news to her I was Irish.

'Yes, both us, both me and both you, both boths.'

''Aw God, yer daft,' she said. 'Away with you.'

We are pulling through the ruins that are Hamburg. 'God, how did people survive?' says Dorita. We all wondered that, yet buses and trams in small numbers, people in grey and black, pushing hand carts and prams with goods and possessions, or goods they possess.

'Poor devils,' says Billy.

'Poor devils,' I said aghast. 'Those out there were trying to do to us what you see them like now.'

'But you can't help feeling sorry for them.'

'Oh, I do,' I said, 'I *do* feel sorry for them, but I don't feel anything else except happy when I see some poor old crippled German woman in rags lying in the gutter, crying. I feel very, very happy, but of course I feel sorry for her.'

'You're a crazy mixed-up kid,' said Billy, who laughed a lot at me.

'Mixed up, yes,' I said. 'But worse – I'm mixed up with you.'

The train is easing itself into the battered station. 'Hamburg – Hamburg!' The voice echoed down the corridors. He's coming back – he's stocked up with them again – the train suddenly halts and Reg gets his suitcase on his head again – 'Oh fuck,' he says, fighting the thing.

'Think of it as an encore, Reg,' I said.

'Fuck it,' he said, feeling his head for blood.

'Never fuck a suitcase,' I said.

'Mother of God, will you not use that word,' said Pat, who meant it.

I'm sorry, Pat, it's the old soldier in me. 'I'll never, cross my heart, ever say suitcase again.'

The train continues its shuddering progress – making us all lurch back and forward like marionettes. 'I suppose this is part of German postwar reprisals.'

'Well, it's not funny,' says Dorita who, preparing herself for debouching, was trying to mascara her eyelashes and now appears to have one black eye. She is spitting mad, and also spitting on her handkerchief and trying to remove the excess.

I suddenly remember that Reg O'List had once told me he

was of Dutch descent, a happier state than of Dutch Cap descent (if the cap fits, wear it, ha-ha-ha). I asked him, while being shunted, to expand on it. 'I thought of it while we were going through Holland, Reg, but I never mentioned it then, in case, seized with latent patriotism, you threw yourself from the train.'

'Well,' he said, keeping an eye on the luggage rack and his arse on the seat, 'well, my people were Jewish, their real name was Augerlist.'

'Augerlist,' I repeated, 'that's not much of a list.'

'Shut up,' he said. 'We came across during a pogrom – I think it was the Huguenots.'

I was surprised. 'Were you a Huguenot?' He didn't know. I told him the Huguenots weren't Jews.

'Weren't they?' he said.

'No,' I said, 'they were worse. They were Protestants.'

He smiles. 'Then perhaps *some* of the Huguenots were Jews, or—' He paused. '—some of the Jews were Protestants.' It was very confusing. Did your parents make lace? No they didn't, they made money, then lost it, he'd been looking for it ever since.

## HAMBURG

The train has finally stopped, and to be amicable, so have we. We must have gone past Hamburg ten times, he's had to keep backing up. 'I've been past it for years,' says Dunlop, peering out the window – he liked a good peer.

I explain the backward and forward motion of the train. 'You see, lots of the rails are missing with the bombing – there are no rails in the Hamburg siding. So he has to back up so they can lift the rails and lay them in the siding. Simple to understand for people of my intelligence, but difficult for people who couldn't make lace.'

'Thank Christ, he's stopped,' said Reg.

'As soon as I see him, I will,' I said. We all stand and grapple with our luggage.

'Can you help me, please, Spike?' says darling, delicious Dorita.

'Stand aside world, I'm helping Dorita.' I ease her suitcase down and get a suspected double hernia. 'Girl alive, what have you got in that case – what is it, a mangle?'

'I like to travel well provided for – you never know.'

Never know what? She doesn't know, now I'll never know. It looks a bit gloomy out there, the lout soldiers go past for a last ogle, carrying great heavy packs, kit bags and rifles. 'Don't forget parade 6 a.m. tomorrow, lucky boys.' They stare at me and look for a dark alley and a pair of my testicles to crush.

'Thish way,' shouts the pissed voice of Major Leslie – who is looking in the opposite direction. 'This way,' we struggle down the corridor and expand on to the platform.

I scream out loud, 'Arrhhh. A PORTER – the camera!' And he has a large trolley.

'I take—' he says. 'I work Pritch Army Velfare.' A big blond giant of a man – not a mark on him, the bombing must have missed him. He certainly couldn't have been in a lift.

'Follow him to the coach,' shez Major Leslie. It's a khaki charabanc with Army Welfare Services on the outside and seats on the inside.

'Oh, see what's on the back,' says Billy. There's a white banner with 'Swinging Along' – a misnomer as the bloody coach won't start.

'Can we all give a push?' sayze Major Leslie. All the men give a giant groin-crippling push – and off it goes, leaving us standing like nanas; he drives a thousand yards and backs up. Girls cheer and clap as we reboard. I dump down in a seat behind Dorita.

'Oh, and you men are so strong,' says Pat – among the best piss-takers I've ever met. 'Whatever would we do without you?'

A voice from the band – 'You'd 'ave to do it to yerself darling!' Bawdy laughter a-much. Through shattered streets, where the odd street lamp is lighting.

'Doesn't this remind you of Catford?' I said.

No, none of this reminds anyone of Catford. Strange, anything reminds me of Catford. We slow to a halt outside a

Police Station. They're going to arrest us. It's more of German postwar reparations – look, when they come for us, I'll say World War Two was all my fault. No, wait a minute, we've broken down. Strangely enough, we all look broken down.

'That suitcase cut my bloody head,' said failed Huguenot.

'Not now, Reg, no good soliciting sympathy now, we've broken down in Hamburg.'

Of course, we'd love to push it again – and stand like nanas for him to back up.

Our driver is an English soldier. 'Sorry about this, ladies and gentlemen – it's never broken down before.'

What's he talking about? We broke down outside the station.

'Ah, we are here,' says Major – sobering up, Leslie stands up and falls back into his seat. 'Whoops,' he says like an old queen, which he turns out to be.

'You all right, Leslie (Leslie?),' says Billy.

'You must try me sometimes,' says the Major.

Hotel Boccaccio – ah, a touch of Italy and a touch of the ruins.

'It's all right inside, I promise,' said the major.

"As the lift been bombed yet?' – a musician.

It has been a splendid, Victorian-style hotel, but dimly lit. Or is it me that's dim? Blue-uniformed staff take our luggage from us and put it down. Behind the reception desk is a female blonde Marlene Dietrich. 'Ve velcome you to the Boccaccio, if you sign the forms our porter vill take you to your rooms.' The lift is working, which is more than half the car workers at Coventry are. My room was obviously a broom cupboard – the porter places my luggage down, hands me a key with a huge Boccaccio key label, does a curt bow and *Danke shön*! Then a maid comes in, she is in Lyons Corner House Nippy uniform. 'Please – I make for your bed.' She's very pretty; yes, she can make for my bed, I'll join her in a minute. Wait! She comes to turn my bed down, will she make up her mind, wait, you evil swine. Chocolate! They told me German women would do anything for chocolate. I rummage through my pockets, chocolate, admitted only half a bar, good for half a fuck – *ja*! *Sieg Heil*! She takes the chocolate and, with an innocent smile, puts it in her pinafore pocket – oh boy, it's true they will do anything for a bar of chocolate. Mine turns down beds, curtsies and leaves. Little devil. She was a temptress incarnate – when she leaned over the bed, she showed the backs of her knees. Arrggg!

It's a simple room, bed, bath, bidet. Back of door notice: Army Welfare Services, Welcome to the Hotel Boccaccio. The management are not responsible for valuables left in the room. Blast, my valuables were at this moment in a pinafore pocket, it had been a near thing – half a bar of chocolate and the backs of knees, oh the temptation, get behind me Satan and give a push.

Reg O'List's room is next to mine, it's identical to mine except for Reg, otherwise identical. Yes, a chambermaid turned down his bed, no, he didn't offer her chocolate because she was sixty. Oh, they have different ages? So people in Germany have different ages like we have back home, so as a people they are very much like us – 'I had a young chambermaid for my bed,' I boasted.

'Oh, good,' said Reg.

'I gave her half a bar of chocolate for turning my bed down. I saw the back of her knees.'

'Well,' said Reg, who was unpacking twenty shillings' worth of clothing, 'I'll be glad to see the back of yours.'

So he could be funny, but this was the first time. I'd keep a check on him for jokes, witticisms, puns and farts, and see which came top of the list. Oh yes, there's a high tea, or rather a low dinner, in a faded but swank dining room – so Victorian. First the huge crystal chandelier, the fluted Corinthian columns, the heavy scarlet and gold curtains, the great floor-to-ceiling windows on to a former garden, straining to be formal save two unfilled bomb craters in which are two ducks (ridiculous!), the moulded and gilt ceilings, and giant Versailles-type mirrors, the waiters all wear evening dress, and pad softly over the giant Larangué carpet, the glass is all crystal, the cutlery heavy silver, none of which will fit my pockets.

Blazing white damask napery, porcelain bowls with flowers, Belgian blinds are half drawn on the windows, the serving trolley tops are all Parian marble (I think), all is sheer faded opulence. We have a trio on a brocade-surround stage with palms almost obscuring the musicians. It's gorgeous stuff, Beethoven. 'This can't be Army Welfare run,' says Reg – well, it isn't, it's a private hotel and we're treated as such. The food is very simple fare, vegetable soup with one vegetable, I think, cabbage, which I see growing in the garden vegetable plot – as a plot, it's as big a failure as Guy Fawkes. Main course, beef, onions, carrots – yes, boiled beef and carrots.

> 'There's the stuff for your Derby Kell—
> Makes you fat and keeps you well—'

I sang to our table, to the concern of the Herr Ober.

'Something wrong mit mein Herr?' he asked.

'No, there's nothing wrong with mein hair, except cascading dandruff.'

'Well, I'm enjoying the stuff,' said Pat. She's enjoying the stuff, I didn't know she was having one, he must be under the table. Good old apple dumplings with thrice-watered custard.

'They must be having a hard time with food,' says Reg.

'So are we,' I said, spooning down my transparent custard.

'Do you hear?' said Head Girl Dorita. 'This used to be a German Officers' brothel.'

'Good heavens, and me a Catholic, a brothel, eh? Well, listen, girls, with a little help from you we could reactivate this place and make a fortune. We'll start after dinner – Miss Joyce and I being good Catholics will go upstairs and have a practice.'

Pat is open-mouthed, wants to laugh. 'Will you listen to him.'

'Hear that, girls, you've got to listen to me, she knows what she's talking about. I'll tell you what she's talking about she's talking about sixteen words a minute, a world record for the Irish.'

Dorita is laughing, 'Spike, you really should be on some tablets.'

I tell her I was on some tablets, the ones Moses brought down from the mountain – I was after, 'Thou shalt not commit adultery' – mine was – BUT SPIKE MILLIGAN CAN, but when he found out I was a Catholic he had me removed; nevertheless, I still keep that commandment whenever I can.

Billy Dunlop has found out something. 'They still got a French letter dispenser in the gents' toilet, but it's empty.' Blast, that means adapting rubber balloons again, oh the agony I'd suffered with them.

Dinner over, coffee – 'It's ersatz,' says Reg.

'No.' I sipped it. 'That's not ersatz, that's coffee.'

'You are *ein Dummkopf*,' said Reg. 'How *do* you keep it up?'

'With string,' I said.

My watch says 10 o'clock. Is it bed or out somewhere? None of us is flush, but Major Leslie, back on gin, is very flushed. 'I'm off to bed, remember rehearsal tomorrow at 10.30.' So saying, he staggered off in several directions.

The receptionist tells us there is a nightclub directly opposite, called the Das Blau Karven. Is it expensive? 'No, not too – if you not drink much and take chocolate or cigarette. If you have silk stockings American, then very good.' So as Dorita and Pat are wearing stockings we take them and our cigarettes. There's a pre-war neon sign trying to stay alight, D-s-lau---ven. Yes, this is the place folks – who wants to go to Das Blau Karven when we can enjoy Ds lau ven. It's down a tunnel of stairs. At the entrance is a bouncer in an ex-German army uniform, he looks like he was responsible for Belsen. 'You want sell chocolate, cigarettes, silk stockings?'

'No *danke*.'

Down the steps coming up, is the sound of a croaky female, an alto sax, a piano and a drum, it's like a converted coal cellar, you can tell by the occasional coalhole above you. 'I hope they don't deliver this time of night.' Smoke, hazy people, candles in bottles, flitting girl waitresses in short skirts. The girl singer is blonde, dressed in black sequins, some hanging off. An upright piano with the front off, musicians in shirt sleeves. Amazing, the alto player is coloured, black, a good colour for a black man.

'Pliss—' a waitress approaches us.

God help me, it's the girl who turned my bed down. 'You,' I smiled at her.

'Yes, me. I do part-time. I have baby, my husband die in war.' She was a plain Jane in my bedroom, but baby look at her now, with make-up and legs, beautiful, her legs are bare, hence the demand for stockings. She shows us a table. 'A table?' she says.

Yes, and chairs please. She puts a menu on the table – it's all drinks – as well we didn't know what was or was not expensive, but we assumed it would be the white Moselle wine that was cheapest – at the bottom of the menu it says, 'Cigarettes, chocolate and silk stockings taken'. *Schwei* (is that how it's spelt?) *bottle Moselle vinen, bitter* (just read, don't check the spelling). The girl singer is singing 'Chattanooga Choo Choo'. 'Parten me poy, is zat zer Chatternooger Chu Chu – Scherwack venty-nine – you swine, giff me ein shine – Glenn Miller, this is more like Max Miller.' I have to bite my lip to stop bursting into laughter. 'Ven you heer zer vistle goink hate to zer par – zen you know zat Tendersee ist nit vary pa – shufel al zer kole him gotta kip hit rollin'.' I would have paid every penny I'd got to have heard this version: 'Zere goink to be ein zertain party hat zer stazion, zatin und lace, zat hi vill korl vunny face' – there can't be anything funnier, my companions think it amusing, but not like me, hysterical – please God, why am I different? When I get over it the band are now playing for dancing, so Dorita and I amble around the smoke-fuzzed dance floor, which is the size of our table. Unfortunately, there's a 'hip' German couple, both the size of tables who are, they think, 'jiving' – a mixture between the Lancers, the Veleta and the Goose-step, even during a waltz they were 'Truckin' On Down'.

Back comes the singer and, thank heavens, sings songs in German, including the classic 'Falling In Love Again' – suddenly she's listenable, it's quite compulsive listening. She sings with this angst that only Germans have, Leider is shot through with it. Even Bix, who was American but German by descent, had it on his playing.

'It's gone one, Spike,' Dorita reminds me; she's late, after four bottles of Moselle I went past one o'clock three hours ago. 'Are we going home?' she says.

I tell her I went home three hours ago.

'Come,' says Reg, 'I'm knackered' – such confidential information at this time of night.

Back to the Boccaccio, and Dorita spurned my advances, she even spurned my retreats. I was dead beat when I reached my turned-down bed and recalled the little darling who turned it down. I really must find some silk stockings and have them filled. I sleep the sleep of a healthy neurotic . . .

It's at some hour when I'm woken by a noise in the room. Was it me, I mean you can let one go in your sleep and never know about it. I turn my bedside light on, there in his pyjamas is an officer of the King, Major Leslie. 'Oh, my dear boy, I'm so sorry, I'm in the wrong bedroom, so sorry,' and he departed. Ah, who said mystery had gone out of life, apart from me only Nelson Eddy and Jeanette MacDonald had found it.

I was telling Reg O'List at breakfast that I had had an Army Major in his pyjamas in my room at five that morning. 'What in God's name was he doing?' giggled Reg.

'It looked like the Polka.'

Dorita and Pat join our table. 'Oh, no more late nights,' said Pat, 'I was never cut out for nightlife. I did six months as a Bluebell Girl in Paris, it nearly killed me and those Frenchmen – all they want is to get you into bed, and that's day or night!'

'Are you better now, Pat?' I said with real artificial concern. Yes, she has recovered, but last night put her back a bit. Oh, which bit had it put back?

'Oh, shut up,' she says, eating her NAAFI-style porridge.

It says on the menu, 'Porridge – English style'. What are they on about, this porridge has no style at all.

'Bergoo, we called it in the army,' says Reg.

I never had to call my porridge, it was always there when I wanted it. Who wants to stand at dawn outside an army tent with a dixie in one hand calling, 'Bergoo – Bergoo, here boy, here boy'?

Ah, boiled eggs – lovely. I asked Reg, 'And what did you call boiled eggs in the army? Eric-Dick, no?'

'No, they were just boiled eggs.'

And bloody lucky to get any – it was mostly powdered egg

yet we were grateful, rationing was on and people were going short. Yes, people did go short on rationing. I know a six-foot man who ended up five foot three on powdered egg; my uncle the glutton vanished completely leaving a wife and four children. The amazing part was how chickens laid powdered eggs.

It's a nice late spring day, warm with a cool wind, and no doubt raining at 3 Leathwell Road, Deptford. We all gather in the foyer with our props, rather like the stock exchange on a busy day. 'The coach is here, people,' the quivering, scrotum-vibrating voice of Major Leslie calls above the babel. 'Do hurry folks, we're running a bit late' – running, no one's moving.

'I slept like a dead ting last night,' said Pat, coughing on her first fag of the day.

I'd done my coughing in the privacy of my bedroom and torn a few off like a gentleman – mind you, I was forced to open a window and pass it on to Hamburg. We are all trooping on to the bus, but wait bus, what's this, Sergeant Joe Baker has arrived to see Dorita, this is her 'it's-all-over-between-us-boyfriend'! I go green with jealousy, scarlet with rage, white with fear and yellow with Chinaman (Eh? What?). They talk a while, then he gets into a jeep and drives away.

'Now then, no tantrums, Mr Milligan,' says Dorita, patting the seat next to her.

'You never told me this creep was in Germany – you never told me he looked Jewish.'

'He *doesn't* look Jewish,' she's smiling.

'Well, he's got a big hooter,' I said.

'You're anti-Semitic, Milligan.'

'Only this once. I've nothing against Jews except Helen of the Candles.'

'Even if he is Jewish – which he's not – what's it to do with you – and stop shouting, the whole coach can hear.'

'Don't stop,' shouted Reg, 'it's getting interesting.'

'How long is this Joe Baker going to be sniffing around?'

'He's not sniffing – don't be so crude – he came to say goodbye, he goes back to England today.'

Oh, what a relief – I can feel myself regaining consciousness.

The Swinging Along Company. Yours truly is marked with an X

Going back to England is he – I hope he goes straight to Catford and gets knocked down by a 74 tram ha-ha – revenge is sweet but not fattening.

We pull up outside the Hamburg Opera House, a miracle survivor from the bombing, the place is huge. 'We'll all get bloody lost in this,' says Eddy Molloy as we all troop from the bus to the stage door, indeed massive, made for Tannhauser not Flat Foot Floogie with the Floy Floy. Again splendid dressing rooms, our band of five look lost in the great orchestra pit – while everyone is milling around getting ready, I try the magnificent piano – a Bechstein – I run through 'A Foggy Day In London Town'. Ah! That's my music says Ann Lenner, who has sauntered over.

'Oh, it's yours is it – I thought it was Gershwin.'

Major Leslie and his voice are calling us to order. 'Beginners, please,' he says from a sumptuous box.

So we run the show through. Eddy Molloy's wife, Beryl, a tall, innocent 'butter wouldn't melt in my mouth' blonde, with chorus sings 'The Fleet's In Port Again' with us all done up as sailors; the result is unintentionally hilarious, with this

Same again, only different

innocent-faced blonde, with a Roedean accent, singing about 'Naughty Sailor Boys,' funnier than 'Chattanooga Choo Choo' in German.

'Oh dear, I'm afraid we're overrunning by thirty minutes, children, we'll have to make cuts.'

How about the throat of the drummer, who is bloody terrible. So a conference with Eddy Molloy – we drop the deaf RAF pilot sketch and Molloy and Dunlop put on drag, among which it goes:

MOLLOY:  My husband has no money.
BILLY:   Don't worry, mine's got piles.

'You'll all have to tighten things,' says the Major, now standing in the box like the turret of a tank. He is using the supplied opera glasses. Lunch and one more run-through. Back to the Boccaccio, through grey Hamburg streets. The sun shines a little, which just illuminated more of the havoc wrought by the RAF. 'There isn't a lift working in the city,' says Reg.

'Never mind the lifts, has he gone yet?'

Dorita puzzles, 'Who's gone yet?'

'Him, the Jewish Sergeant.'

'Oh dear, you still on about him.'

'Yes, I'm on about him.'

'How do I know if he's gone – oh give over, Spike.'

'I'm sorry, Dorita, I'll forget all about him being run over by a tram in Catford, but I'll watch the obituary columns . . . Jewish Sergeant killed by 74 Lewisham tram.'

Lunch at the Boccaccio is a rearrangement of yesterday's high tea. The pea soup has been rewatered and heated, the main course, the meat, has been turned over and by hammering with a mallet made into a larger steak, yesterday's boiled potatoes had been baked, and the leftover carrots mashed. Ah! I chewed my way through it, a warm sense of *déjà vu*, and, of course, I recognised the custard, it was so familiar it should have recognised me.

'How did you think the show looked?' Eddy Molloy is leaning over me.

'I? – Me? Well, it looked good, but I think the Opera has won – it's so bloody big.'

'Well, we could do the show in the gents' toilet and let the audience in three at a time.'

He laughed. 'We'll just have to lump it.'

'So will the audience,' I added.

'It'll be all right,' said Reg. 'Soldier audiences are always marvellous.'

Wouldn't it be hell if this time they weren't.

'He must be there by now,' said Dorita.

'Who?'

'The Jewish Sergeant,' she said and ran off laughing.

'What do we do about that drummer?' said Ann. We agree that he doesn't play during our act, except on 'Quiet Town In Cross Bone County', our finale.

'I bet', said Reg, 'he finishes before us.' A prophecy that was to come true.

'Blast, I've run out of my Sweet Aftons. Pat – beautiful Celtic Goddess,' I said.

'Is it a fag you're after?' she says.

'You are more beautiful', I fall and clasp her round the

177

knees, 'than the dawn over Bernard Shaw's landlady – and can you lend me three?'

She takes three cigarettes and drops them on me like a benediction.

'I'll never be able to repay you for this,' I said.

'You bloody well will,' she said.

'Wrong,' I said.

The coach – the coach. We all scramble in. 'Well, how does everybody feel?' says Major Leslie, standing at the front of the coach.

We all chorus, 'OK.'

'Well, I think we've got a jolly good show. Now sit down.'

Another run-through – Jack Jordan sees Molloy and Leslie. 'It's no good, we'll have to send the drummer home. The dancers are complaining about the tempo.'

So Alf Maunders from East Acton is sent home. 'I'll report this to the Musicians' Union – I've been a drummer for forty years.' He's almost in tears and he's almost sixty, it's time he was run over by a 74 tram in Catford.

Being a musician myself I tried to commiserate with him; as he speaks with a squeaky North Country accent it's hard to keep a straight face. 'Your trouble is, Alf, you keep getting faster and faster.'

'Aye, I know, but I t'can't t'help it, Spak, as I got t'older, I've got t'faster. They called me the Gene Kruper of Dudley.'

Hard luck, Alf, you've done your best, been honest and hard working, there's only one thing left, fuck off. So he did. By now, if he went on getting faster, he must have finally disappeared in a blur leaving behind a widow and three children to take over the drumming. So the final rehearsal. Molloy is satisfied and Major Leslie, with his opera glasses focused on the girls' limbs and a stopwatch, says the show is dead on time.

Curtain up at 7.30. Reg, Billy Dunlop and I share the same opulent dressing room – our jockey pants hanging on gilt coat hooks look as out of place as Hitler in a synagogue. Aren't men's willies ridiculous? Apart from doing the procreation bit they look totally meaningless, all day long they just hang there hoping for work – on a rough estimate I'd say nine-tenths of a willy's life is spent just hanging down, getting caught in zip fasteners, getting sniffed by labradors, hit by young children or crushed when you cross your legs, even when you don't know they're doing anything your cobblers go up and down according to the heat and you don't know they're doing it. I see Reg's willy, it's got a bend on it, what?! Don't tell me he fucks round corners! What a wonderful disguise, the poor girl round the corner will be given a quick one, two three and never know it's happened.

'Do you know you've got a bend in your willy?' I said.

'Yes, I know,' said Reg. 'I got it from my father.'

'Really, what's he using?'

'He had a bigger bend than mine, in fact it nearly went sideways.'

'I see, there must have been quite a few times he missed,' I said.

'Yes,' said Reg, 'it's a wonder I got here. And I object to my prick being a topic of conversation.'

I tell him he's lucky, no one's ever spoken to anyone else about mine. 'You don't want your prick to go to its grave unsung, do you?'

'This conversation is impossible.'

The Opera House stage manager is shouting. There's the overture, soon the entire cast are in lines on stage.

> We're here, we're here.
> We're here to entertain you
> For an hour or two.
> We've comedy and dancing and singing
> We'll set the rafters ringing.

Now the walk-down by Eddy Molloy in a check suit, a white trilby turn-up hat. Billy Dunlop has to cross talk with him.

MOLLOY:   My dog's got no nose.
DUNLOP:   How does he smell?
MOLLOY:   Terrible.
CHORUS:   Oh we're here, we're here,
          We're here to entertain
          You – you – you you you.

And so to the first dance routine, then sketches, then the Lenner Trio – so on to the grand finale.

> Goodbye – Goodbye
> We hope you've enjoyed the show
> Goodbye. Goodbye
> Goodnight as off we go.

Uggg! Show business. After the show the old routine – the Town Major, John Ball, invites us all (the girls really) to the Officers' Mess for 'restorative cordials'. It means the females are taken over by young officers. I have a jolly colonel, with bravery medals galore. 'Jolly good show – men really enjoyed it – jolly funny – where do you go next? Really? I was stationed – nice place – yes, jolly good show. Had an auntie on the stage – with Ivor – what's the chap's name? ["Patel?"] No-no-no – "Novello" – yes, that's the chap – she was trained at RADA—'

'Really?'

'Yes, but she's the only one – none of us were inclined – father was regular army.'

'Listen, I think I hear a number 74 tram approaching from Catford.' I ease away without him noticing.

'Yes, served in India . . .'

I join a group with Reg and Molloy. Soul-crushing small talk about the Russian zone, the American zone, the French zone, the black market, chocolate, cigarettes, silk stockings, that seems to be what Germany is all about. By midnight all the girls have avoided being fucked by the officers of Hamburg, though they've been heavily pressed.

'Oh dear,' said Dorita as we entered the coach, 'I've been eye-raped for the last hour.'

'Don't worry, Dorita, you're safe with me.'

She'd be safer still with Reg and his bent willy.

'I suppose you'll be starting next,' said Dorita.

Starting, I've never left off. I smoke my last fag and plead with Pat Joyce. 'Just one for the night, Pat, tomorrow we get paid and I'll repay—'

She puts her hand over my mouth, rummages in her bag and gives me one. 'Hold your breath – here – anything to KEEP YOU QUIET!' The trip's getting to her.

The Boccaccio – we sit up and let the night staff bring us coffee in the deserted dining room – the German staff are so servile – servile to the point of embarrassment, something spookey about it. 'No – zer is no charge,' says the waiter, 'kompliments.'

'They must feel guilty about the food they serve, this coffee is in the nature of a peace-offering,' said Reg, who still insists it's ersatz. 'It's made from some kind of bean like soya.'

Dorita and Pat rise to leave, 'You're not going,' I said.

'I'm just about going,' said Pat in an exhausted voice.

'Goodnight, boys,' says Dorita taking Pat's hand and leading her away.

'Well, darling,' says Reg, 'beddy-byes.'

We run the show for a week, the form is much the same as I have described. We don't mix with the Germans and they don't mix much with us, cultures don't mix, one destroys the other and makes a watered-down third. Our next town is Celle. We play the Garrison Theatre, like a shoebox with a roof on. I pop into the girls' dressing room to wish them luck and see if I can catch them naked, success: 'Get out, you dirty little devil,' amid false screams.

'Dorita's got the best pair,' I told Reg. Knock on our door; it's Dorita now dressed.

'You're a naughty, naughty boy Mr Milligan – do you know what he did, Reg?'

Yes, Reg knew. 'He said yours were the best.'

She throws a packet of ten Players at me. 'To keep you going,' she said and left.

She must be mistaken, I wasn't going, I was contracted to stay with the show. Another successful week, then Hanover, then north of that, Kronenberg. The last two are mixed military and civilian audiences and one can tell because the reaction from the Germans is much more restrained.

'They need bombing again,' says Dunlop whose drag act died a death. 'Nobody loves a fairy when she's forty,' he lamented.

There is one more date, Klagenfurt in Austria – for this we are entrained at Hanover – it's an overnight trip and we have sleeping berths. I'm bunked in with Reg.

'Very comfortable,' he said, trying the berth.

I explained that the upper berth was for the upper classes and the lower for lower classes, so any wild beast getting into the carriage would eat the lower classes first, thus ensuring the survival of the upper classes.

## KLAGENFURT

The train chugs off at midnight, I fall asleep to the rhythm of the rails. It was that rhythm that inspired passages in 'Rhapsody In Blue', the theme runs through my head, what a talent, and why isn't Dorita here? In the distance I hear the train's mournful hooter. In the night we have passed through Vienna. I heard official voices from time to time when the train halts, some sound Russian. When I awake it's 7.15, I clamber down to look but I'm caught in the corridor by Jack Jordan, also in his pyjamas. 'Great minds,' he said as we pass. Where are we – the countryside is bathed in early morning sun. A waiter is shouting, 'Brickfast – Brickfast now.' Reg is awake sitting on his bunk scratching his arse. I raise the carriage blind, sunlight floods in. 'Oh dear,' he says, the sun does that to people. In the restaurant car I join Ann Lenner. 'Hello – nice and early.' She's having toast and coffee, what a good idea. 'And it's *real* coffee,' she smiles. She looks at her watch, 'We're due in at 8.50, Major Leslie said so.'

My God, Klagenfurt, where Toni Pontani and I were young and in love and lay by the Wörther See, will I ever see Toni again? Klagenfurt is a British garrison town where there's ten soldiers to one civilian. It's a smallish station – we can't get all the train into the platform, we all have to exit from one carriage – a railway transport officer is waiting, he waves us all towards him and a few soldiers, 'Just leave your luggage, my men will bring it.' Oh, great slaves. Another coach through lovely rural countryside along the Lake Wörther See and into the grounds of a simple country hotel with chalets in the grounds. I recognise it all. 'I was here before,' I told Reg, 'with the love of my life.' Reg says don't worry, there's plenty more waiting in the wings. We are all allocated rooms, I'm in a garden chalet on my own – at last my night manipulations can be carried out unheard. There's no let-up – the show is tonight at the Alexander Theatre as the old Koenig Theatre is called, conqueror's rights. It's always theatres and bridges, you never hear of a Field Marshal Montgomery phone or letter box.

We spend the day by the lake, some playing cards, some just throwing stones in the water, a high tide of excitement. Reg and I reminisce on old times. I've known him since Army days in Naples*. 'Who'd have thought,' he said, 'that distant day at the Bellini Theatre, Naples, when I first saw you in the Bill Hall Trio, we'd be lying by a lake in Austria.'

'Well, Reg, when I first saw you, I said to Bill Hall – see that man, the last thing I want to do is lie by a lake with him in Austria.'

Reg laughs out loud. 'Oh Spike, what are we going to do with you?'

We? What's he talking about 'we', he's on his own, he must be suffering from schizophrenia, to think there's two of him and only one change of underwear. God, if he has an accident now, I'll have to lend him mine – yes shitzophrenia! The afternoon dozes on and we doze. 'Wake up – look at the time.' We hurry back to the hotel and just make the coach.

'We were getting worried about you two,' said Ann. Us *two*? She meant us three – did she know tonight she'd be a quartet?

'You've caught the sun,' said Dorita.

'Yes, I've got it in a box in my room – I'm going to let it out to start tomorrow.'

We've all been invited to the *Bürgermeister*'s home after the show in the Feldpark. Great; never seen a *Bürgermeister*. I wonder what shape they are. The show goes a bundle. In the walkdown the Trio get the best applause, and I have a feeling I might be a big part of it, hope so, an ego needs hand feeding. Such a lovely house, the *Bürgermeister's*, so he's like the town mayor. '*Ach so*! I am liking your show very much. I like much zer jazz, *ja*!' I wonder if he knows the 'Chattanooga Choo Choo'.

*See *Mussolini: His Part In My Downfall* (Penguin Books, 1980).

The food is what the yuppies today call a 'fork supper', it used to be supper, but now, now, fork, why? Why fork – what did they think you were going to use, a shovel? Another yuppie crappie, 'finger buffet'. Ugh. Knife, fork and spoon dinner – hand sandwiches. Anyways, it's a super spread. Word is that he's in the black market – I suppose that's what they called the Negro slave trade, ha ha. I stay close to Dorita all evening, there's even a balcony on to the lake, but it's crowded with crowds. Dorita is making signs that my shares on the stock exchange are going up. We are drinking white wine when, from out of the blue, she said, 'Milligan, I think it's time I visited you in your chalet.'

Oohh oooh – I can feel my swommicles revolving. 'Okay kid,' I said as calmly as I could. 'I'll be waiting.'

Well, that's the story of how we finally got into bed with each other, it was only a single bed, but I think we used both sides of the mattress and the walls – she left me softly as the dawn cometh up – and lo he was sore afraid and verily, I say unto you, he was shagged out. Oh, Dorita, I didn't know what bliss was, in fact, when I woke up I didn't know what anything was. Oh, and I didn't use up my chocolate ration – as she left me, I whispered, do you think the 74 tram got him? So, one night of bliss and one day of lightheadedness and occasional fainting. I spent most of the day in bed. Dorita brought me a cheese sandwich and we did it again – more cheese, nurse.

We are to catch the night train back to Hanover – it's the journey in reverse but this time Dorita and I share the same cabin – and as the poor stoker is shovelling coal in, pouring with sweat, we too are shovelling away and covered with sweat. No, I don't believe it! – it must be the greatest coitus interruptus since Héloïse and Abelard, a hoarse German voice is saying, '*Feuer in zer Wagen*'. No, there's a fire in the wagon – Dorita is struggling to get dressed. I take deep breaths to reduce the swelling – we are all out of the train on the embankment. The brake box under our carriage is glowing red hot, they douse it with extinguishers, a great hissing sound, or is that mine? Dorita says, 'See what we started.'

*I stop the book here, because as I wrote this page I received a phone call, it was Dorita, she's in Britain on holiday. I told her what I was writing, she started to laugh – yes, she remembers it, wow what a coincidence. With my wife Shelagh's permission, she's coming to see me.*

They have to wait for the brake to cool, then refill it with oil and off we go, the train, that is. We'd had enough for the night. Oh, yes.

It was midnight when the train restarted so I managed a night's sleep with swollen balls. Back in Hanover we play another week at the Theatre. My diary would read, slept all day, theatre in evening, screwed all night. I was starting to get double vision and shaking fits – I must get some sleeping tablets for Dorita or I'm a dead man. Thank God, the trip is at an end, it's nearly mine, oh help, come back Sergeant Joe Baker and help take the strain, let me help that No. 74 tram off you.

We're all packed for the return journey. What of the future: I can't see the Ann Lenner Trio lasting. Well, I'm not lasting. Dorita has put on six pounds and it's mine!!! The train journey to the Hook starts at the unearthly hour of 7 a.m. so it's a dawn rising, down boy.

The night before, Dorita and I resisted the raving mad, red-hot mindless surge. A sort of post-show gloom has settled over the cast. We sit in our rail compartments as quiet as chastened schoolchildren, but soon the breakfast car is put on and it's a good, *very* good menu, eggs and bacon. Having seen how the Germans were living, one could not but feel guilty; nevertheless, I need it, I've lost six pounds and she's sitting opposite.

'So, all over,' she says.

'Yes, all over – it's all gone so quick,' I said, 'especially, madame, this past week.'

She grins and I think she must be one of the most attractive girls I've ever seen, but there's still the ghost of Toni Pontani to lay. If I can lay it like I've laid Dorita it should be easy.

# HOME

It's all anti-climactic – the ferry back is better, the sea calm like polished steel. Dorita and I stand at the rail, we seem to be in love and we ask each other are we or is it that blinder, sexual attraction? We decided it was love. What a responsibility! Oh Toni – Toni – forgive me, *Mea Culpa* – And Dorita's! It's all finally ending as the boat train from Harwich steams into Liverpool Street Station. Suddenly it's over, there's last-minute exchange of addresses and phone numbers. Yes, Dorita, I'll phone as soon as I can. No, I haven't any phone so I can't give you a phone number. So 3 Leathwell Road here I come. 'My son, my son.' Good, she still remembers me, and she hasn't let my room. She kept it exactly as I left it, filthy.

What now Spike Milligan? I don't know what happened to the Ann Lenner Trio, we never actually broke up. Reg died, he must have, they buried him. I would like to go solo but I was so frightened I would hide most of my career behind a typewriter.

After a week at home I got gastritis, ten days later I feel better, 'I feel better, Mother,' I said.

She crossed herself. 'You look terrible, you really must shave.'

So I had a must shave; what agony, my face is a mass of cuts and blotches. 'How's that, I look?' I said.

'Worse,' she said, and crossed herself yet again, she'll have to get a crossing built there, then we can all do it together.

I must get up to London. I phone the Grafton Arms, Abbey 3266, 'Hello, Grafton Arms.' I press button B and get my money back one more time. 'Hello, Grafton—' I do it again. It can only be the Irish in me.

'Hello – got it right this time,' says the cheery voice of Jimmy Grafton.

'Yes, is Harry around?' Yes, Harry has a week out from variety, I can get him on Gerrard 0081. I dial out, a lady answers, 'Kilston Villas'.

'Can I speak to Harry Secombe?'

'Just a minute.'

I hear her call Mr Secombe – Mr Secombe – I hear his distant chattering.

'Coming – Coming – Hello, Hello, Secombe here.' His voice is expectant. 'Hello, Hello,' he repeats in a police voice.

I say, 'Mr Selcon, it's about this thirteen-year-old girl.'

'You swine, Milligan, where are you?'

I am in a phone box directly between the Rialto Cinema and the public karzi, I don't know who is showing the best programme, they say one stinks. We arrange to meet at Jimmy's that evening.

'I'll tell Jimmy we're coming,' says Secombe.

When we do arrive Jimmy invites us up to his lounge for dinner – his wife Dorothy serves us. 'What's the matter with your face?' says Jimmy.

I said, 'I shaved.'

Jimmy laughed, 'Well, I shave but that doesn't happen to my face.'

'Well, it bloody well happened to mine – Mine.' I arose from the table clawing the air and speaking like a ham actor.

'I told you, you shouldn't have let him come,' giggled Secombe.

'You, Secombe,' I pointed with quivering finger, 'you shall be accursed, all your sons will have wives with moustaches and three legs.'

Dinner now proceeded. 'Is he always like this, dear?' said Dot to her husband.

'When there's an "R" in the month,' said Jimmy. Jimmy is acting as Harry's manager with an agent called Frank Barnard, who has balls the size of Israel melons due to some lymphatic malfunction. He cannot cross his legs without screaming; he has a 'girlfriend': a sixty-year-old lubricator who once played for the 8th Army, she is nicknamed the desert pianist. Harry is doing variety whenever he can, his name very small on the bill.

Jimmy is writing scripts for an ex-Geraldo singer, called Derek Roy, who fancied himself as a comic, that he was alone was no mystery. Somehow or other I found myself sleeping in Jimmy's attic office and whenever, writing scripts; it was a pretty mad establishment, with two young children James and Sally whom I told stories to. To add to it there was a rhesus monkey, 'Jacko', and a bulldog, Buller, plus Minty, a Siamese cat. The pub was very popular and served meals, Jacko seemed a bit dispossessed, so I put a rug atop a hot water tank and it became his refuge. Alas, it was right over the kitchen stove, a lethal position when food for the pub lunches was simmering on top, and I actually saw Jacko pee – and watched it land, of all things – in the Pea Soup where Louis the cook stirred it in: mind you, this wasn't a regular occurrence. However, there are people alive today who lunched there, good luck I say!!!!

Harry is due to appear at the Hackney Empire so all of us arrange to see him including Hall and Mulgrew. However, Hall says no, 'I'm not going to that fucking death hole – I'll never forget how we died the bloody death there.'

Cheer up, woeful fellow, come and see Harry Secombe die there. But, no. In the bar of the Empire I meet Peter Sellers again; he is plump-faced and wearing gloves, all a cut above the rest of us tramps. We get to know each other, I got to know each other, and each other got to know I.

The pit band strikes up 'I'm Just Wild About Harry'. Secombe is on! He does his lunatic shaving act and ends up as Jeanette MacDonald and Nelson Eddy singing a duet, falling on his back to finish.

We all go backstage to his dressing room where he's packing up. He does a looney continuation of this, having put his props away he then removes the light bulbs, leaving the room in darkness. He then says, 'Now why are you all persecuting me like this, are you from the Church?'

Sellers says, 'No we are poor travelling Jews of no fixed income.'

Secombe says, 'Oh, just a minute,' and restores the light bulb. At the switching on we all gasp at the wonder of light.

'See – see the light – it is a sign,' says Bentine.

Secombe says, 'You must help me escape from here, I'm being kept prisoner against my Dick.'

'You mean Will.'

'No, Dick, Will died last week.' He then unpacks his large travelling zip bag and gets in. He protrudes from the top, so sitting waist-up in the bag we carry him to a taxi and on to the Grafton Arms.

We form a clique and throw jokes around. Bentine says from his scientific knowledge that gold can be made from liquorice if transported at speed strapped to a lady's bike. The liquorice must be pumped in liquid form into the tubular frame, then driven at twice the speed of sound; the element missing is a man who can cycle at that speed. I say I could do it but I refuse to on religious grounds. How about Brands Hatch, that's not a religious ground. I explain I am a seventh son of a seventh son sworn never to travel in the company of liquorice. There was a curse on the family. What was that curse? Haricot beans – even that was a codeword, that codeword could only be released by the drinking of a pint of old and mild. It is forthcoming. I reveal the family curse. It is – piles, hereditary piles, passed down through the male line since Niall of the seven hostages.

'That's a load of cobblers,' says Mulgrew.

'You're so right, Johnny, they're so big they do look like a load of cobblers; but! now, honestly, when did anyone here last actually see a load of cobblers – come on.'

Peter Sellers puts on an official BBC voice, 'I think I speak for the entire company when I say none of us have actually seen a load of cobblers, one or two maybe in rare instances three, but a load, never.'

Then, I said, as the potential liquorice cyclist I must ask brother Mulgrew for the sake of the brotherhood to withdraw a load of cobblers. Mulgrew is laughing, 'If that wasn't a load of cobblers I don't know what is.'

'You see, brothers,' I said, 'he can't tell the difference between a load of cobblers and he doesn't know what is.'

Bentine suddenly says, 'Shhhh.' We wait, his finger still to his mouth. 'Shhhh,' again.

'Listen,' says Sellers, 'the poor man is trying to tell us something.'

'Shhhhh.'

'What is it, man?' says Secombe, pulling Bentine's bottom eyelid down and peering in.

'Shhhhh,' says Bentine. 'It's no good, you're bound to find out eventually, it's my impression of a train getting up steam, so there.'

Sellers puts on a military voice, 'While you were away this arrived.' He held out his hand.

Bentine took the hand and held it palm upwards, then pretended to scrutinise it with a jeweller's glass. 'It's a hand,' he said finally.

'Yes, it arrived by runner, I was told to report to HQ.'

'Yes,' I said, 'because, Carstairs, on this hand is written a secret message in invisible ink. Mornington, this is your speciality.'

Secombe salutes like an idiot.

'What's that?' I snap.

'A clumsy idiot salute, we don't want people to suggest we're intelligent.' He then takes Sellers' hand and examines the palm. 'Ah yes, a strong heart line, three children and two marriages.' 'It's not what we were expecting; is there some invisible writing?'

I say, 'Yes, but I can't see it.'

'Fools,' says Bentine, 'this is all it needs.' He dips a finger in the beer then runs it across Sellers' palm. 'There, it says, the natives are revolting. Oh yes, especially the women.'

'But', says Secombe in a very sexy, slimy voice, 'not Tondalayo.'

We all chorus, 'Not Tondalayo.'

Well folks, this stuff went on at every meeting.

When Sellers hears I have to get back to Deptford, he says I could spend the night at his place. 'We've got a blow-up mattress.' Fine. He has a car, Sellers always had a car, it was an American Hudson. 'Only had it a week.'

'Does it go back now?'

'No,' he laughed. 'No, I love cars – cars mean freedom.'

As a travel slave I agreed, but I was poor, I would never ever be able to afford a car.

Peter lives on the second floor of a block of flats off Finchley Road. Peter was already foot in the door with the BBC and earning MONEY, but he spent, all his life he spent, all cars were on HP. Peg, his mother, would say, never pay the lot, HP – if you drop dead you're in the clear. So I meet Peg and Bill, his father, who was like a ghost in the flat.

'You're very welcome, Spike,' she says.

'I hope I'm not too much trouble.'

'You just make it like your own home,' she says.

Right, I'll start by tearing the curtains and install gas lighting, then I'll use heavy sandpaper to shred the sofa, just snip the strapping, let out a few springs.

'This is your mattress.' Peter holds up a red rubber lilo. 'It is flat as a pancake, you blow in here,' he says, with an evil grin points to a little matchstick-thin tube, he's already in his pyjamas.

'I've made you both scrambled egg on toast,' says Peg. We sit in the small kitchen overlooking the back gardens of Limes Avenue and the washing. 'What are you doing at the moment, Spike?'

Well, apart from eating this scrambled egg, nothing. No, I was fully occupied egg-eating after that nebbish for ever. 'I'm doing some scriptwriting for Derek Roy for which I get £2.10.0 but Jimmy Grafton is arranging for me to get more, maybe £10.' Oh good. Wait, they have a print on the wall of a hare by Dürer. That's a Dürer, I said.

'It's only a print,' says Bill, who chain-smokes and like all smokers it will one day do for him. 'Uncle Bert's got the original.'

I gasp, 'It must be worth a fortune, an original Dürer is well . . .'

Peg sits up. 'Are you sure, Spike?'

Yes, I'm sure, Spike.

'Worth a fortune you say.'

Yes.

Peg phones Uncle Bert, yes, he's still got the picture of a

hare, he hasn't got any but there's a hare in a frame – signed? Looks like Dürer. Will he wait there, we're all coming round. So we bundle into Peter's Hudson. 'Worth a fortune,' Peg kept saying, her Jewish blood bubbling. Well it's not an original, we took it out of the frame, printed by the Wishing Well Print Company, Ohio. Of course, by the time we returned the egg was cold. 'Shall I warm it up for you?'

No, no, Mrs Sellers, warm food no, I don't want to get used to luxuries.

Peter is in his bed, I start to blow mine up. Goodnights from Bill and Peg.

'It shouldn't take you long,' says Peter, as he turns to go asleep. It took half an hour then I stripped to my ragged army pants and vest – if they were people they'd be in the poor house. I snuggle under the blanket, as I doze off there is a soft distant hiss, my bed has a puncture – I had started sleeping four inches off the ground, I awake flush with it.

Peter awakes first; he calls out in a pitiful wail, 'Pe-eggy – Pe-eggy.'

I'm still a-doze doing floor impression, I'm not so sure I haven't made an impression on the floor.

'Pe-egg.'

Pe-egg comes.

'What is it, darling?'

'Tea, Mum.'

'You want some tea, Spikey?' (Spikey, that's new.)

Yes, Spikey would like tea and a crowbar to prise him from the floor.

'How did you sleep?'

I explained how the mattress leaked, how over an hour it slowly lowered me to mother earth.

'Oh, I am sorry,' says Peter.

*He's* sorry. Today he's going to the BBC to see the producer, Pat Dixon, he can drop me at the tube, no why can't I come with him. Okay. 'But I'm going for an audition so you'll have to wait outside.'

Outside where? I mean the Bank of England? The Tower. He's a bit nervous me coming . . . so I go over to the Grafton Arms and Jimmy is happy that I continue writing part-time with him for Derek Roy. 'I don't want to be rude, Jimmy.'

'Then don't be,' he interrupted with a giggle.

'I was going to say that I don't think Derek Roy is very funny.'

Jimmy agrees, then says perhaps the scripts are bad? Not so, I had seen Derek Roy perform at the Gaumont State, Kilburn; he was a nice unfunny fellow with a jolly singing voice.

'Well, it's up to us to make him funny, there's money in it.'

I suggest he should wear a Harpo Marx wig and a red nose. *Variety Bandbox* on BBC is the biggest entertainment show of the week, Roy alternates with Frankie Howerd, who is much funnier.

At the same time as writing, Jimmy is trying to progress the career of one Harry Secombe, our perambulating, chattering Welshman, also in the pipeline is a possible series for Roy. As Jimmy's writing times are erratic, he works in the cracks between running the pub. He has also put himself up as a Conservative Councillor, so usually we work at nights on the living-room table when his wife, Dorothy (long suffering), and two children James and Sally, along as I say with Buller the bulldog, Minty the cat, and Jacko the monkey, are abed. By the time we've finished writing, it's too late to catch a train home, so I sleep on a mattress in Jimmy's attic using one blanket and overcoats. In rush hours I sometimes help behind the bar.

Jimmy, now with no movement from the Ann Lenner Trio, tries to get me odd dates. He gets me one at the Nuffield Services Club, first I have to meet Mary Cook to vet me. With my affair with Dorita going like a piston the last thing I needed was a vet. Mary Cook is a well-educated, terribly well-spoken lady with enormous hips, it looks like a thin person has been slid into someone else's bottom half. 'Now, Mr Milligan, or do they all call you Spike?'

No, she can call me Spike, normally I'm called 'Hey you' or on bad days 'Stop thief'.

Is my act clean, yes, that means I'll have to drop the joke about the monkey, the elephant and the sore arse. So on the Friday night, wearing a velvet jacket I've knocked off from Army Welfare Service Wardrobe, I do an act doing imitations of wallpaper and end up singing 'Body And Soul' as a coloured girl. I go down okay, but nothing to write home about. But a singer, David Hughes, goes and sings 'The Desert Song'; he gets an ovation, so fuck him.

So back to the attic and scriptwriting. Margaret Lockwood is to be Derek Roy's guest – now his gimmick is to be billed as 'The Laughter Doctor', opening his act with 'hello patients', they all were by the end of his act – so we have to write a script with her as the nurse. We work all night on the script, in fact, I haven't shaved for three, then there's a panic: Miss Lockwood must see the scripts right away, so first thing in the morning I shave at speed, cut myself to pieces. Off I go to somewhere on the outskirts of London to a posh block of flats. ''Ere, where you goin'?' said a grotty hall porter.

'I'm going to see Miss Lockwood.'

He savages me with his crust-edged eyes. 'No, you're bloody not,' he said. He picked up the phone, 'Miss Lockwood, there's a man here says he's got a script for you from the . . .' He looks at me, 'Where is it?'

'The BBC – Derek Roy.'

He repeats it down the phone. 'Okay. Second floor, room 118, the lift's not working,' he said gleefully.

The RAF? I thud up the stairs two at a time. I'm in fine fettle, in fact I've never been fettler. I press a polished, polished bell on a gleaming white door. Wow, Miss Lockwood opens it with her beauty spot.

'Oh,' I said surprised. 'No coloured footman.'

She gave me a Rank Charm School smile, took the script, said a Rank Charm School thank you and shut the door; it was all of one-minute fifty.

'Oh Jimmy,' I say, 'is it worth £10 scriptwriting for Derek Roy, the man who kills 99 per cent of all known jokes?'

Jimmy said, 'Patience, it can lead to bigger things.'

I tell him I don't need bigger things, mine are big enough, ask any heavy plant operator.

'There could be a series,' says Jimmy.

'What of disasters? Roy is *not* funny.'

'It'll put money in your shatteringly hollow account,' he says.

Things to come. The Goons, which it was all leading up to, in 1951. From left to right, front row: Dennis Maine-Wilson (producer); Jimmy Grafton; me; Larry Stephens (co-writer). Back row: Secombe; Bentine; Sellers

So when he's in the bar serving I bang away at the jokes. I remember an early one: Man says to doctor, 'My wife thinks I'm mad because I prefer brown boots to black.' Doctor says, 'How silly, I myself prefer brown boots to black.' Man says, 'How do you like them, boiled or fried?' Now that's how a normal joke would end; not me, with me the Doctor says, 'I like mine boiled, my wife thinks I'm mad too.'

Jimmy organises a night with The Goons, as we have decided to call ourselves. So one evening, after hours, we have an ad-lib session. Bentine starts the ball rolling, 'Gentlemen, now you know why I've called you here?'

'No, we don't,' we murmur.

195

'Very well, we've been besieged in this fort for, does anybody know?'

'Forty days,' says one.

'Fifty,' says another.

Any advance on fifty—?

Seventy.

'Right, we've been besieged forty, fifty and seventy days. Gentlemen, you will synchronise watches.'

They all adjust their watches, but never say a word, the phone supposedly rings, Secombe answers, 'Hello, Fort Agra, hello? Just a minute.' He holds his hand over the phone, 'Does a Mrs Gladys Stokes live here?' No, sorry Mrs Stokes doesn't live here.

SELLERS: Someone has got to go and get reinforcements.

ME: Yes, someone has to.

BENTINE: Yes someone has to.

SECOMBE: Yes gentlemen, someone has to go and get reinforcements.

*Pause*

SELLERS: Good, well that's settled.

ME: Run up the Union Jack.

SELLERS: Right, sir.

ME: Wait, that flag should be red, white and blue.

SELLERS: Yes, I thought I'd run up the white part first.

BENTINE: It's these night attacks that worry me, one more night attack and I'll have to change the sheets.

It went on for an hour, with all four of us crawling on our stomachs in the desert dying of thirst.

ME: Water.

BENTINE: Water, for God's sake.

SECOMBE: Yes, water—

SELLERS [drunk]: Scotch and Soda.

I suppose it would only be a matter of time before someone in

the BBC might use us. There was one enlightened producer
streets ahead in perspicacity, Pat Dixon, totally unrevered by
the BBC but directly responsible for giving us the break.
Already we had introduced the first comedy show on the new
Third Programme (for unknown reason now called Radio 3),
they can't leave alone can they, using Harry Secombe, Peter
Sellers, Benny Hill. It was the first comedy show without an
audience, I used to go and listen through the studio door, I was
desperate to be given a break as such on the media; it never
did, the three, Secombe, Sellers, Bentine are all working and
earning. If I hadn't written myself into *The Goon Show*, I'd
never have been heard of.

Peter Sellers is courting a girl called Anne Howe, his mother
is dead against it. 'She only wants your body,' she kept saying
to Peter. Actually, I think it was the other way round, Peter
was hooked on blondes, unfortunately his mother wasn't, it's a
wonder she didn't wear a blonde wig to keep him. I was
awakened from my flat, deflated, Sellers ritual torture mattress
with Peter Sellers calling, 'Pe-eg, ba-ba-ba Pe-eg.' Well, it
sounded like it.

'Did you sleep well, Spike darling?' said Peg.

Yes, darling, as sound as possible on a cold, hard wooden
floor with knots in, mostly mine.

'Do you feel like scrambled eggs?' she said.

Not only felt like but looked like scrambled eggs. As I don't
travel pyjamas, I sleep in my long johns, in the mornings I
looked like Worzel Gummidge without the stuffing.

Today Peter is to see a new car; I must come along for the
only reason I must come along, 'You'll love it, Spike', says
car-haunted Sellers. 'Pe-eg ba-ba-ba Pe-eg ba-ba. More tea,
Peg.'

As usual the house is full of Peg, Peter; father Bill, I think, is
kept in the clothes cupboard, I see his cigarette smoke filtering
through the keyhole. Poor Bill, the original man who never
was, he looked a pasty white and reminded me of those people
at Belsen. He was a concert party pianist, once he played the
piano, I think it was with Peg's permission; anyway he played a
tune he claimed to have written, 'If I Had The Lamp Of
Aladdin'. I hated to tell him I'd heard my mother and father

singing it in India twenty years before; perhaps he did write it but it reached India twenty years previously. So the car. We drive to the Star Garage, Golders Green, and there a car salesman so Jewish in appearance as to make Jewish people look European. 'Ah, Mr Sellern,' he pounced on Peter; 'she's all ready for you I say.' He brushed past me like Dante heading for Beatrice, 'You'll love it, Mr Sellern, I say, love it!' Peter's face is set as though the Second Coming is nigh – there, centre car showroom, the car is draped in a white cloth, 'I seen no dust got on it, Mr Sellern.' The atmosphere is like the Pope about to take communion. 'There, Mr Sellern – there.' The Jewish car salesman, who really had two Jewish noses, struck a dramatic pose before the shrouded prize. 'Shall I?' he said, offering to remove the shroud. By now Mr 'Sellern' is in a trance, it is for him Christmas time, he nods his head, Jewish car salesman takes one corner and sensuously slides it off the car. '*Voilà*,' he said and 'Oh dear,' as it stuck on the far bumper. Holding the taut end he appealed to me, 'Could you?' Mr Sellern was rooted to the spot staring at his promised bride, I hurried, acting like Quasimodo and shouting Esmeralda, all my comic effort being ignored by my two terror-stricken companions. Reciting a Hail Mary, I unhooked the snagged end, the shroud slipped off like a snake shedding its skin. There stood a racing green Jaguar saloon. I couldn't resist it, I knelt down and sang Handel's *Hallelujah*!. The car was polished like a dressage gelding at the Dublin.

Sellers, still mute, opened the driving door as though a hosanna of angels would come forth. He slid behind the driving seat, then placed both hands like a benediction on the steering wheel, Sellers grinned through the window at the salesman, who is now holding an HP document – 'I told you you'd love it,' he said. Alas, the window is up, on top of that Sellers has started the engine, Sellers lowers the window and he spake, 'Can I take it for a trial spin?'

'Of course, anything, Mr Sellern.' He shouldn't have said that.

Sellers backed the car out and, stopping only to pick up Peg and Bill, drove it to Brighton. As we drove through the Sussex countryside I thought I'd mention the Jewish salesman.

'Oh, fuck him,' said Peter, 'did you hear what he kept calling me? Mr bloody Sellern – *Sellern*, at least you can get the bloody customer's name right.' So we lunch at the Grand and Peter signs an overdraft cheque.

'Peter darling, that's very naughty, will it bounce?' says Peg.

Sellers relates his relationship with his bank. 'He keeps writing the bloody letters about my overdraft, I write and thank him for reminding me. He writes back and says when will I clear it? I said, look once a month I write all my creditors' names on pieces of paper, screw them up and put them in a hat, I then draw one out and pay it, if you don't stop bothering me I won't even put your name in the hat.'

We arrive back at the Star Garage at six, Jewish salesman is in a state of shock – as he sees it draw to a halt – he runs round the car looking for damage. He's very sorry, Mr Sellern, but he's alerted the police that the car is stolen. 'So sorry, Mr Sellern, but my managing director made me do it . . . did you like the car, Mr Sellern?' Yes, Peter likes it, would he like to step in the office and sign the agreement. No, he has to sell the Hudson first. Collapse of Jewish salesman – like many people he ended up on the Peter Sellers scrapheap.

# GERMANY III

At last a solo booking! It came via a certain Joe Rocaroni in the music business – it was a tour of Germany, in the United States zone. Backing the acts was Frank Weir and his orchestra, with brilliant pianist, Bill MacGuffie, singer Helen Mack, Canadian comic Danny Arnold, plus a troupe of girl dancers. The Company Manager was Jack Delroy.

We all meet at a rehearsal room in Goldhawk Road, shake hands, knees and boomps-a-daisy and all that. Jack Delroy is a prat, a know-all with a mid-Atlantic accent, 'Okay, everybody, I'm Jack Delroy.'

'What a memory you have for names,' I shout.

'Okay, now serious,' he explains. 'We will fly out from Greenham Common to Berlin, then Stuttgart and Munich.'

'Oh great, Munich, Nazis!'

I get along very well with Danny Arnold. 'By descent I'm French Canadian, by descent I mean I was lowered down a cliff. I also have Indian blood, I've got three bottles of it in the freezer.'

Good, I am of Irish descent, I came down by green parachute, I was brought up by the nuns and brought down by Miss Muriel Body, I am a man of letters, I use nothing else while speaking. I shape up with some of the girls, Ellen, a petite blonde from Wales, and her friend, Trixie, raven-haired, also Welsh, both very street-wise, so I'll avoid the streets and use the alleys. 'I seem', she said, 'to 'ave been dancing since I was six.'

'You must be tired,' I said.

'That's a bloody old joke,' she said.

Yes, I knew it was old, I only brought it out for its annual airing.

The company leaving London for Germany. Marked are Danny Arnold and me

'We're both from mining families,' says Trixie.

Ah, was it gold, silver? Marry me from the waist down and I'll be faithful to you for ever until tomorrow.

Trixie raises her eyebrows, 'Ohhhh, what have we got here – a nut,' she says to Ellen. 'I think he's trying to impress.'

Yes, I like impressing girls, there are some walking the streets with my impressions all over them.

Trixie, raven-haired, sloe-eyed, rolls her own cigarettes. It's cheaper you see, it takes longer to roll one – and you smoke less, would I like one?

I'd love her to roll mine for me.

'You don't mind inhaling my spit do you?' she said as she wet the Rizla paper. No, I didn't mind spit, as long as it wasn't in the eye of the beholder, no, spit was all right, I had a lot of it myself.

We all meet, Sunday morning, outside Victoria Coach

Station, the poor man's Orient Express Station. It's a cold blustery Sunday, we can hear the great bells going from Westminster RC Cathedral. I can't help but grin at the thought of all those campanologists shooting up and down like human yo-yos – all going like the clappers for Jesus. Two large American Army coaches bear down. 'Okay everybody,' says I'm-in-charge Delroy, 'keep together in your separate groups.' Whereupon we all broke up into separate groups. Danny and I sat in the seat adjacent to Ellen and Trixie, they both have the same surname Roberts, but are not related. Danny is great fun, he wants to 'make it in England'. Right now he's off to make it in Germany. He hasn't said what he wants to make, but I think it's money. No, no, no, he says, he wants fame, not fortune. I tell him he's on the wrong bus, I tell him in Berlin he could be famous with chocolate, cigarettes and silk stockings. Yes he knows, he's come loaded, he's done the trip before, but he says the real gold is coffee beans. Oh, I'm learning. There's a change in airfield now it's Lakenheath. Jack Delroy explains it's a security measure, 'Okay folks, sorry but it's a security measure.'

. . . Security measure, Oxford Dictionary: the extent or dimensions of a thing, as determined by measuring. So, the extent of my security was five feet eleven. Dwarfs are much more secure, they don't have so far to fall. After documentation, we go aboard.

The plane is a C-54, four-engine bomber with bench seats.

'Oh, I trust four engines more than I trust two,' said Ellen.

'Ah, Ellen, would you trust me more than two engines?'

No, she doesn't trust men, she's got a husband in the RAF who's buggered off, he's a pilot, so he buggered off on one engine, now she only trusts two.

Why did he bugger off?

'Someone else.'

Ah, there's lots of those around, I told her, I was someone else, and as far as I was concerned so was she, in fact, everyone was someone else, there was a wide choice. It's a cold evening but the plane has heaters, 'You done this flight before, Danny?' I said. Yes, several times, never mind several, how many? Twice he tells me.

'The accommodation is all military but very good. The chow is great, steak every dinner.' Steaks eh? With my Belsen body it's what I need.

We are landing at Tempelhof. 'Okay folks,' says Jack-I'm-in-charge. 'Keep in your individual groups.' I was an individual group so I kept there. It's night-time, we are driven through bombed streets trying to look normal, to the Barre Hotel, modern, but everything very efficient. Porters in dark blue run out to take our luggage. 'Okay, folks, listen, when you've finished, chow is served.' He points to the dining room sign, DINING ROOM.

Get the hint? said Danny. Danny and I get a room together; he, unlike Mulgrew, doesn't smoke, unlike Danny, I do. Danny has a strange habit, he would count all his money on to a table, the notes first, then stack his change in little pagodas. 'My father used to do this.'

Oh, did he kneel in front of it?

Don't be silly. It was something to do with insecurity, he was afraid of being poor.

Poor? I told him my poor grandfather was poor, only spoke Gaelic, he came to Britain, but he became rich, yet only spoke three words of English, 'Stick 'em up'. What was Canada like?

'Well,' said Danny, 'as far as showbiz was concerned the Indians are still in charge, anybody who's anybody goes to America.'

I was an anybody, I'd do well there. How come he was here?

'Well, I was in the Canadian Army.'

'Canadian? My regiment declared war on you in 1940, we were always having fights with you.'

'Shall we stop now,' he said.

Why is he living in lousy London?

'I just like England, it's got something, this girl with big tits.'

Not Bexhill Betty with bursting boobs, no, this was Thunder Tits Theresa from Tyneside. He had done stand-up comedy in the States.

Never sitting down? He said, 'Just one performance, Spike, should get the VC, the only thing worse would be pulling your balls through a mangle.'

What's this? Oh no! could I *not* smoke in the bedroom, please? Look here, Danny, I can be pushed so far.

'Right,' he says and pushes me into the toilet. 'Smoke in there.'

It says in the Book of Job: Verily thou shall not argue with a six foot three Canadian. Yes, *not* smoking is *good* for me, I just have to get used to screaming convulsions and wanking.

Dinner in a hall mixed with US Servicemen, we queue up for chow. They give us strange looks, I already had one. Afterwards in the bar, we sit around drinking Moselle wine and are introduced to our entertainments officer, Major Evelyn May, who makes a beeline for our singer Helen Mack; poor girl, is there no let-up? He stands so close, Trixie said, 'I couldn't get this fag paper between them.' He's a middle-aged used-up Airforce Officer, no, he's never flown a plane, no, he was never in action. Tennis then? 'But I was bombed once and, Spike, that was enough. [I didn't think it was], as a result I'm deaf in one ear.' That's the one he'll use when Helen says no. 'If there's anything you want, you just ask Uncle Evelyn.'

Pardon.

'Okay, okay, you hear that folks?' echoes Delroy. 'Anything you want, just ask.' You little arse licker.

It's Sunday night, all tired, Danny and I turn in. We lie in bed working out cross-overs, I gave him my original. The invisible man wants to see you. Tell him I can't see him or quick, duck behind the couch. You're a liar, there's no duck behind the couch. Elephant then? He has a great opening gag, he unbuttons his jacket and a tie unrolls across the footlights into the orchestra pit. 'It's my brother's, he's taller than I am.' I tell him I've an idea, we auction the theatre to someone in the audience, for say a dollar, someone would bid, thereafter if the audience didn't react, we'd blame him for booking the act. We did this, in fact, and dragged the 'owner' on stage and made him apologise for each act. 'Go on, say sorry, you mean swine, with your money you could have got Bob Hope.' We got unstuck one night, the owner was drunk and punched Danny and me, causing hysterical laughing as we tried to avoid the onslaught. Even giving him his dollar back, he snatched, tearing it in half; this infuriated him. 'God dammit, I'll kill you,

you limey bastard. No one does that to [whatever his name was] from Texas.' At this there were 'Remember The Alamo' shouts and the band busked 'The Yellow Rose Of Texas'. Two white-helmeted Military Police took him, struggling, from the stage.

As I lay in bed I was dying for a smoke, trouble was I didn't. 'Danny, if I just had three puffs.'

Hell no, he's not sleeping in a room full of three puffs, hell no!

So hell no, what a pathetic idiot figure I made sitting on the loo, just smoking. If my poor parents could see me now. 'There he is,' they'd say. Cigarettes are really hell, yet I'm loving it, maybe if I strain I could have a crap as well and make it official! After a good night's coughing I am awakened by Jack Delroy, who wants a meeting of the principals; that's Helen Mack, Frank Weir, Danny and me. He tells us this opening night is special as General Dempsey, the British General, and the French General LeClerc are guests of honour. It's at the Opera House again. *Sieg Heil*!

I don't know about the audience, but for me it was a disaster. I spoke and acted so fast that no one understood me. I was nearly in tears. Danny Arnold comforted me, 'Boy, did you die a death.' He comforted me, 'That wasn't an audience.'

I said, that was the Nazi Party waiting for Hitler.

'Wait on,' said Danny, 'they're Americans, you speak too fast for them.'

'But that's me, my act wasn't meant for dolts. I bet the fucking lot together couldn't spell cat, only one guy laughed and that was LeClerc, *he* thought I was funny and he doesn't speak English.'

'Slow up your act,' said Danny, 'and they'll get it.'

'Get it?' I said, in a rage now. 'They've already got it, brain damage, they're all from a Home.' When I cooled down (a month later) I did do the act slower, but taking the piss out of the audience, 'Gooood . . . eve-en-ing . . .' Long pause. 'I'm – not – going – too – fast for you – am – I – to get laughs from the men?' I would address it to the officers in the front row.

Mine was a wild act; I'd bounce across the back half of the stage like a kangaroo making strange idiot noises, I'd circle the

Rhine Maine

stage a few times, stop and give an idiot grin at the audience and say, 'Not long now.' Finally, when it reached breaking point I'd say, 'I must be a great disappointment to you' – then I'd do 'My impression of General Eisenhower.' I would then just curl up in a ball, I'd then explain, 'Mind you, that's only my impression.' Then my impression of Paul Robeson: here the stage would black out, in the dark I'd sing a few bars of 'Old Man River', then I'd say my impression of Mrs Gladys Lurks of Penge. I'd pull a face, then say you'll just have to believe me, then I'd put a blindfold on and say anyone give a number between one and a hundred, someone would shout a number and I'd say correct! I ended up singing 'Laura' but with comic interjections (sing), 'Laura is the face in the misty night.' When the mist cleared, ARGGGGGGGG that face! Like Tommy Cooper's pulled inside out! And so on. I was a good singer (was folks) so it was a very good ending to the act. It's a pity I stopped to concentrate more on writing.

Day; Danny, Ellen, Trixie and I go walking to one of the

(ABOVE) The Opera House at Hanover, where we appeared
(OPPOSITE) In mid-act with Bill MacGuffie at the piano

black market squares, there are people selling their household belongings, all very sad really. Women with all kinds, selling trinkets of family jewellery, pots, pans, statuettes, mirrors, and saddest, framed family photos. I bought, just for the sake of passing them money, two little tin pepper and salt containers, which I still have. Every time I use them I remember the face of the woman and child I brought them from, where is that little child now? Has she a salt and pepper pot? 'If we'd have lost the war,' said Ellen, 'this could have been us.'

Yes, in fact, if the truth be known only *one* soldier won the war, that was Montgomery! *He* won the war, who did Churchill invite to the Victory banquet – L/Bdr Milligan? No, Montgomery – in fact, Churchill, the King, the Queen, Eisenhower all ignored me personally, do you know who I am? I'm the Unknown Soldier! They just forgot to bury me. Who knows, when I die my friend Prince Charles may grant me an NHS state funeral and my tombstone.

L. BDR MILLIGAN
950024
Another Unknown Soldier

Danny Arnold is doing well, he's selling his imported coffee beans and has a wallet full of marks, 'Isn't all this a touch illegal?'

'A touch,' he says; 'it's totally illegal and authorised by the four powers, smuggling, stealing, selling, secreting. God bless democracy, Spike.'

So as not to be excluded I 'sold' a piece of Cadbury's chocolate to a young girl, she immediately started to eat it, I couldn't take the money. 'She might be putting on a sympathy act,' said Danny.

'Well, it went down better than my bloody act.'

'Who's to know,' I said, 'in the strange atmosphere of

Berlin, that young girl wasn't a British soldier in drag who was a chocolate freak who did this to get extra rations?'

'The one thing', said Trixie, laughing and rolling one, 'they don't buy is rolled cigarettes.'

Now a strange change in the fortunes of Milligan. Trixie, all of her, stood in front of me blocking the way, 'You, Spike, darling, could sell me *anything*.'

Oh, how about a harmonium? Wow, was there something on here?

'Here, try one of these,' she said, taking her rolled cigarette and placing it between my lips.

'Ohhhh!'

Ellen pipes up, 'She thinks your act is great.'

Oh! Danny doesn't notice, he's selling silk stockings.

'You're another Danny Kaye,' says Trixie, lighting my cigarette. What's happened to her since yesterday? Was it the food? Something in the water, like crocodiles, or was it me? I think I'd better start describing this chick; as I said, she is saturnine, raven black hair, eyes like black Cyprus olives, she's tall for a showgirl, short for a guardsman. She has an angular face, high cheekbones, small boobs, but legs for ever and alarmingly small hands and feet. When I first saw them, I sounded the alarm, I rang a bell shouting, 'Beware, small hands and feet'. When she walked it was like one of those Okovango women carrying water pots, she spoke with a slow, silken Welsh drawl and, when I told her I played rugby, our mutual fate was sealed. She stood very close and felt my muscles, I hadn't got any.

'No, I wasn't big, I was fast, on the wing.'

All the while Danny and Ellen are black marketing.

'Did you score many tries?' she said, like, have you done brain operations?

'Yes, I had, I was top try scorer for my battery.' Twenty-one points in one game.

She shook her head all the while fixing me with those sloe eyes. 'Oh, I've been looking for you,' she said. Well, she didn't have to look far, I was right there with twenty-one points in one game.

'Come on you two,' said Ellen. 'Getting on well are we?' she said with a knowing smile that turned into a bed. Help, I'd only come out to sell chocolate.

Trixie linked arms as we walked the market. 'Now,' she said, 'I want you all to hear this.'

Danny puts a hand to his ear.

'Listen,' says Trixie, 'Spike here and I are going to have a tempestuous affair.' Then turning to me says, 'I want you to save yourself just for me.'

Of course, anything to help. This is all new and I was getting it free on the black market! We take a horse-drawn landau to the Wiener Park Gardens, for a bombed city a splendid winter garden, what grabs us is the absence of litter, the pond has a mixture of wildfowl. Danny looks at the ducks and shouts, 'In this town you're lucky you're not all hanging in the butchers.'

'*Gut* afternoon, sir.' This from a smart-uniformed park attendant, not without a touch of the Nazi, or Prussian. 'You are liking our park?' Oh yes. 'In zer war all bombed, here nothing, there nothing, nothing everywhere.' A lot of nothing. 'Me und mein men we make it all, no money, just volunteer, now ve get money but first nix in der winkel.'

'Nick in der Winkel???'

He explains. 'Means nothing in the corner.' He marched off with a slight salute no doubt modified from a Nazi one.

'Who knows, that bastard,' said Danny, who'd been wounded in action, 'who's on another day on the Sangro\*, he would have filled me.' I feel uneasy about anyone with a military bearing. I had a military bearing once, I'd lost it through a hole in my pocket. Trixie asks, 'Now listen everybody, I don't want any whispers behind my back, Spike have you a bedroom of your own?' Yes, but it's back in Leathwell Road, Deptford, with the harmonium. Why? Never mind, she has a: 'Single bedroom, so darling I'll await you after the show.' My God, this all sounds like a Town Crier standing on the steps shouting, 'Fucking tonight, Spike Milligan and Miss Trixie Roberts, O-yez.'

That evening I do as Danny suggested, I calmed the act down, slow delivery, almost Caesarean, and I went very well. During singing 'Laura' I knocked the mike into the pit, I dived

---

\* River Sangro, Italy, where Danny was in action.

after it. 'You all right, Laura?' got a big laugh, yes a success, now I'd finished 'Laura' it was time for thermonic Trixie. After the show it's the usual invitation to the Officers' Mess, snacks and drinks galore, all gratis. Oh, those Americans they know how to live, of course, they know how to die as well, even as I write some might be doing just that. Fancy. I mean Reagan's getting on, I doubt if he can get off. So the officers ogle the girls, some very fine ogling went on that evening. That night I gave Trixie a real good ogling. What was all this rubbish about chocolate, now if Trixie was a fruit she'd be a peach but stoned! No, that's it folks, no juicy bits, I had all of those. Life is a repeatable formula, we did the show, wandered around Berlin; always present, the four-power military patrols, the bullshit! Each national representative vied with each other for smartness, the Russians and French wearing white gloves. 'It's to stop them biting their nails,' I said. Trixie and I are in a trance over our affair.

'You know, darling, this is all coming to an end, but,' she looked away and smiled, 'you never know.'

Oh yes, I specialise in never know, I never know anything, yet, I knew there were no dry cleaners in Peru, things like that, and Mary Queen of Scots thought Rizzo was a rice dish till they killed him.

The show moves on to our last date, Munich. I have a room with a balcony and I had to be stopped by order of Major May from doing Hitler speeches at all times of day and night. Given a bit more backing I think I could have revived the Third Reich, I mean people did stop and listen! '*Gersplatzen! Guzunder – Gershitzen hauser – Pileszen Gott Himmel!*' How did Hitler get away with it?

'Listen, Spike,' Danny sounds like a vicar, 'no, listen.' I know he's going to say something serious. 'This business with Trixie.' It isn't a business, we don't have a shop or a stall, what's he mean, business? 'Well, do you know she's married?' he says.

Married? 'You're joking.' If she is, it's not getting a laugh.

'I thought you knew.'

Strange, she doesn't wear a wedding ring. Her poor husband. I confront her.

'Yes, I'm married,' she said, blowing a long stream of smoke into my face. 'Does it make any difference, darling?' I don't know, when I try again tonight I'll let her know. Her husband is a policeman, a Detective Sergeant. Oh Christ, my fingerprints are all over her, all he needs is aluminium powder and a magnifying glass. 'Look,' she said, 'he never suspects a thing.' Sounds like one of our police.

'Why don't you wear a wedding ring?' I said, just curious.

'I took it off the moment I saw you.'

Help! that's not all she took off for me.

We took Wiesbaden by storm, by then the show was broken in and I had the hang of how to handle an audience and Trixie. Helpppppp! The whole tour is like 'Swinging Along Part II' but with Trixie instead of Dorita, though I still missed her. So the time comes and we wind up the show. 'Okay folks,' says Delroy, 'it's been a great tour, a real success, tonight.' After the show Major May invites us to an onstage party . . . Where have I heard this all before? I was getting tired, this was my third trip to Germany; it was like being on a conveyor, we were all about to come off the production line. I wanted home, that little back room in 3 Leathwell Road.

The flight from Tempelhof is very early. I board the flight reeking of Trixie's last-night perfume. I think it was called 'Kill'. We sit together on the flight, she feels for and holds my hand, she's wearing a wedding ring. 'What must you think of me?'

Dare I say, a good fuck? 'These affairs do happen,' I say, 'but never before has it been so organised.' I suppose I'd like to go on seeing her till the gas ran out, but no, she to Wales and her policeman. She'll say how much she missed him . . .

So ended my final tour of Germany, getting paid was a bonus.

Back home I made my way to the Grafton Arms to Jimmy Grafton, Arnhem hero and landlord extraordinary, who was helping Charlie the barman wash the glasses; it was after closing hours so the place was full.

'Last drinks,' Charlie kept calling as he filled another glass.

The company, Frank Weir and his orchestra et al, before embarking for home

'Hello Spike,' said Arnhem hero, 'welcome home, have a drink.'

'No thanks, I don't feel like a drink except a brandy.' Yes, Jimmy, the tour was over – I was over. What about the Ann Lenner Trio? They were over too, I think – everything was over, even my dandruff was over, over my jacket. Was there any work going, no, not cleaning the glasses, writing? Yes, along with Derek Roy there were others coming along. Chubby Chattering Harry Secombe, Bill Kerr the latter, an Australian, also Alfred Marks and Graham Stark. My life became one that kept me writing up in Jimmy's attic by day and sleeping on a mattress at night; it was the life of a drone, but it was all I had, of course, I was on the fringe of the radio world, and lived in hope. Sometimes I would sleep on the floor at Peter Sellers'. Some writing was for money, some on spec. for an unknown comic like Dick Emery, who would pay when he could. Emery had a narrow escape from death. Desperately poor, unable to pay the rent, he sealed his bedroom, stuffing newspapers in any vents or cracks. He then lay down, put his head in the gas oven – almost at once the gas ran out and he had no more money for the meter. What terrible luck.

A new 'star' whom we wrote for has appeared on *Variety Bandbox*, Robert Moreton, a droll, who told 'Merry Japes' from his Bumper Fun Book; he was like a lot of five-minute wonders, as soon as he'd been aired enough, he would be gently left off the BBC star list. Not finding work, he committed suicide, no one from the BBC was at his funeral, still he was and that's what mattered.

I visit Reg O'List, he too realises that the Ann Lenner Trio is finished. He's looking for work, won't be easy, he thinks that he and his girlfriend Jennifer can be a double act – can I write something? Yes, I can, I type out, 'To Whom it May Concern – I, Terence Alan Milligan, being of sound mind, declare that Reg O'List and Jennifer Lautrec are both free from infection and suitable for employment as entertainers.' Very funny they say, now drop dead. So I write an act, it must have been appalling; as I recall they got one day in which they were billed bigger than Harry Secombe.

'We died, Spike,' they said. 'We and your bloody script died.'

'Well, that's showbiz,' I said with an embarrassed cough, I often had one of those. Thank heaven, I'd written the script free to see how it went; well, it ended the brief career of Reg O'List and Jennifer.

'I don't think we've got it,' said Reg, fist clenched; not only haven't got but, but had it!

So I decided to have a 'fiesta' that meant chicken and chips and a bottle of wine in the bedroom, we sat eating and drinking.

We had invited Mulgrew, 'Och, you should hear the guitar player we got now – oh dear – he's like George Formby.'

How was the act doing?

'Well, we're doing the rounds, not bad for a bunch of squares.'

(OPPOSITE) Reg O'List and Jennifer hit the bill bigger than Harry Secombe. Find it if you can. Jennifer O'List is on the right. Unknown person at her side

And Bill Hall?

'He just lives for Arsenal football team, if they lose he plays badly, every Saturday I have to look up the football scores to see how he's going to play on a Monday.'

Reg is worried about work. 'It's a worry, I'm not young, I'm forty, it's late to start again.'

I said, 'Don't start again, carry on from where you are. Tell 'em you're thirty.'

He huffed, 'But I look forty.'

Then tell them not to look, I said.

He tried to kill me.

For no reason I said, 'I have a guilty conscience about eating chickens – I think I'll become a vegetarian.'

'But you love meat,' said Jennifer.

'Okay, I'll only eat animals that eat grass.'

'It's cruel to kill animals,' says Jennifer.

'I couldn't bear to see them killed in a slaughter home.'

'Then the best way', I said, 'is to eat meat blindfolded.'

We talk about the good times we had in Italy. 'I'll never get over Sorrento,' said Reg. 'The Officers Rest Camp, it was marvellous, *bella*,' he kissed his fingers into the air. '*Bella*', he repeated. Had I got over Italy?

Me? I hadn't got over Catford, I'd need a long convalescence, maybe life.

'Why are you always on about Catford?' said Reg.

'Well, I lived there when I was alive, it's the name I find funny, and you can never ever find the *centre* of Catford, it has no centre, it's everywhere except the centre.'

We were passing the wine around, at a late hour we split. It was lovely to have such friends.


Dorita lived at Chingford, miles away, you had to change buses three times, the same people seemed to be on the same bus! I spent so long on one bus they thought I was the conductor.

I met her mother Flossie, dad Reg, sister Olive and brother Edward, who is retarded. They let me stay the night in the little front spare bedroom. They all stayed up late, so our love life came to a halt.

Work! Alfred Marks is due to do a new revue at Brighton

written by Jimmy Grafton; music by Jack Jordan and bits by me – it's all hours all guns go. It's got to be finished by the 1st October – oh dear, here it was, only September and I was finished already. At night I bus off to see Dorita. Her father Reg starts to borrow money from me, 'I'm sorry – I've miscalculated my monthly allowance – and I'm just off to the pub and I've discovered I've got no money.'

So it was a quid here, a quid there, in fact a quid anywhere, then Dorita says, 'Has my father been borrowing money off you?'

Yes.

'The bastard – I should have warned you about him.'

Yes, the warning has come £20 too late.

'I'll see he gives you back every penny,' she said, with great determination in her voice. 'And,' she added, 'the interest.'

It's 1990 now and I've lost all interest. He didn't stop, he made innuendos, 'Lend us ten shillings, and I'll see me and mother get to bed early,' nudge-wink. It worked well, he and his wife had an early night and Dorita and I a late one and ten shillings worth! By now Dorita and I got really serious – but it was not to be.

The Alfred Marks revue was called 'Panama' and set in that quarter. The theatre was the old Grand (now demolished), Brighton. The week before opening, the rehearsal at the Grand. The last night of rehearsal I booked a room for Dorita and me at an hotel, 'a single door with adjoining rooms'. Horrors, in bed that night she refused to let me make love to her, had she heard about the ten shillings? Wasn't it enough? So there, between the hotel bedsheets, it all stopped, my first coitus interruptus, don't ask me why, I arose from the bed crippled by non-coitus. I dressed, went down to the lounge and entertained a Jewish family of twelve, who had never had coitus interruptus. Dorita left next morning. I stayed for the first night, it was a flop. It ran for a week and finis. What now, Milligan?

How could Dorita be so cruel. The cost of the hotel room – I'd spent my life savings on her, £17 – God knows that money could have been put to better use, for a start I needed a new sock, one of mine was like a mitten and the ragged state of my underwear, my long johns, had such holes I could get into them via the legs. My mother had cut up her bloomers to sew new collars on my shirts. My swimming trunks, I had had them since I was sixteen and the elastic was gone, I had to dive in holding them on. Likewise, if I sneezed all the wedding tackle dropped into sight, so I also chose swimming baths where the water was cold so they all shrivelled up out of sight. Dorita also says I don't seem to reciprocate her feelings, is she mad? I've felt all her reciprocals and she's been well pleased. I even let her feel mine and they pleased her no end, well, it did end, but very late.

At last, another breakthrough! The BBC have commissioned Jimmy Grafton to write a series for Derek Roy – Jimmy asked me to write it with him, I really wasn't up to it yet, I could drum up a few one-liners but a whole half hour was behind me. But in we go, we both work long hours, split with Jimmy in the bar, then he's running as a Conservative Councillor and he gets me going round putting his election leaflets in letter boxes, all this and writing with visits from the monkey. At night Jacko was locked in the attic next to me. Out of curiosity I wondered what he was doing and I looked through the keyhole only to see his eye looking at me. To keep himself going Jimmy took pep-up pills, consequently he could stay awake when I was falling asleep. The show was very well received. I have included the entire script to show what level comedy was in those days forty years ago. I've underlined some of the jokes that were mine.

Well, folks, that's where I was at on Wednesday, 5 October 1949. I went on writing for the series, which was far from being a success when it ended. I was back where I started, though I had been paid £30 a week and I'd saved nearly all of it, except I bought my very first radio, hoping one day I would be on it with my own show.

# HIP HIP HOO ROY (1)
## (THE DEREK ROY SHOW)

With

DEREK ROY
SPIKE MILLIGAN
ROBERT MORETON
JIMMY LAVALL
CHERRY LIND
THE STARGAZERS

THE DANCE ORCHESTRA CONDUCTED BY
STANLEY BLACK

*Script by*       JAMES DOUGLAS and SPIKE MILLIGAN

*Musical Links*   JACK JORDAN

*Producer*        LESLIE BRIDGMONT, 421 AEOLIAN


*Rehearsal*       Wednesday, 5 October 1949 3.00–6.00 p.m.
                  Aeolian 1

*Transmission*    Wednesday, 5 October 1949 7.30–8.00 p.m.
                  GOS/LIGHT

*Rec. Reps*       Thursday, 6 October 1949 2.30–3.00 a.m. GOS
                  Sunday, 9 October 1949 1.30–2.00 p.m. GOS


*Rec. No*         SOX 28611

| | | |
|---|---|---|
| 1. | ANNOUNCER | The Derek Roy Show! |
| | ORCHESTRA & QUARTET | SIGNATURE TUNE |

2.

'Hip hip hoo Roy,
Take time out to play,
And cheer your blues away,
Hip hip hoo Roy.
Come and spend a half an hour of joy.' You
might have been –

ANNOUNCER   (OVER MUSIC) (WITH CHEERS IN B/G)

3.

at an angling contest – where fish after fish
was being caught. Big fish – little fish –
they're jerking at the end of everyone's line;
but there's one competitor who can only
catch poor fish. His line has a jerk at *both*
ends – and here he is—

ORCHESTRA & QUARTET   'Hip hip hip hip hip who? Roy.'

4.   DEREK

Well, hello, patients. This is a very happy
occasion for me, and I hope for you. Here I
am with my own radio show – at last they've
persuaded me to do it, and it's happened so
quickly I hardly had time to get off my
knees. Of course, I won't say I haven't
dropped an occasional hint to Leslie Bridgmont – but now it's all settled and I can
move my bed out of his office – and let
Frankie Howerd move his back in.

As a matter of fact I was in the South of
France when I first heard the news. I was
sitting in my hotel in Monte Carlo, telling
the proprietor how much I appreciated the
warm friendly sun – and the warm friendly
daughter. He, on his part, congratulated me
on my polish – and the number of shoes I
was doing to the tin. Suddenly the phone
rang.

(PHONE BELL)

1. DEREK      Hello – Derek Roy here.
   DEREK      Hello patients, and thank you – it's nice to
              be back on the air and see in front of me all
              those happy smiling faces – and behind me
              Stanley Black and his boys (ORCHESTRA
              'BOOS') – still full of boos. Ah yes, it's good
              to take the mike again. So much has hap-
              pened since I've been away. They've given
              collars and ties to the police force – and
              they're thinking of doing the same for the
              House of Lords. Then there's been the
              heatwave – it was so hot last month, I was
              passing a field and I saw a cow on its back
              trying to give itself a shower. Still, the
              fashions have been very bright all summer,
              although I read that twenty-thousand
              women had to go without dresses this year.
              I spent half my holiday trying to find out
              where they were going.

                 And at Radiolympia they're trying to find
              out how many people are watching tele-
              vision. Somebody phoned me the other day
              and said, 'Have you got your television set
              on?' I said, 'No', and he said, 'Well, put it
              on and see how it fits.'

                 And everybody's working so hard – per-
              haps because it costs so much to have a loaf.
              I worked hard myself while I was away. I
              got a job in one of the old shadow factories,
              but it closed down. People just won't buy
              shadows. Then this programme was sug-
              gested. Of course, it's a worry. I'm so
              worried I'm on a diet – fingernails three
              times a day. Even tonight – well, you know
              how it is – I've got butterflies in my
              stomach. I took a pill to get rid of them –
              now they're playing ping pong with it. But
              I'm very grateful to the BBC for giving me
              this chance. Of course, I won't say I haven't

dropped an occasional hint to Leslie Bridgmont, but now it's all settled and I can move
my bed out of his office and let Richard
Murdoch move his back in.

| | | |
|---|---|---|
| 1. | CHERRY | (FRENCH VOICE) (TELEPHONE VOICE) M'sieur Roy? I have a call for you from London. They weesh for you to accept ze charge. |
| 2. | DEREK | <u>Accept ze charge? What do they think I am – a bull fighter?</u> (ASIDE) <u>Now who could be so mean</u> – Oh yes. (LOUD) Tell the BBC I'll take the call. Hello . . . |
| 3. | BRIDGMONT | Hello – Derek – This is Leslie Bridgmont calling from London – nice of you to accept the charge. |
| 4. | DEREK | That's quite all right Leslie. Call me any time – always happy to— |
| 5. | CHERRY | Your time is up, do you wish for further time? |
| 6. | DEREK | No— (INCOMPREHENSIBLE MUMBLE) (PIPS: VOICE CEASES ABRUPTLY) |
| 7. | DEREK | Yes, it was the great Bridgmont himself. He wanted me to come back and carry on with my radio work – there were still seventeen sets to be repaired. Well before I left Monte Carlo <u>I took a gander round the town – I thought the exercise would do it good.</u> I remember it was one of those heavy days— |
| 8. | BOB | (COCKNEY) Ooh blimey, it must weigh 'arf a ton. |
| 9. | DEREK | And I – I was in a heavy daze. |
| 10. | BOB | (COCKNEY) Ooh blimey, it must weigh— |
| 11. | DEREK | Thank you, we had that. |
| 12. | BOB | (COCKNEY) Sorry. |
| 13. | DEREK | Almost without realising it I found myself inside the Casino. I approached a gentleman sitting at the roulette table. Excuse me, sir . . . |

| | | |
|---|---|---|
| 1. | LAVAL | (FRENCH VOICE) *Oui, monsieur?* |
| 2. | DEREK | Tell me, are the stakes very high here? |
| 3. | LAVAL | (FRENCH VOICE) Very high, I wouldn't eat one if I were you. |
| 4. | DEREK | I walked over to the dicing table. They seemed to be having trouble with an American gentleman. |
| 5. | SPIKE | (AMERICAN VOICE) Hey, these dice. |
| 6. | LAVAL | (FRENCH VOICE) What is wrong with them, *monsieur*? |
| 7. | SPIKE | (AMERICAN VOICE) They're loaded, that's what. |
| 8. | LAVAL | (FRENCH VOICE LAUGHINGLY) But no, *monsieur*, loaded dice in the Casino? Nevair! Throw zem and see. |
| 9. | SPIKE | (AMERICAN VOICE) OK. (NOISE DICE ROLLING – TWO SHOTS) |
| 10. | SPIKE | (AMERICAN VOICE) There I told you they were loaded. |
| 11. | DEREK | I lost heavily and was summoned to the manager's office. (DOOR EFFECT) |
| 12. | LAVAL | (SECOND FRENCH VOICE) *Monsieur* – you owe the Casino two hundred thousand francs. |
| 13. | DEREK | Er, what's that in sterling? |
| 14. | LAVAL | About two hundred and twenty-three pounds, *M'sieur*. |
| 15. | DEREK | Well – I'm sorry – but all I have left is this ten-dollar bill. |
| 16. | LAVAL | That is quite all right, *M'sieur* – we can give you change. |
| 17. | DEREK | Stunned, I walked out into the night – misfortune seemed to dog my footsteps. |
| 18. | CHERRY | Hello, *Chèri*—(YAP YAP AS DOG) |
| 19. | DEREK | What do you want? |
| 20. | CHERRY | I'm Miss Fortune. |
| 21. | DEREK | The Casino was still only a stone's throw away – I decided to have one last fling. |

(WHISTLE AND CRASH OF GLASS)

1. DEREK  That'll teach them to take my money. Well, that ended a very exciting stay in Monte Carlo – and my last recollection is of a fellow passenger on the train, as we were leaving, waving farewell to Monte.

(TRAIN NOISE)

2. DEREK  (COCKNEY) Goodbye, Monty – see you at the Alamein Reunion.

3. BOB  (BERET) (REFINED VOICE) Right-ho, press on regardless.

4. DEREK  We couldn't press on because although the carriages were there, the engine had gone – so I went up to a porter – 'I say Porter—'

5. LAVAL  (FRENCH VOICE) *Oui, M'sieur?*

6. DEREK  What's happened to the engine?

7. LAVAL  (FRENCH VOICE) Well, *M'sieur*, the engine got here early, the carriages were late, so the engine went off in a huff.

8. DEREK  HUFF
(BOTH CARRY ON HUFFING TRAIN NOISE)
(STARGAZERS – 'TROLLEY SONG')

9. DEREK  Fascinating – that little transport song – especially the go slow movement in the middle. Well, patients – to ensure the success of this show, I've engaged the services of a very competent gag man – he even admits it himself – and here he is, with his Bumper Fun Book tucked underneath his arm – Robert Moreton . . .

(APPLAUSE)

10. MORETON  A jolly good evening to one and all, and let joy be unconfined.

11. DEREK  She is – they let her out of gaol yesterday. (COD LAUGH) Now Moreton, I hope you have the script read.

12. MORETON  Oh yes, and a funnier one you've never seen.

| | | |
|---|---|---|
| 1. | DEREK | I haven't seen this one yet – but I'm all ears. |
| 2. | MORETON | (CHUCKLE) So I've noticed. (LAUGH) Oh, I say – that was rather crisp wasn't it? |
| 3. | DEREK | (FORCED LAUGH) No. |
| 4. | MORETON | Oh – well listen to this convulsively, hilarious opening joke. |
| 5. | DEREK | Yes, yes, yes. |
| 6. | MORETON | I say to you, 'Derek, why did the chicken cross the road?' |
| 7. | DEREK | But Moreton, that gag's older than Bernard Shaw. |
| 8. | MORETON | I know, but I have rather a cunning twist to the answer. |
| 9. | DEREK | Pity you haven't one for your neck. |
| 10. | MORETON | Well, when I say, 'Why does the chicken cross the road?', you *don't* say, 'To get to the other side.' |
| 11. | DEREK | What *do* I say? To see Gregory Peck? |
| 12. | MORETON | No – you say, 'But Moreton, that gag's older than Bernard Shaw.' |
| 13. | DEREK | I *said* that. |
| 14. | MORETON | Ah – but here's the extremely funny climax. *I* say – 'I know – it's got whiskers on it.' Hmm,mm. You see, Bernard Shaw has a beard. (CHUCKLES) |
| 15. | DEREK | (LOOK IN DISGUST) And you worked that out all by yourself? |
| 16. | MORETON | Yes. |
| 17. | DEREK | Well. |
| 18. | MORETON | I'm glad you enjoyed it – though I must confess a certain amount of credit is due to my Bumper Fun— |
| 19. | DEREK | (INTERRUPTING) Moreton, have you succeeded at *any*thing? |
| 20. | MORETON | You mean at anything else? Oh yes – I was very successful as a submarine commander during the war. |
| 21. | DEREK | You were? |

| | | |
|---|---|---|
| 1. | MORETON | Oh yes, indeed. In fact, I'm the only British Submarine commander to have been awarded the German Iron Cross. |
| 2. | DEREK | How was that? |
| 3. | MORETON | I sank a British battleship. |
| 4. | DEREK | Thank you, Moreton – I'll always give time for wit in this programme. |
| 5. | SPIKE | Da – Mister Roy! |
| 6. | DEREK | Pardon me – I should have said time and a half, because here's our resident half of it – Spike Milligan. |
| 7. | SPIKE | Da – gee thanks, Mister Roy. |
| 8. | DEREK | Well, Spike – what brings you here? |
| 9. | SPIKE | Da – der fifty-three bus – it goes up there by der— |
| 10. | DEREK | No, no, what are you here *for*? |
| 11. | SPIKE | Da – I brought dis telegram. |
| 12. | DEREK | Well read it. |
| 13. | SPIKE | Ha – it's from Frankie Howerd – da – To der BBC, care of Derink Roy. |
| 14. | DEREK | Hm – could be. |
| 15. | SPIKE | Dear Derink – good luck to your programme. When you get this my mudder will be listening – and I will be listening to— |
| 16. | DEREK | Now isn't that nice of him. |
| 17. | SPIKE | Da – I ain't finished yet – da – and I will be listening to *Take It From Here*. |
| 18. | DEREK | I might have known – that Frankie Howerd— (ELECTRICIAN GAG) |
| 19. | SPIKE | Da – what's the matter? |
| 20. | DEREK | Well, you read what he said, didn't you? |
| 21. | SPIKE | Da – yeah, but I wasn't listening. (LAUGH) |
| 22. | DEREK | Stop acting like an idiot, Spike. |
| 23. | SPIKE | (INDIGNANT) Da – I ain't acting. |
| 24. | DEREK | Just you go and sit down and rest your brains. Oh dear, if only that agent would show up with the singer he promised. |
| 25. | LAVAL | You looking for me, Mister Roy? |

| | | |
|---|---|---|
| 1. | DEREK | That depends who you are. |
| 2. | LAVAL | Britain's leading theatrical agency boy, that's me. 'Ere's me card, read for yourself. |
| 3. | DEREK | (READS) Hm, Rabinowitz, Levinski and McTavish. Which are you? |
| 4. | LAVAL | I'm McTavish. |
| 5. | DEREK | Oh – er – where are your partners? |
| 6. | LAVAL | They're tied up at the office. |
| 7. | DEREK | You mean they're busy? |
| 8. | LAVAL | No – tied up – just a little precaution I take whenever I go out. |
| 9. | DEREK | I see – and what's that you've got under your coat – the safe? |
| 10. | LAVAL | No – that's a box of chocolates boy, I'm very fond of chocolates. 'Ere, look. |
| 11. | DEREK | Why Mr McTavish, they look simply scrumptious – ha ha – they're making my mouth water. |
| 12. | LAVAL | Well, I'm a big-hearted feller. 'Ere – 'ere's a bit of blotting paper. |
| 13. | DEREK | Such meanness – just like an agent – not one man in a hundred would be as mean as you. |
| 14. | LAVAL | That's what I like about you, Derek boy. You've got a good head for figures, and talking of figures – here's the young lady I promised to get for you – Miss Cherry Lind. (APPLAUSE) |
| 15. | CHERRY | Hello . . . |
| 16. | DEREK | Hallo . . . Why Cherry – you look so ripe. |
| 17. | CHERRY | Why Derek – you talk such tripe – McTavish, I thought you said he was the answer to a maiden's prayer. |
| 18. | LAVAL | Yes, I did, but I didn't say it was the right answer. Ha ha, ain't I cruel – ha ha – go on tell me I'm cruel. |
| 19. | DEREK | You are – to look at. Miss Lind, where I come from the women tear out their hair for me. |
| 20. | CHERRY | Why don't you go back? |

| 1. | DEREK | I don't like bald-headed women. |
|----|-------|--------------------------------|
| 2. | DEREK | But you, Cherry, you're so— |
| 3. | CHERRY | Beautiful. |
| 4. | DEREK | Yes – and you're so— |
| 5. | CHERRY | Charming? |
| 6. | DEREK | Yes – and you're so – |
| 7. | CHERRY | Understanding? |
| 8. | DEREK | Yes. |
| 9. | CHERRY | Derek – you say the nicest things. |
| 10. | DEREK | Yes – don't I. Haven't you something nice to say to *me*? |
| 11. | CHERRY | Well, a modest girl doesn't make advances to the man. |
| 12. | DEREK | No – and a mousetrap doesn't make advances to the mouse. Can't you think of *something* nice? |
| 13. | CHERRY | Of course, Derek. I think you're so – so— |
| 14. | DEREK | What? |
| 15. | CHERRY | Nothing – just so-so. |
| 16. | DEREK | So-so! Well that's enough to give anyone the needle. And after I've paid you such compliments. |
| 17. | CHERRY | Oh Derek – if only girls could see themselves as you see them. |
| 18. | DEREK | Oh, I don't know – it's not much fun peeping through keyholes. Cherry, don't I mean anything to you? |
| 19. | CHERRY | Well yes – you amuse me – you take me out of myself. |
| 20. | DEREK | Like a winkle. |
| 21. | CHERRY | Yes – no. Like a child— <br> (MUSIC INTRO. SONG 'I LIKE TO DO THINGS FOR YOU') |
| 22. | CHERRY | (SING) Though you are a great big grown-up, You are like a child to me. |
| 23. | DEREK | Tell me more— |
| 24. | CHERRY | And somehow or other you make me want to mother you. |
| 25. | DEREK | Mammy. |

| | | |
|---|---|---|
| 1. | CHERRY | Every now and then I'll own up – I want to take you on my knee. |
| 2. | DEREK | She thinks I'm Archie Andrews. |
| 3. | CHERRY | The hardest thing for me to do – is to keep my hands off you. |
| 4. | DEREK CHORUS | Why bother? |
| 5. | CHERRY | I'd like to fix your tie – smooth your hair— Put things in order here and there 'Cause I'd like to do things for you. |
| 6. | CHERRY | I'd like to tie your shoes – brush your suit. |
| 7. | DEREK | (SING) I'm beginning to think you're rather cute 'Cause you like to do things for me. |
| 8. | CHERRY | There doesn't seem to be need for me to mention— |
| 9. | DEREK | Mention what? |
| 10. | CHERRY | That I'm the party who can give you attention. |
| 11. | DEREK | Oh, shoot me while I'm happy. |
| 12. | CHERRY | I'd like to find your gloves, dust your hat. |
| 13. | DEREK | Go on and tell me, Cherry – why do that? |
| 14. | CHERRY | 'Cause I like to do things for you. (SPEAK OVER LINK) Come along now gentlemen – what would you like to do for me? You first, Derek. |
| 15. | DEREK | I'd like to take you along to some quiet spot And tell you confidentially I like you a lot 'Cause I like to do things for you |
| 16. | CHERRY | Mm – hm. McTavish? |
| 17. | LAVAL | I'd like to see you get the stardom for which you're meant. With a great big salary less 10 per cent 'Cause I've got an interest in you |
| 18. | CHERRY | Moreton? |
| 19. | MORETON | Miss Cherry, yes, I must confess that one look Decided me that you were the one girl who Should share my Bumper Fun Book. |
| 20. | CHERRY | And what about you, Spike? |

| 1. | SPIKE | Da – well you see – I just like for you to do things for me |
|---|---|---|
| 2. | CHERRY | And I like |
| 3. | DEREK | I like |
| 4. | CHERRY | I like |
| 5. | DEREK | I like |
| 6. | BOTH | To do things for you. |
| 7. | SPIKE | Me too. (END OF SONG) |
| 8. | DEREK | That was lovely, Cherry. You're engaged. |
| 9. | CHERRY | Derek – this is so sudden. |
| 10. | MORETON | Oh, I say – congratulations you two. |
| 11. | DEREK | What do you mean – congratulations? |
| 12. | MORETON | Well I couldn't help overhearing your conversation. |
| 13. | DEREK | Peeping Tom. |
| 14. | MORETON | Oh really. I hope you don't think that I'm the sort of drop who eavesdrips – er – drip who eavesdrops? |
| 15. | DEREK | In that case you'd better take that key out of your ear. If you must know – the engagement mentioned is purely a business one – I'm afraid. |
| 16. | CHERRY | Did you like my singing, Spike? |
| 17. | SPIKE | <u>Da – yeah – da I love the sound of a female voice – da especially when it's a woman.</u> |
| 18. | CHERRY | You know Derek – I like Spike. He looks the sort who's good to his parents. |
| 19. | DEREK | He is – <u>he never goes home.</u> |
| 20. | CHERRY | I mean he looks quite a caveman— |
| 21. | DEREK | Oh, positively pre-historic. |
| 22. | CHERRY | And yet there's something rather noble about him. |
| 23. | MORETON | Miss Lind – I have a portrait of one of my ancestors executed in oil. |
| 24. | DEREK | Why didn't they just hang him? |
| 25. | MORETON | No, no – I mean he was painted *with* oil. |
| 26. | DEREK | Oh – a Channel swimmer? |
| 27. | CHERRY | What about you, Spike. Have you any antecedents? |

| | | |
|---|---|---|
| 1. | SPIKE | Any anty cedents? Let me see – Anty Rosie, Anty Mary, Anty Minnie – da no – no anty cedents. |
| 2. | CHERRY | What about your family tree, Derek? |
| 3. | DEREK | Well – of course, it has a lot of branches – if you twig what I mean. (LAUGH) |
| 4. | MORETON | Oh crisp – very crisp. As a matter of fact, Derek – I've been investigating your genealogy— |
| 5. | DEREK | Moreton – please – there's a lady present. |
| 6. | MORETON | And I've discovered that one of your ancestors was the first Baron FitzRoy— |
| 7. | CHERRY | FitzRoy? How did he get a name like that? |
| 8. | MORETON | Well you see – he used to wear the King's cast-off clothing – and the King used to say— |
| 9. | DEREK & MORETON | What fits me – fits Roy. |
| 10. | DEREK | Moreton! You're not in *Variety Bandbox* now. |
| 11. | MORETON | That was just one of my little jokes. |
| 12. | DEREK & MORETON | What are you, one of your father's? |
| 13. | DEREK | Okay. That makes us quits. But what about this Baron FitzRoy? |
| 14. | MORETON | Well – his father was a knight errant. |
| 15. | SPIKE | Da – *my* father was a night watchman. |
| 16. | DEREK | Oh, shut up, Spike – or I shan't give you your bonus this week. |
| 17. | SPIKE | I don't care – you can keep your old bonus – dey ain't never got any meat on dem anyway. |
| 18. | DEREK | Oh – somebody hit him on the head. (CRASH) |
| 19. | SPIKE | Da – come in. |
| 20. | CHERRY | Please don't hit Spike like that. |
| 21. | DEREK | No? |
| 22. | CHERRY | No – hit him like this. (LOUDER CRASH) |

| | | |
|---|---|---|
| 1. | SPIKE | Da – I accept your apology. |
| 2. | DEREK | Tell me more about the Baron Moreton. |
| 3. | CHERRY | Yes – was he at the signing of Magna Carta? |
| 4. | MORETON | Yes – in fact, he played a most important part. I've written a short historical sketch on the subject if you'd care to read it. |
| 5 | DEREK | Read it? We'll act it. Come on everybody. J. Arthur Moreton presents 'History in the Making'. (FANFARE) |
| 6. | MORETON | Runnymede – and the time is twelve or twelve— |
| 7. | DEREK | Twelve-fifteen? |
| 8. | MORETON | No, it's quarter to eight. No – er what I mean is – Runnymede in the year twelve hundred and – er – twelve hundred and – er – Runnymede early in the thirteenth century. The Barons are gathered together awaiting the arrival of King John. He is coming in on— |
| 9. | DEREK | A wing and a player? |
| 10. | MORETON | Yes – no – he's coming on a steed — |
| 11. | DEREK | Come on steed! |
| 12. | MORETON | Chief among the waiting Barons is FitzRoy. He is their leader by virtue of the fact that he was once an Earl. In fact, his mother still calls him Early. Oh I say – that was rather crisp. The Barons are talking amongst themselves. (BABBLE OF VOICES) – but FitzRoy's voice rings out above the noise. (ASIDE) That's you, Derek. |
| 13. | DEREK | Oh yes. (ALOUD) Noble Barons, silence I pray, silence while I call your names. Page? |
| 14. | LAVAL | Sire? |
| 15. | DEREK | Have you the roll? |
| 16. | LAVAL | Aye, Sire. |
| 17. | DEREK | Well – slice it up – we're getting hungry. (LAUGHTER AND CRIES OF 'A JEST – A JEST') |

| 1. | MORETON | Oh crisp, Sire – very crisp. |
|---|---|---|
| 2. | DEREK | What's this – another page? |
| 3. | MORETON | Yes – Sure, Page two. |
| 4. | DEREK | Dog – if I but thoughtst that thou takest the mickey – I'd — (IMPATIENT MURMUR FROM BARONS) Contain yourselves gentlemen – until King John arrives. |
| 5. | SPIKE | King John! I spit. |
| | | (CRY OF AYE, AYE, AYE) |
| 6. | DEREK | 'Tis agreed then – we spit in his eye. |
| | | (CHEERS) |
| 7. | SPIKE | Why is he keeping us waiting? |
| | | (CRIES OF RAGE) |
| 8. | DEREK | Patience, gentlemen. We must have patience. |
| 9. | CHERRY | Patience has gone – will I do? |
| 10. | DEREK | (ASIDE) Later wench – later. |
| | | (TRUMPET FANFARE) |
| 11. | ? | Hist – list – here come King John now. |
| | | (HORSES' HOOVES) |
| | | Be not afraid. |
| | | (CRIES OF 'NEVER'. KNOCKING ON DOOR) |
| | | He's at the door. |
| | | (LOUD KNOCKING) |
| | | He's getting annoyed. |
| | | (BANGING AND CRASH) |
| 12. | LAVAL | Can I come in? Ho there, Barons – what would you? |
| 13. | DEREK | Your signature, Sire – on the Magna Carta. |
| 14. | LAVAL | And where is the Carta? |
| 15. | DEREK | Outside with his cart. |
| | | (CRIES OF 'A JEST – A JEST') |
| 16. | ? | Here, Sire – here is the Magna Carta. Read it. |
| 17. | DEREK | Ah – red petrol – no we can't use that. I have it – we'll burn something we've all been trying to get rid of. |
| 18. | LAVAL | What's that? |

1. DEREK — Moreton's Bumper Fun Book.
   (CHEERS. MUSIC LEAD IN TO SONG TIME)
2. STARGAZERS — It's song time – song time etc.
3. ANNOUNCER — Yes – it's song time – and each week we invite our listeners to send in their requests for Derek Roy to sing their favourite song – and this week's choice is 'Home Girl'.
   (DEREK SING. APPLAUSE)
4. ANNOUNCER — Roy is a man of many parts – some of them very nearly in working order. He is an entertainer, singer, comedi – er singer – entertainer – but it is not widely known that he has another side—
5. DEREK — That's right – every man has two sides – his front side and his—
6. ANNOUNCER — In this case we refer to his talent as a writer – and it is with pride that we tell you of his latest book on travel – entitled 'Round The World With Roy' – or 'Where The Heck Are We Now'. This outstanding book has been widely reviewed in the Press. Listen to the Birmingham Express.
   (TRAIN NOISE)
7. — The Battersea Bugle.
   (BUGLE CALL)
8. — Now hear what the *Manchester Post* had to say.
9. LAVAL — (LANCASHIRE) Parcel for Mrs Ramsbottom. Thank yer, luv.
10. ANNOUNCER — Here is another report.
    (PISTOL SHOT)
11. — Perhaps the general reaction to this book is best summed up in the words of eminent book reviewer, Professor Blurb.
12. LAVAL — I have studied Roy's book with considerable interest and I am prepared to claim that I now know it backwards. Now I am about to embark on the more difficult task of reading it forwards. Let us then open the volume

haphazardly – say at page one – and what do we find – Chapter One – entitled – 'In the footsteps of Livingstone, Stanley and ENSA' – And this is what Roy has to say on reaching Darkest Africa.

| | | |
|---|---|---|
| 1. | DEREK | Strike a light somebody – I can't see a flipping thing. |
| 2. | LAVAL | (READS) Mmmmmm – 'and free all serfs'. Do the serfs wish this? |
| 3. | DEREK | Let one speak for himself. Come here, Serf! |
| 4. | LAVAL | So you're a serf. |
| 5. | SPIKE | Da – yeah. |
| 6. | LAVAL | Tell me, why do you wear a saddle on your back? |
| 7. | SPIKE | Da – for surf riding, Sire. |
| 8. | LAVAL | Very well – I will sign. There – it is done. (CHEERS) |
| 9. | DEREK | Sire – you will go down in history. |
| 10. | LAVAL | How do you know? |
| 11. | DEREK | I saw your school report. |
| 12. | LAVAL | Have a care, Baron FitzRoy. My archers are outside. |
| 13. | DEREK | Hm. I thought you were walking a little flat-footed. |
| 14. | LAVAL | As a matter of fact, FitzRoy old man – I *am* without my supports. As you may have heard, I lost quite a lot of stuff in the Wash. |
| 15. | MORETON | I lost a garment at *my* laundry too. (CRIES OF 'A JEST – A JEST') |
| 16. | MORETON | No – a vest – a vest. Oh I say that *was* crisp. |
| 17. | DEREK | You dog-eared page. I warned you – now you shall pay for this insult. Is there a bookbinder here? |
| 18. | SPIKE | Yea, Sire. |
| 19. | DEREK | Well bind this page. |
| 20. | MORETON | No, no, Sire – have mercy – help. |
| 21. | DEREK | Be careful, men – he is tall and will need much binding. |

| | | |
|---|---|---|
| 1. | LAVAL | (COSTA) Good morning, Sir – was there something? |
| 2. | DEREK | There was – but not now. Come, men – tie the page to a stake, and burn him. |
| 3. | SPIKE | But, Sire – we have no stake. |
| 4. | DEREK | Then lash him to a lamb chop, and grill him. |
| 5. | MORETON | Oh dear – it looks as though I've had my chips. |
| 6. | SPIKE | I have it – we'll roast him on a spit. |
| 7. | DEREK | Capital – and I shall turn the page. Tell me page, how do you wish to be burnt. |
| 8. | MORETON | Oh crisp, Sire – very crisp. |
| 9. | SPIKE | But, Sire – what shall we burn him with? All we have is a few old pound notes. |
| 10. | DEREK | Hm – they won't go very far. Anything else? |
| 11. | SPIKE | A container of strange spirit from the Far East. |
| 12. | LAVAL | Quickly, Roy organises his party of fellow travellers. |
| 13. | DEREK | Oh Spike— |
| 14. | SPIKE | Da yeah? |
| 15. | DEREK | Light some fires round the camp. |
| 16. | SPIKE | Da – what for? |
| 17. | DEREK | Lions, of course. |
| 18. | SPIKE | Da – lions. Why can't they light their own fires? |
| 19. | MORETON | I say – listen. What's that? |
| 20. | LAVAL | (PARROT LIKE) Manana manana manana. |
| 21. | MORETON | That's funny – what's Edmundo Ros doing here? |
| 22. | DEREK | Don't be silly Moreton – that's the Korbili bird. |
| 23. | MORETON | The Korbili bird? What's that? |
| 24. | DEREK | The Korbili bird is a bird that leaves its warm nest at six in the morning, plunges into an icy pool, and screams 'Korbi limey ain't it cold.' |
| 25. | SPIKE | (DISTANT) Da Mister Roy. |

| | | |
|---|---|---|
| 1. | DEREK | (CALLING) Yes, Spike. |
| 2. | SPIKE | I've lit der fires for der lions but dey won't come near them. Da – I'll try and coax one – Puss puss puss. |
| | | (LIONS ROAR MIXED WITH CRIES FROM SPIKE) |
| 3. | DEREK | Moreton, Cherry, quick – Spike's in trouble with a lion. |
| 4. | CHERRY | Clawed? |
| 5. | DEREK | No – Spike. Come quickly. (SCREAM) Oh look. |
| 6. | CHERRY | How horrible. |
| 7. | DEREK | Quick – carry him over here – you take his legs Moreton. |
| 8. | MORETON | (GRUNTS) I can't. |
| 9. | DEREK | Why? |
| 10. | MORETON | They appear to be attached to his body. |
| 11. | DEREK | Gently now – put him down here. |
| 12. | CHERRY | Do you think he'll be all right? |
| 13. | DEREK | Well, I think with a little rest and a feed of raw meat he'll be fit enough to rejoin the other lions. |
| 14. | LAVAL | Suddenly into the middle of the group an unseen hand throws a spear. |
| | | (EFFECT) |
| 15. | CHERRY | What's that? |
| 16. | MORETON | It looks like an assegai. |
| 17. | DEREK | Yes – and assegai that threw it. |
| 18. | MORETON | Do you think the natives are revolting? |
| 19. | CHERRY | Oh no – some of them are rather nice. |
| 20. | LAVAL | Suddenly their worst fears are confirmed as they hear the sound of a native rising. |
| | | (ALARM CLOCK) |
| 21. | DEREK | (AS NATIVE) (YAWN) What a time to get up. |
| 22. | LAVAL | Fleeing from the menace of the savages, the brave little band forge on into the interior. Even the great Ubangi River is no obstacle to the initiative and enterprise of the dauntless Roy, who immediately builds a boat. |

| | | |
|---|---|---|
| 1. | DEREK | (SING. 'LIFE ON THE OCEAN WAVE') Hard on the tiller there. |
| 2. | CHERRY | Aye aye, Sir. |
| 3. | MORETON | By jove – this brings out the Drake in me. Quack quack. |
| 4. | SPIKE | Oh Derink. |
| 5. | DEREK | What is it, Spike? |
| 6. | SPIKE | Da – I feel sea sick. |
| 7. | DEREK | All right – everybody out of the boat – tomorrow we'll take it down to the river and see if it floats. |
| 8. | LAVAL | Having decided *not* to cross the river – the expedition plunges deeper into the jungle. The only contact they have with the outside world is through the Morse key. <u>One day a message is received.</u> (MORSE TRUMPET) |
| 9. | DEREK | Quick, Spike – take down that message. |
| 10. | SPIKE | Da – Okay. <u>(MORSE CONTINUES, STOPS)</u> |
| 11. | DEREK | Did you get it? |
| 12. | SPIKE | Da – yeah. |
| 13. | DEREK | What did it say? |
| 14. | SPIKE | It said <u>(MORSE NOISE)</u> |
| 15. | DEREK | Sounds like a message from Coney's mother. |
| 16. | CHERRY | Who's Coney's mother? |
| 17. | DEREK | Marconi. Listen – there's another one coming through. (TRUMPETS. MORSE SABRE DANCE) |
| 18. | | That wasn't Morse. |
| 19. | CHERRY | No – it's coming from somewhere near. |
| 20. | MORETON | I say – quick everybody, look through your binoculars over there. |
| 21. | SPIKE | Da – I can't see a thing. |
| 22. | MORETON | It looks like a group of the natives Livingstone wrote about. |
| 23. | DEREK | No it's not. |
| 24. | CHERRY | What is it! – cannibals? |

| 1. | DEREK | No – yes! It's a band of Stanley Blacks! This is the end. |
|---|---|---|
| 2. | CHERRY | (SCREAMS) Look, it's that horrible-looking savage in the front row. |
| 3. | DEREK | I think he's going to speak. |
| 4. | FRANKIE | Ladies and gentlemen. |

ORCHESTRA    CLOSING SIG. 'HIP HIP HOO ROY'

ANNOUNCER    (OVER) Frankie Howerd nearly put paid to Derek Roy in Hip Hip Hoo Roy.

Yes, this is the end of 'HIP HIP HOO ROY' for this week, but we'll be on the air again next week at the same time, with Derek Roy, Robert Moreton, Cherry Lind, Spike Milligan, Jimmy Lavall and The Stargazers, with the Dance Orchestra conducted by Stanley Black.

Script by James Douglas and Spike Milligan.

Musical links by Jack Jordan.

Produced by Leslie Bridgmont.

ORCHESTRA &    SIGNATURE TUNE UP TO FINISH.

STARGAZERS:    PLAYOUT